D1150642

Redlegs

by Chris Dolan

Vagabond Voices
Glasgow

© Chris Dolan 2012

First published in June 2012 by
Vagabond Voices Publishing Ltd.,
Glasgow,
Scotland

ISBN 978-1-908251-07-7

The author's right to be identified as author of this book under the
Copyright, Designs and Patents Act 1988 has been asserted.

Printed and bound in Poland

Cover design by Mark Mechan

Typeset by Park Productions

The publisher acknowledges subsidy towards
this publication from Creative Scotland

For further information on Vagabond Voices, see the website,
www.vagabondvoices.co.uk

For Moira Leven

Redlegs

In an old house in the remotest corner of this island, I found the book printed here below. How I came to be interested in the Rosies is of little interest. The poor whites of the Caribbean are a vanishing people; both in the sense of diminishing numbers, and in their invisibility. If noticed at all, in the streets, or in the market or rumshop, by their countrymen or a visitor like me, they're mistaken for bedraggled tourists perhaps after a night out before going back to their beach hotel for a change of clothes. Generally, though, they simply escape notice. But if poor whites are indistinct, blurred, the Rosies are covert and imperceptible. Partly because no one wants to see them; partly because they do not want to be seen. But their land was of value, in an island almost totally developed for tourism, which was how I came to learn of them. A group of people living, forgotten, in an obscure, nearly inaccessible, headland of Barbados.

Early in March last year I drove up a stony, overgrown lane that led to a broken-down old plantation house. Tucked away next to North Point, beyond the Scotland District, along a promontory where the land has been steadily eaten away by a powerful sea, lies Roseneythe. Over the years it had been all but cut off from the life of the island. The Rosies' homeland was no longer viable, and it was the community itself that had invited offers for their few hundred acres of land, unprofitable cane fields and the dilapidated house.

Mrs. Martha Ruddock, a tiny elderly woman, sunburned an alarming, cancerous shade of orange, welcomed me as if I had been expected. The house was spick and span, hardly lived in. Martha, like a professional estate agent, showed me round, providing details about ownership rights, dwellings (there were twenty wooden chattel-houses on the estate, hidden by trees and a hill to the front of the main property) and potential amenities.

"Place useless for livin' in, but worth top dollar for wheeler-dealers."

The windows upstairs gave a good panorama of the real estate: a pretty bay lying north-east of the plantation house and a wooded area planted, apparently, a couple of hundred years back. Apart from that, the terrain was mostly flat. Martha was right – a gift for contractors. Ideal for a five-star compound, links course, watersports. I warned her she'd never recognise the place once they'd done with it.

"They'll strip away the fields, the houses, even that hill there – it'll just get in the way. Take the whole place right down to the coral rock, flat as a pancake. Then they'll build it all the way back up again. Widen the bay. Pull down the house and throw up a concrete replica. Time those guys are done you won't know you're on the same island."

She took me into a large room, furnished with a mahogany table and twenty or so chairs, perfectly polished. The room was unchanged, probably, in over a century. Around the walls was a series of portraits, painted, I guessed, by an amateur hand. The subjects – all women on the side walls – were a little racily depicted, dresses and shawls pulled down to reveal pink shoulders. They ranged from late teens to early thirties, all dressed in nineteenth-century peasant women's Sunday best. There was no artist's signature, no dates, and no subjects' names.

"They our ancestors, or so I was learned."

Each of them stared directly out of the canvas, with the same blank expression. Despite the décolletés and the attempts at seductive smirks, all of them looked a little careworn: the older ones tense, the younger apprehensive. Most had been given dark brown hair, pulled back from their faces, bunched under a white cloth bonnet; one was burdened with a particularly unlikely shade of ginger hair and plain, bordering on ugly, features. Their faces were pale to the point of ghoulishness, especially those in the direct line of the sun from the window.

Martha walked me back to the opposite end of the room.

"This un's called Lord Albert. Over there, Cap'n Shaw." She stood in front of the middle portrait. "Elspeth Baillie, the actress." Like I should've heard of her.

The titled gentleman had thick, damp lips and drooping eyelids. Maybe forty–fifty years old. His clothes seemed to date from an earlier epoch than the other subjects. The captain was thin, could've been any age, uniformed, riding a horse. A nag so emaciated it buckled under its rider, skinny as he was, stooping over his saddle, beard straggly and clothes soiled. The pony was being led by a young black boy, a Huckleberry Finn character, expression full of helpless resignation.

The woman in the middle was the most successful of the collection. At least, she'd been treated to more care and greater detail. I suppose she was meant to be beautiful – the artist had favoured her over the others with shinier hair and brighter eyes. A kind of archetypal English rose. Blush cheeks, snub nose, full lips. But it hadn't quite come off. None of these portraits would add any value to the property. Miss Baillie sat on a large, high-backed chair, in front of the window, Roseneythe cove stretching out into the distance behind her.

"She the mother of we all. Now there be a story you don' hear often. Life like an anancy tale."

Martha led me through to the kitchen where she opened a trapdoor in the floor. Below it extended wooden stairs leading down into a basement. It was pleasantly cooler down there and the walls had been comparatively recently replastered and painted. A little arch led into a small room, perhaps once a large closet. Inside there was an old escritoire, which Martha opened and took out two books. One of them she laid aside, but I noticed it was written by an Alexander Kinmont. The second she handed to me. There was no title on the damp, mottled leather binding, nor was there a name of any author. Opening it, the pages weren't stitched in, but loose leaf. The manuscript inside was written in pen, in a fine hand. Martha knew nothing of its origins, only that it had been here all her life and for many years before. She allowed me to take it away. "Understand, sir. We ent quite north, and we ent quite south."

On my return to Bridgetown I read it through at a sitting. At the very end it was signed simply "Jean Alexander". I spent the next few weeks keying it into my laptop. When I returned it to Roseneythe, Martha put it back in the desk in the basement and said: "Small garden got bitter weed."

I

There was never a happier day for Elspeth Baillie than the day she was plucked from her old life, the only life she had thought possible, nipped in the bud and transported across oceans to be planted again in the warmth of the sun. She had been a poor stunted bramble in her home ground: nineteen wearying years that felt like forty. Then, on the eve of her second decade, she was unearthed and grafted onto a new vine. The husbandry was performed by the Right Honourable Albert Lord Coak: he it was who stripped away the mildew and mould that had formed on her soul, pared her down, and restored her to youth.

That eminent person's presence in a cantankerous port – by chance the same town which was playing host to Elspeth and her family – caused several days' worth of muttering, suspicion and some quite splendid Scotch shrugging. They already had their own dandies of course, the good folk of Greenock, but these were homespun and old hat compared to this newcomer. The sheen of his hand-tooled suit, his blue wool over-cloak and the splash of marigold on his collar, as he weaved his way through their midst, added a watercolourist's daintiness to the dark oil canvas of the town. The interloper journeyed between the Harbour Master's office, shipping agents' premises, and the sugar refinery, ending his afternoon's travails as a guest in the grand house of a more commonplace, native moneybags. He then caused a considerable stir when he reappeared, at seven o'clock sharp, at the hall of the Seamen's Mission, and took his seat for "An Evening of Sketches, Songs and Monologues Performed by Mr. Charles Baillie, his Wife Helena, daughter Elspeth, and Sundry Talented Nieces, Nephews and Cousins of the Baillie Theatrical Clan" – not least amongst the family of performers themselves, peeking out from behind their home-made curtain. He sat alone in the theatre, patiently waiting for the show to begin, whilst the rest of the audience remained outside drinking and jostling until the last possible moment when they could no longer put off the entertainment.

"Who could he be?" whispered Elspeth's mother, agitated.

"Pay him no mind," replied her husband. "Another swaggering knab who'll uptail and awa' long before we're done."

"He seems comfortable enough in his pew," said Elspeth. "Maybe he's from the Edinburgh theatre."

"We'll ken soon enough. If he gloats at you, we can be sure he's not."

Elspeth pirouetted away expertly from her father: his blindness to her genius no longer offended her. She would wait till the end of the performance when, as happened after every show, she would be showered with compliments and surrounded by admirers, while her parents kept four keen eyes out for wandering hands and all ears open for impudent propositions.

The entertainment that night began, as it always did, with the players struggling to be heard above the turmoil and din of the drunken crowd. Tender verses of Gaelic-inspired poetry had to be yelled out at the top of the voice; the subtle love-lines of Messrs Shakespeare and Scott earned only lewd responses from stevedores in the front rows; carefully crafted choreographies were turned into stomps in a bid to secure a smidgeon of attention. Elspeth didn't mind: the fine gentleman seated towards the back sat still and attentive. She knew from experience that once the evening's repertoire reached her Cleopatra soliloquy there would be a hush throughout the house.

Helen Baillie, turbaned and tunicked, set down at the feet of her daughter the basket containing the pretty worm of the Nile that kills and pains not. Some jester in the back row cried out – as one always did in every audience from Ayr to Musselburgh – "I've got one of yon too!" And, as ever, the rest of Helen Baillie's speech was drowned out by laughter. But Elspeth knew how to win them over. She stood stock still. For so long that the audience wondered if she had forgotten her lines, and they fell into silence out of curiosity. Finally she took three slow tentative steps towards the fatal casket.

She sank to her knees and spoke in a near-whisper. "Will it eat me?"

She looked up, seemingly blind but scanning the faces in front of her, checking that the gentleman was leaning forward in his seat, which he was. She knelt in front of the snake's basket, and braved the tips of the fingers of her left hand into the deadly lair. She let slip the most restrained of yelps, but held her hand heroically inside, pulling it out at last, dripping with poison – in reality, soured milk. "I have immortal longings in me." She stood up, and with her right hand loosed the laces of her shift, let one single drop fall slowly from her fingertip between the swell of her breasts. She let the communal intake of breath from the audience pass before wilting, swaying. The audience was entranced; the jokes and quarrels of a moment ago forgotten at the sight of a beautiful young queen dying, and, better still, showing a good measure of cleavage.

Through the glaur of the candle-smoke, in the penumbra of the Seaman's Mission, she felt the visitor's scrutiny as much as observed it. A warmth on her skin on a cold night, as if the moon had begun to heat. Men had always stared, gawked, as she tiptoed or paraded in front of them, less voluminously dressed – depending on the scene – than they were used to seeing a woman. Certainly there was lust in the fine gentleman's eyes too: she could detect craving even in the back pews; but there was something else. Something different. Emptying. His gaze gouged at her insides, like a fishwife's knife, leaving a drained space, ready to be filled with some new, unfamiliar element.

When she reappeared – after the applause that persisted throughout her exit and for a full two minutes after – to sing in duet with her father "The Shepherd Lass o' Aberlour", a ribald verse penned by Edward Baillie himself in his youth, the crowd were amazed to see that the beautiful queen, who only a moment before had lain piteously dead, was now transformed into an uncouth country maid. Her father, behind his greasepaint, scowled at the loosened lacings of her bodice which she had omitted to retie, and at her excessive winking and histrionics, but no one was paying him any mind. All were shouting encouragement at the shepherdess as she sang of her peccadilloes, and laughing at her indelicate turns of phrase. But even that rude piece had its melodramatic finale, when the farmer scolds the maid for her sinful ways and she promises to be good for evermore. Elspeth found a catch in her voice, stooped her stance, and altered the story of a woman reformed to one of a woman defeated.

She did not need to wait until the company had dressed and left the hall to come face to face with the man who – the rumour had by now reached the dressing rooms – was a lord of the realm, in Greenock for sugar business, English and with money to burn. There was a time when any such personage would be immediately tracked down and pursued by her father and subjected to boasts of his talents. But Edward knew that his moment had passed and now went out his way to avoid any contact with the promise of what might have been. So when Lord Coak invited the entire family to share a jug of wine with him, he shrugged and let his family go on ahead. "You ken fine what he's wanting," her father shouted to Elspeth, as he struggled with Mark Antony's chain mail shirt which no longer fitted him.

"Breeding will oot," her mother liked to say and Coak was proof of the adage. He diligently spoke to each and every member of the company, from Aunties Jessie and Nanie, who toured with their sons and daughters and kept the company's wardrobe in order, to Mr. Nicol of the Seaman's Mission, thanking him profusely for opening his premises to such pleasurable and important events as theatre and song. He complimented the cast from the youngest to the oldest, saving his most exuberant praise for Mr. and Mrs. Edward Baillie themselves. He only nodded in passing to Elspeth. She didn't fret that he was ignoring her: he was saving her up to last. She watched him as he made his rounds, bowing slightly to the most menial of those present, smiling when required, tut-tutting when it was expected, talking as little as possible about himself, making light of a lord's presence in such a humble venue. He was a smallish man, his hair receding, a pot-belly burrowing out from under his coat like a mole searching for daylight. But his manners were cut as finely as his clothes, and his voice beguiled – the accent a mix of high English rank in its vowels and Colonial oddity in its consonants. He was not an attractive man, yet there was attraction in him, even beyond the lure of his status. Elspeth liked the way he modestly infiltrated the company, speaking to one person at a time, as if he were the privileged party.

He spent a little too long, she thought, with her sister Peggy. Peggy made a meal of him, curtsying and laughing and stretching her head up to show off her slender neck. The gentleman patted her on the back, which Elspeth was pleased to see, it being an act of open condescension. Then he turned abruptly away from Peggy, stepping directly and unexpectedly up to Elspeth. He did not introduce himself. Omitted to make polite conversation. He did not even address her by name. He simply placed himself in front of her and stated bluntly, "You have a faculty for finding beauty in the commonplace."

Elspeth was wrong-footed by the suddenness of his arrival and the directness of his compliment. She curtsied, said Thank you, reddened in the cheek, and kicked herself for being so unprepared. "Yours is a natural gift, my dear. One that has managed to survive whatever nonsense you've been taught. Will you come and see me tomorrow? Can you find a way to do so without, as yet, anyone knowing? I assure you, I wish only to speak of matters professional."

Elspeth found herself nodding dumbly. The pretty words she had rehearsed for this interview were defunct; the practised rejections of his flattery of no use, and she stood like a child being sent an errand by a strict uncle. And yet, there was warmth in Coak's eyes, and his bearing was amiable. If she was a child to him then it was an especially favoured one. She had received similar invitations in the past, but this was free, she reckoned, of any impropriety. As he gave her the details of his lodgings and suggested the hour of their meeting, she had that emptying feeling again. Stronger now that he was so close to her and addressing her intimately. Elspeth Baillie – the girl she had been, the young woman she was now – was being reduced, as water over a fire is boiled away, leaving her drained and ready for the life that was to come.

She turned and left the Seamen's mission, the day turning out just as she had expected. That morning when she had risen, before sun-up, and long before news of a Lord's presence in town had reached her ears, she had seen through the window of the room at the inn where she shared a bed with her sister and two of her cousins, a ripple of light in the sky. Perhaps a fire somewhere distantly flickering, or a trace of the Northern Lights. But Elspeth recognised it as a sign. She had seen such signs before and had gone back to bed at the end of the day wondering if she had missed some covert opportunity. Not tonight. The Fates had long had her in their sights, and now she would give herself over entirely to their power.

Where was the beauty in the little scene she found herself playing now? Black rain fell from a muddy sky. Perhaps she should think of the night as smouldering embers, doused by God's tears? The tree she was pinned against was hard and cold, its leaves, under the sickly moon, grey and damp. A proper poet would see it differently: silvery boughs danced upon by tiny elves. But even a poet would be hard pressed to make a dashing hero out of Thomas. Perhaps, if ever she were to tell the story, she could portray the grunting, red-faced boy as an ardent young suitor, his jupe and breeks the honest uniform of a decent, manly drover; his popping eyes, as he tried to squint inside the shift he was tearing at, aglow with passion, startled by the grace of her youthful, innocent breast.

The rarest of gifts, said his lordship. A faculty for finding beauty in the commonplace. The Fates had played kindly with Thomas tonight, too. Elspeth's brisk exchange with a Lord had left her hankering.

The west coast ports in festivities were full to the gunwales of randy callants in second-hand flannel and hand-me-down compliments. Sailors whose fortune would be spent before the night was out; engineers and harbour-boys who hoped their wages would go further with an actress than in the bawdy-house. In society like that, Thomas was as reasonable a suitor as any, and she let him lead her away into the park where other unidentified couples could be heard wooing in the gloaming.

The eternal in the momentary. That's what the gentleman had said. An actual gentleman. In clean clothes. And the subtlest whiff of perfume – an exotic tincture, that for all Elspeth knew, might well be the natural smell of the well born. Only the best-educated could speak as he did without the aid of a script. An English Lord, travelled all the way from the Colonies, solely to find her, Elspeth Baillie, on stage at the most shambolic of penny gaffs. Judgement like that, surely, could be trusted.

Try as she might, though, she could not convert a farm-loon into a cavalier, sonsie Tam into a dashing swain. The tree felt just like a tree, and if the raindrops were tears, they weren't God's. Thomas's choice of amatory words were a far cry from poetry: between grunts, he employed the only names he knew for parts of her body and his, and his intentions were described in humble, if honest enough, terms. Poor Thomas only managed to increase the hollowness she felt inside. She felt sorry for him, bringing him to the verge of his dreams only to push him back again. But this she did, and with a certain violence. The boy, surprised and convulsing dangerously, could only let out a stricken cry.

"Tom. Go see Peggy."

"It's no' Peggy I want."

The Right Honourable Albert Coak was not in the habit – at least, not lately – of attending cheap burlesques in Seamen's Missions. He had become accustomed in recent years to more civilised and lavish spectacles at La Scala, or London's Adelphi or Strand. But he had found himself alone on business and on his birthday, and the Baillie Family were the only show in town. After a day of wearying engagements – talking sugar tonnage and refining requirements – the prospect of rude humour and gauche performances enticed.

Unlike Elspeth, Albert had not seen any special light in the sky that morning; even had he done so, he would have attached no importance to it.

As he took his seat in the Seamen's Mission, his weariness grew more oppressive. This, most assuredly, would not – could not – be the place where he would find what he had been looking for. If La Scala had failed him, and Drury Lane, and all the arenas, both exalted and profane, of New York, Berlin and Havana, had not produced the talent he sought, then Greenock, he doubted, would come to his rescue. But the moment that girl walked onto the stage – actually, a clearing in the chairs – Coak's eyes, and heart, widened. Who would have thought? And isn't it always the way that the thing you are looking for turns up in the last place you look? He caught his breath at his first sighting of Elspeth Baillie, fought his own incredulity, dampened down his hopes, and sat in rapt attention for the rest of the evening trying to convince himself he was wrong. But there she stood in front of him – comely, hearty, pleasingly presumptuous and certainly affordable – the best candidate he had seen for his project. After so many years in countless theatres and concert halls, he had seen prettier girls. Better actresses, or, at the very least, better schooled in the dramatic arts. Finer singers; performers even more brazen and assured than the Baillie girl. Yet her voice was strong and sweet and convincing; her acting surprisingly proficient but still, he was sure, susceptible to tuition and improvement. And her looks, as the night grew on, struck him at every moment as more remarkable. There had been contenders in the past whose rejection of his offer had irked him: Italian singers who earned, or were confident they would one day earn, more than he could pay; Londoners who had no wish to exchange the mother country for a colony they thought fit only for convicts and fallen women. He was thankful now that these women had turned him down. The fresh, authentic voice that would breathe life into West Indian theatre was found at last, in the middle of nowhere, deep in the slender neck of young Elspeth Baillie.

He did what was necessary: stayed behind in that mean and dispiriting little hall; let his lips touch the "wine" offered to him, and made polite conversation with the entire dreary Baillie family, the vulgar father and feeble-minded mother, all the many cousins, aunts and menials that surrounded the nugget he was about to pluck from their midst. Doubtless, he could have avoided the whole tedious business, put his proposition to her directly, and sent her off on a boat the very next morning, her hampered little heart bursting with gratitude. But he was in no rush. The ship he had just that day chartered would not sail for nearly a month and, being a cautious man, he saw no reason not to double-check a contemplated acquisition.

The following morning, armed with a telescope, he spied on the family from behind a tree in a thicket of poplars some distance from the harbourside inn the players had leased. He was Galileo inspecting the moons of Jupiter from a million miles away; Napoleon at the head of his Armée d'Orient reconnoitring the unruly malcontents of Cairo. And there was Cleopatra amongst them – more Queen of the Nile this morning, as she shouted and remonstrated with father, mother, cousin and aunt, and stamped her feet on the cobbles of the embankment, than during her death scene the night before. The entourage were taking out the company's wardrobe, stacking shirts and dresses, tunics and robes, wigs and hats, on to a cart which would trundle them and their owners two hundred yards to the ferry which in turn would take them all to their next engagement, in Helensburgh, across the estuary. The scene was delicious to the watcher: to facilitate their task each member of the company carried a pile of clothes, but also wore wigs on their heads covered by two or three hats, draped cloaks around their shoulders, and stuffed props under their arms. Thus there was an elderly cavalier sporting a judge's thatch and carrying a Redcoat's musket. An elderly woman with Rapunzel's locks brandished a Turk's scimitar. Helen Baillie wore several false beards around her neck and a stack of tricorns on her head, while bearing a severed head under one arm and a life-size puppet that dangled like a sacrifice under the other. Albert warmed to them immediately, and all the more so to the aggravated Elspeth who, flushed with exertion and temper, looked more theatrical in life than she did on stage. Presumably her petulance derived from an argument over her insistence on absenting herself, without providing any good reason, for an hour on so busy a day. Her excuses, he could imagine, would be naive but forceful; this girl would not let him down, and he began to look forward to their meeting.

Lord Coak was a perfect gentleman during the exclusive performance. He sat at the far side of the room and listened intently to her Lady of the Lake – sometimes, to Elspeth's consternation, closing his eyes in appreciation for just a little too long.

The family flitting followed by lengthy wrangling with her father to let her escape for an hour, thereby delaying their ferry crossing to Helensburgh, had agitated her. No one was convinced that she had fallen so in love with the northerly views over the Clyde – a panorama she had never been seen to notice before – that she had to spend time on her own contemplating it. She was met with all kinds of accusations, the most foul coming from her father himself, who had no notion of the whereabouts of her tryst but knew perfectly well whom she would be seeing there.

Her discomfort increased on arriving at the mansion of a shipper – an associate of Coak's – set high above the port of Greenock, and being treated by the servants as a scullery maid applying for a position she had no hope of securing. But on being led into a finely furnished room, almost as large as the auditoriums she was used to playing in, where her patron welcomed her with an amiable smile, all disquiet immediately left her. As on the previous night, Lord Coak did not waste time with preliminaries, but set at once to business, asking her to perform some little piece for him. Elspeth sang out the opening lines of Sir Walter Scott's poem with all the lilt and drama she had in her.

"Harp of the North! that mouldering long hast hung
On the witch-elm that shades Saint Fillan's spring!"

The colonial gent – as immaculately groomed as before – nodded his way through the recitation, smiling here, frowning there. She did not recite the fiction in its entirety – that would have taken long past the hour the ferry was due to leave, and besides would only give her more scope to make a mistake. The version she used had been edited by her father, who had included as much lyricism, and as much battle and death, as any audience needed. She finished boldly, in a strong and steady voice with the subtlest hint of Gaelic in her accent, on lines that she hoped would draw attention to herself, rather than Scott's heroine:

"A chieftain's daughter seemed the maid;
Her satin snood, her silken plaid,
Her golden brooch, such birth betrayed."

She gave a little bow and found that, now that she had stopped performing, the trepidation she had felt at the start returned. Lord Coak sat still, nodding quietly to himself, and stared out the window onto the river below, for such a protracted period that she began to worry that she had disappointed.

"A native talent. You would be surprised, Miss Baillie, at how many – if I may say so – far more experienced actors fail to convey their own comfortableness before an audience and delight in performing."

He looked back out the window until Elspeth wondered if her presence was no longer required. As she moved towards the door, however, he stirred, raising an arm. As if on a spontaneous whim, he asked her to delay a moment. She stood, watching him while he lost himself again in some unfathomable thought. At last, he spoke the thoughts out loud: "I will understand if you judge my next request as scurrilous. You must not think it so and, if you decide not to comply, I hope you will not think ill of me."

His lordship did not have any particular quality to his voice that demanded obedience; on the contrary, there was a softness about his manner and his speech. His position and title, though imposing, gave him no authority over her. She felt he was a shy man – regardless of what he was about to request – and one over whom she began to feel a little power. She said nothing, but looked attentive.

"You would not, I don't suppose, consider speaking the opening stanzas again for me, Miss Baillie, but on this occasion disrobed?"

He looked, for a moment, as if he might explain his flagrant proposition, and then waved it aside, turning away once more, and leaving her to decide without further inducements or justification. Elspeth felt her colour rising, though her awkwardness was not caused by any sense of outrage. She would have been more scandalised if a man – of any rank – did not wish to gaze more fully at her. No, the difficulty at this not entirely unsuspected turn of events, was more a matter of policy. If the request were granted would it lead to a further, unwanted, pass? Though she had no objection, now that she considered it, to having her nakedness looked upon, she was quite unwilling to have to return the gaze at any disrobed part of the old man. More importantly, if she were to decline, would any offer he was considering making be lost to her?

He waited until she had made a move, noting that it was not towards the door, before speaking again.

"Great actors, my lady, must lay themselves bare before their audiences. You must not construe any other meaning into my suggestion – strange, I grant, as it must seem."

All she had done was shift from one foot to another, but from that he had deduced that she was agreeable to his suggestion. He knew before she did. Despite the differences between them she felt this stranger understood her in a way she did not yet understand herself and knew that he spoke not to convince her or defend himself but to cover the embarrassment between them as she began to undress. He let her do so without once glancing at her. As she unbuttoned her dress she decided to make her voice heard.

"I suggest, your honour, that you retreat further into the bay of the window while I stand closer to the door. You can assure me, I hope, that no one will come in in the meantime?"

"No one shall disturb you either from within or outside the room. You have my word."

As he spoke he got up and pushed his armchair so close to the windowpanes that she feared he and it might tumble through them. Elspeth placed herself behind the door, and turned away from him.

Privacy, she told herself, unlacing her chemisette, was a luxury to which travelling players, dressing together in sheds behind halls and barns, should not become accustomed. However, looking now at her underlinen, a new worry caused her to colour again: what must such a perfectly tailored man think of her poor, greyed, and stained clothing? To be sure her mother had always seen to it that her simmit and unmentionables were regularly scrubbed, but they were a far cry from new and crisp. It was too late to go back now, though; nothing to do but hope that her blushing did not cover her like a rash and conceal the bonny cherry-blossom tone of her skin of which she was so proud.

When she was quite bare she turned and looked in his direction. Coak waited a moment then turned to her. He kept his glance markedly above her neckline, gawking even at some point above her head, which gave her the chance to inspect him. She satisfied herself he was not an impostor: his weather-beaten face and wild hair spoke plainly of long voyages and hot, distant lands. His clothes could be afforded only by the wealthy, and there was none of Thomas's wheezing and ruddiness in the presence of feminine flesh. She had lost the fledgling feeling of power while taking off her faded underclothes, but naked now, and he so resolutely looking above her, it returned to her. She let a hiatus open up between them: she would not begin her recital until she had his full attention, so she stood straight and dignified until he was forced to glance at her.

"When you are ready."

Hearing her own voice speaking the first stanza of the poem she recognised it to be even stronger and more masterful than before. Unrestrained by shifts and chemises, and in the full knowledge of having nothing further to shed or lose, she limited her gestures but sensed each one to be all the more graceful and effective in its restraint. She chose other verses rather than repeat herself, leaving in only those which she felt lent themselves to her particular talents, and choosing more menacing phrases from elsewhere in the epic. She let the words and the images build, not so much in volume or drama, but in intensity, and finished with an almost pained flourish:

"The wizard note has not been touched in vain.

Then silent be no more! Enchantress, wake again!"

Throughout, his lordship had continued to take care not to let his eyes drop too often or too conspicuously below her shoulder, and, once she had reached her finale, he managed a smile that she suspected masked tears. He clapped quietly and murmured, "Bravo."

"There is the most exquisite cadence in your delivery, child. Quite natural, and quite remarkable."

He spoke on in this vein as each turned their back on the other, his words complimentary but serving merely to bridge the tricky business of her dressing and the announcement he was getting ready to make. He rehearsed over again the argument of acting being a stripping away of layers and false coverings, this time, she thought, a touch more apologetically. Once the matter of making herself decent was accomplished and out the way – her jacket and skirts fixed and tattered shoes replaced – the arrangements were immediately concluded for her passage on a cargo vessel to the island of Barbadoes, in one month's time.

II

She had heard tales of desperate voyages to the Americas. Reports of mountainous seas and sad, cold drownings. Of disease and slave ships, and pirates and mutinies and death by drinking the sea's brine. From the girls who would later follow her, she heard more complaint. Cold nights and burning days, the sadness of leaving mother and father and family, a whole world, behind. But when Elspeth Baillie stood on board her ship her hand was raised, not to wave a tearful farewell, but to push that damned, wet, disappointing land away from her. If they had made her row the boat single-handed to the West Indies, by God she would have done it.

Elspeth Baillie's journey was not cold, or wet or frightening, and it was not nearly long enough. She learned the wisdom in the old dictum of her father's, that anticipation is preferable to arrival. ("Ye're as weel t' gang as t' get there.") The journeys she had been in the habit of making were not ones anyone would wish to prolong – manky drudges through bog and rain, forty miles for one night's show at the cattle tryst, thirty more to a rabble of drunks in the brawling western ports. Father drinking too much, mother on her last legs, brothers and sisters and people she called aunts and cousins bickering and whining in the cold and the mirk and the smir. All for a few moments' begrudged applause, and not enough money to feed half the Company. Such was her juvenile certainty of the voyage she was undertaking that she dared in her mind to change the words and sense even of Mister Shakespeare's Tempest: "Nor would I give a thousand furlongs of sea for an acre of barren ground, long heath, brown furze, any thing!"

Lord Coak delivered her from all that. He had seen the colour of her petal, understood she was a genus cultivated in the wrong climate. He unearthed her, set her on the high seas to blow away her impurities before replanting his precious bloom by the lapping lazuli of the Caribbean Sea.

Miss Elspeth Baillie's Return to Greenock had the ring of a strathspey about it – perhaps one day in the future, when her name was celebrated across the globe, a fiddler or piper would compose the tune, a bard pen words to it, and plans would be made to perform it for her homecoming, though they would wait long enough for she swore never to set foot in this nation again. From the moment she stepped on to the quayside, her schooner sitting majestically in dock, sails billowing, her expedition had all the tumult and drama of a penny romance. There were stevedores and cargo, mainsails and harbour hubbub, and the smell of tar and sea and sweat, and masts stirring the very clouds.

Elspeth re-entered Greenock just a little over three weeks after her performance as Cleopatra and the Shepherd Lass o' Aberlour, alone in a new dress and crinoline, with a trunkful more – of pilot-cloth and silks, with bustles and pelerines, tiered skirts, and satin, button and Balmoral boots to match – waiting for her on the ship Lord Coak had chartered. This time, her voyage would last weeks, enough time to shuck off the old Elspeth and let the seeds of the new one germinate.

At the far side of the world there waited a new theatre for her. Her patron had described the Lyric – an arena as grand as the Lyceum, more modern than anything London itself had to offer, already staffed with writers and designers, actors and seamstresses, all standing ready, waiting for her to add the Promethean spark to set their dramas ablaze. It had been built specially for her – her actual name unknown until now, but she was the one, chosen from all the companies of Europe, fated to be its star.

As if to mark the momentousness of the occasion, a man died moments before her ship broke from land. The captain of the Alba – to Elspeth's eyes a rude, salt-cured and imperious fellow – was nevertheless a Jacobin and a Democrat. News had just arrived of the July Revolution in France, and the abdication and expulsion of King Charles. Captain Douglas ordered the firing of a salute, and not one shot but two, to celebrate the success of the insurrection. He explained to her that even trade ships must arm themselves against over-enthusiastic privateering. He had a sailor set the guns high enough to make sure the wadding would clear the sheds, while Elspeth and the captain and crew stood in line along the deck, and the folk on the quay fell silent, eagerly awaiting the blasts. The first volley shot cleanly enough, causing the ship to bounce on the agitated waters, prompting squeals of delight from the land-bound onlookers. The able seaman sponged out the gun, but the wadding must have ignited the second charge prematurely, for the man's right hand came flying off and sailed over the heads of the crowds like a bird heading south. His leg dropped into the sea a moment before the rest of him hit the water's surface with a dull, dead thud.

The captain showed no sense of loss. He ordered the sailor's remains to be fetched from the water and handed over to the port authorities for disposal. He brooked no argument, and the boat set sail before the one o'clock gun sounded. Elspeth felt no sadness. She had never met the dead man and his demise was so sudden and strange that grief was not possible. This, after all, was the port from which the notorious Captain Kidd first set out, and such barbarities were to be expected. Elspeth stood on the deck, wind funnelling upriver and through her hair, like a pirate captain scanning the horizon for adventures to come. The death of the unknown sailor felt like a sacrifice, the end of his days marking new life for her.

She was the only passenger, the captain's guest on the elegant, fast-moving trading ship, carrying goods back to the Indies, in exchange for American tobacco and sugar and rum, the last of which the deck and the hull still reeked, as though the entire vessel had been tempered in distilled spirit. The mahogany furniture in the captain's dining room and the ash-wood of her own quarters were impregnated with molasses, the sweet hopeful scent of sugar.

The bonny ship the Alba cut through the waves as if the Atlantic Ocean were silk of the finest denier. It took Elspeth one or two days to find her sea legs, but even the nausea she felt from time to time was welcome, purging the old Elspeth from the new. When, after a brace of days, the last of the British Isles was finally cast adrift, she waved again, her arm like an oar in the air, propelling her beautiful boat and manly crew away, yonder, beyond. For the next few weeks she would play the part of intrepid sailor – throwing her cap as she would hang it on the horns o' the moon! She stood on deck as the evening sun melted, and calculated that the Baillie Family Itinerant Players, famous at every fair, assizes and cattle show from Falkirk to Dumfries, were about to take the stage at Perth for the first of three nights' performance. Not one of them had come to wish her bon voyage. Mr. Baillie had not tried to restrain her – Lord Coak had ensured that her departure was economically indisputable – but he guaranteed to the assembled company that his wayward oldest daughter would become little more than a "weel-travelled, wide-spread hoor".

But here was Elspeth, upon the wide ocean. A girl drowned for nineteen years by Scotland's rains that quenched her, its fogs and haar dimmed her, bogs and quags pulling her down. But the sea! – now quiet as a lamb, mild and shy; now restless and pitching, full of business and scurry. By day, singing a gentle lullaby, and on the night following, swirling, tossing, muttering, annoyed, to itself. Then under the evening sun she caught glimpses of its underwear in the deep coral and seaflowers, and she thought of the woman she might become. The shadow of her form rippled on the surface, constantly changing shape. How could a single entity be so many things? Elspeth talked so confidently to the captain and his crew about her future life but, truthfully, she could not picture the world she was heading for, nor her place in it. Possible future Elspeth Baillies were just as multiple as the sea's moods. Already she was Cleopatra and Ophelia, Queen of the Night and Lady of the Lake. She was Clarinda and the Shepherdess o' Aberlour.

The crew of the Alba were as perplexed as she was. Each day they waited to see who it was they were dealing with – Anne Bonny, the Irish lady pirate, lady-in-waiting to a Lord of the Realm, fearful Scots lassie far from home. Elspeth herself didn't know whether she would be douce or voluble, a sea-sick maiden or tomboy mucker-in, until she had uttered her first words of the day. She kept the crew, and herself, waiting for three full weeks to discover if she preferred the power of the captain or the more polished first mate. For another month she played merry hell with their expectations and cravings, until finally they landed at Bridgetown.

*   *   *   *

The image of herself stepping off the ship – greeted by a small party headed by Lord Coak – burned itself indelibly on Elspeth's mind. It would hang there for the rest of her life, like a portrait or a daguerreotype on a wall, seldom acknowledged but always on show. And there was, truly, something photographic about the event: as if time had stopped and only Elspeth moved through a suspended world. Behind her, Captain Douglas and his superior officers stood rooted to the deck. Before her, Coak and some gentlemen and ladies she was yet to know, stared, hands held up in mid-wave, jackets and shawls rippling gently in the breeze. She inched towards them as if giving a portraitist time to capture the scene: the sea beneath the gangplank murmuring but still; little fish, impossibly colourful, ogled her, lulled by the moment. She alone moved, and her movement arrested the rest of the world's.

The spell was broken by the first words she heard in her new land. The General Manager of the Lyric Theatre – a Mr. Philbrick, she discovered later – addressed his lordship, but kept his eyes on Elspeth.

"Your valuation, Albert, is as ever quite faultless."

She had chosen to disembark in a simple white dress, without parasol or shawl. The correct choice as the scene was already bursting with colour. A late afternoon sun, itself a yellow polka-dot in a powerfully blue sky, amplified all the hues below it. The green sea, pink stone harbour, creamy white houses beyond the port. The group come to welcome her was a little patchwork of pink and grey hats, striped skirts and blue knee-breeches. No sight imaginable could be so different from the port she had left behind.

Philbrick, in indigo waistcoat and high starched collar, glowed with practiced wonder at her. She knew his type at once: a professional of the theatre who had long since ceased to marvel at any production, actor or performance, but whose function was to smile when required. She would have trouble with him. Not a minute off the boat and the perfect path to success she had daydreamed of across the Atlantic already had an obstacle. Lord Coak stepped away from the lady by his side – older than Elspeth, rouged to hide a natural plainness – and spoke as he approached. Elspeth thought she heard a note of doubt in his words.

"Miss Baillie more than lives up to my remembrance."

He looked different to her. The balding head and little pot belly were the same, and he remained the authoritative figure in the group, but he seemed more businesslike, even as he smiled and reached out for her hand, taken up perhaps with the little worries of everyday life. He introduced her to the rest of the party. While she curtsied and smiled at the embellished Miss Constance Sturges, bowed to Mr. Overton and his wife. The formalities completed, the party walked in twos and threes towards carriages waiting for them. Mrs. Overton and her sister took up each side of the newcomer; Coak fell in behind and spoke quietly to Philbrick. Elspeth recounted tales of her journey to Mrs. Overton and Miss Sturges. She was startled by her own accent, in contrast to the other ladies' plainer English, stabbed though it was with a hint of a more metallic, cruder sound. Elspeth liked the difference. Her own voice sounded clear and vivacious – soft watery vowels running over the sharp pebbles of consonants.

"Frightening? Not at all! A wee bit exciting at times, yes. But, oh, when you're alone on deck with nothing but sky and sea, you're mistress of the entire world. Especially with a dram of rum in you."

She made only limited use of Scots words, but gave her Western Scots free reign. They entered the carriages, and the drivers were instructed to make for the Overtons' – not, she noted, the residence of Lord Coak. The dust they kicked up rained back down in ochres and reds like fireworks. The air was warm, even at this late hour. The houses they passed gleamed white and imposing, as if they would be hot to the touch. Most astonishing of all was the encroaching night's music.

"Frogs," laughed Constance Sturges, seeing Elspeth listen with wonder. "They sing all night long. In no time you won't even notice them."

"And cicadas," said Mrs. Overton, with a shudder. Elspeth had never heard of a cicada, but could not believe anything terrible could make such a sweet sound or be the cause of such a shudder.

At the impromptu celebration organised in her honour at Teddy Overton's town house, everyone scurried around her.

"You are most welcome, my dear," said portly ladies. "Everything we have heard about you is true," offered portlier gents, though few, it seemed, could remember her name, if they had ever been told it. Lord Coak himself was as much a focus of attention as she was.

"Northpoint isn't in the habit of throwing parties," Mrs. Overton's sister whispered to her. Northpoint, Elspeth gathered, was the name of Coak's sugar plantation, too far from town to be a locus for social gatherings. Everyone showed polite interest in the new arrival, however, promising to show her around, give her the benefit of their advice and, of course, attend her future performances.

"I know you will be very happy here, my dear."

"So long as you manage a trip away once or twice a year. Mr. Thomson and I simply could not get by without returning to London every season."

Elspeth nodded and smiled and curtsied. These society people would have interested her more – after all, she was now at the heart of a gathering she had only glimpsed before through windows – were it not for the servant girls. They were not the first darkies she had seen: Macumbo the Witch Doctor had been a regular at circuses and country fairs where the Baillie Family had performed on the same bill; Daurama the African Queen had regaled audiences with her stories of rain-dances and bloody wars, bewitching them with her dark eyes and bright robes. The girls who proffered trays of snacks and glasses of planter's punch, therefore, struck Elspeth as dull in comparison. They wore ordinary servants' clothes – not a tiger's tooth or a leopard's paw between them. The male servants at each of the doors of the grand house had no face-paint or scars on their faces. Yet still she was fascinated by them all. They seemed turned in on themselves, their eyes looking at the guests but refusing to see them; the girls' spiky hair like hedgehogs, bristling.

There were two interruptions to the evening's proceedings, both in the form of unexpected arrivals. The first was a tall and stately gentleman to whom everyone deferred in subtle ways: hunching their shoulders a little; greeting him and quickly moving back again. The second was quite the opposite, a roughly dressed man, as tall as the first, but so thin that his lack of breadth nullified his height. Whiskered, and with that shadow of ingrained earth that those who labour in the elements can never wash away.

The first gentleman was introduced to her: Mr. Reginald Lisle. He smiled at her amiably enough, but said little. In his eyes, however, she saw the customary desire she inspired in certain men.

"Lisle's about the richest man you and me'll ever come across." With a few rums taken, Constance – or Nonie, as her fellow actress insisted Elspeth call her – betrayed her Irish roots. The West Indian twang gave way every second word to relatively recent Dublin brogue. "Puts money into the Lyric, so he does."

"He puts money into everything," added Christian Bloom, the young man to whom she had first been introduced at the Careenage and, she now realised, was Nonie's beau. "It's an insurance policy: he wants a bit of everything, just in case."

"And anyway, he only invests because of Georgie."

"Georgie," Christian explained "is his son."

"Now wait till you meet him, Ellie," laughed the Irish girl.

The look she received from the thin, whiskered man, had that hint of desire too. It was the yen that all older men hold for young women, but there was a childish shame there too, in the recognition of it: a kind of huffiness. She was not introduced to him, nor even discovered who he was. Plainly, he was not a guest, but had come to see Lord Coak on some matter of business, for he spoke to no one else. Nor did anyone mention him, though Elspeth felt that all were aware of him. Perhaps even frightened of him. She couldn't see why – he was of inferior caste and, apart from his gauntness, unimposing. Yet, when he turned to leave, his business with Coak quickly concluded, the room seemed to lighten and gaiety return.

After the excitement of the day, Elspeth began to wilt. She was led, by Mrs. Overton and Lord Coak, to her chamber, and she roused again at the sight of a four-postered bed in a magnificent room. She walked around, touching the heavy drapes on the windows and bed, feeling the sturdy, bright wood. Coak and Mrs. Overton watched her wordlessly, as if in a swoon themselves.

As she drifted off to sleep on the largest and softest bed she had ever known, the faint echo of a billowing sea at her window, an entrancing lullaby of cicadas and frogs from the gardens, Elspeth considered that she had not merely changed localities, but the very nature of life itself. In this heat, a person could not possibly stay the same. These new faces and accents and sounds and sensations belonged to a different realm. The old laws of her old world would not apply here. Nothing she had understood until now had any meaning. In this place, life could only unfold in unexpected and dreamlike ways.

III

The first week passed like hours, minutes. It seemed she skipped off the Alba and struck her new life into flame like a Lucifer match.

The Coak plantation was somewhere north of Bridgetown – a day's uncomfortable journey, inconveniently far from town and the Lyric. The planter saw no reason for Elspeth even to visit such an incommodious place, much less reside there when she would be needed on a daily basis at the theatre. It was agreed that she stay at the Overtons' for the time being, though not in the grand room they had given her on her first night. Instead, she was lodged at the back of the house in a suite of rooms designed, most likely, for a major-domo or a steward, or some other domestic assistant. Lord Coak agreed with Mr. and Mrs. Overton that a suite of rooms, cut off from the rest of the house and thus ensuring a degree of privacy would, in the long term, be more agreeable to Elspeth's needs. But with the flurry of activities and duties that descended upon her from the first day in Bridgetown, Elspeth scarcely noticed her new quarters.

Nor did she see much of her patron, who had business to attend to at his Northpoint estate, returning to town only when he was directly needed. Before he left, however, he sent a brougham to the Overtons to collect her in order to show her round the Lyric Theatre. She passed through an elegant arch and rode alongside the Careenage – bustling, noisy and exhilarating, with men of many races and all classes shouting and working, and smells as pungent as they were unidentifiable. The buildings in this part of Bridgetown were grand and bright and weightless-looking in the sunny light. At the far end of a broad street sat the Lyric – as large a playhouse as Elspeth had ever seen. Its bright new stone, smooth and silvery, glinted like steel in the sun, a dark-windowed dome crowning the whole. The entrance looked like those she had seen in drawings of London theatres: pillared and stately, the gateway to a better organised and more exciting world.

Coak was waiting for her on the street outside, accompanied by Mr. Philbrick. The owner welcomed her and rushed inside, like a child eager to show off his new toy. The company manager sniffed to her, when Coak was out of eashot. "Lord Albert is quite the expert on poetics but not, regrettably, an authority on architecture."

"I like it," replied Elspeth firmly.

"Good for you, dearie."

Inside, stage and stalls and ceilings were painted in every colour imaginable – dark greens and indigo, scarlet, crimson and maroon – with depictions of King George riding in a carriage over the sea, Arthur and Excalibur, Henry V at Agincourt. The seats were leather-upholstered and even the curtain and backcloths were sumptuous and enchanting, embroidered in gold and silver thread with seahorses, stars, snowflakes, sugar crystals, and birds of paradise. Coak watched his new recruit run from stage to stalls, up onto the balcony, and back down through the wings into the dressing-rooms, her childishness a joy to witness.

Lord Coak left that first afternoon. At the stage door of the Lyric, where a gang of slaves en route to somewhere Elspeth could not imagine sat heavily eating fruit doled out by a gaffer, he doffed his hat at Elspeth, like he might to a stranger in the street. "I shall be back Friday to see how your initiation is going. Until then, my dear, all you need do is watch, listen, learn and enjoy."

Elspeth attended her first performance at the Lyric with Mr. Philbrick and Mrs. Overton. Some nonsense cobbled together by Philbrick himself and Frederick Denholm – the Lyric's leading man and budding writer – on the theme of colonial childhood. Nonie struggled in her part as a girl clearly a decade younger than herself. Elspeth genuinely marvelled at the production's professionalism and the sophistication of its theatrical engineering. The play itself mattered less to her than the audience. The performance was not full, yet there must still have been nearly five hundred people in that hall. The rough trade in the stalls seemed aristocracy compared to the rabble who used to congregate in front of her in Falkirk and Glasgow. Stevedores, shop attendants and even agricultural workers they may have been, but they didn't bay and curse like the Scots, and were very smartly turned out. The balcony and box seats were occupied by the island's bejewelled, well-fed, if slightly sleepy, upper crust. The play itself made hardly any impact on her, but the beauty of the new costumes, the sheer size of the cast, and the effect of modern stage-lighting – gas-pumped! – were a wonder to her. She was not so overawed, however, that she felt the need to keep her criticisms to herself in the lounge after the curtain came down.

"I wondered if there couldn't a bit more movement about it. Everyone stood around a lot."

Mrs. Bartleby – who topped the bill alongside Mr. Denholm – paled at the impudence. "I think you'll find, my dear, our public prefer to mull over a drama's significance undistracted by clumping and dashing around."

Nonie rescued her from a dressing-down at the hands of Mrs. Bartleby, flanked and supported on either side by the Misters Denholm and Philbrick, and took her off to a room behind the prop store which the younger members of the cast had made their hideaway. Christian Bloom made coffee on a little open range, and laced it with rum. As the three of them sipped – Nonie and Christian still in costume as sixteen-year-olds but, in the lamp-light, actually looking ten years older than their true selves – other members of the cast popped in and out, shook Elspeth's hand, downed drams of straight rum, laughed and swore, and went out again. The names of these visitors were thrown at her – in the gloom, each caller indistinguishable from the next – snippets of advice were given her, and more spirit was added to her coffee. At the end of the night, Nonie took her back to her actress's lodgings in a dark and noisy street somewhere behind the city's main thoroughfares.

"Baxter's Road. I don't know the part of the world that you come from, Ellie, but I imagine you'll feel more at home here than anywhere else."

Nonie was right: the smell of cheap food and alcohol, the shadows and muffled noises, clandestine activities being played out up side streets and beyond the doors of rowdie-houses took her back to Greenock, Glasgow and Leith. In a way, she was glad to be reminded that life everywhere has its givens and constants; yet at the same time she was disheartened that every part of her new world was not utterly different and contrary to the life she'd left behind. Nonie's lodgings were akin to those Elspeth had suffered in countless towns from Dumfries to Dundee: a single room, filled with the sickly smell of tallow candle, an awkward landlady and boisterous neighbours. Sleep was made all the more difficult by the heat that lay on her like a heavy blanket. But the excitement of the day, a shared cup of rum with Nonie, and an hour or two's whispered chattering soon saw both ladies unconscious for the night.

The next three days followed the pattern set down on the first. Rehearsals in the morning, lunch at the Lyric with Mr. Philbrick and the senior cast, a stroll round Bridgetown in the afternoon – the shiny new town and steady hot sun reviving her. She helped stagehands rearrange scenery before the next performance, sorted scripts with prompters, and assisted Nonie into her costume, before sitting through the show again.

Elspeth followed Philbrick, Denholm or Mrs. Bartleby around, like a five-year-old too uncomprehending to do much more. Inwardly, however, she made her judgements on the Lyric Company. Its super-intendence – comprised of Philbrick, and Denholm and Bartleby as the senior players – disappointed her. Coak himself, who had shown such acumen and taste in Greenock, was much less involved in the venture than she had hoped. Philbrick, despite his puffed-up English, reminded her of her father: stale brandy ill-concealed by lavender water; yoked to a frustrated career that made him critical of all around him. Their artistic vision was limited and – in the opinion of a young lady who had never entered even an Edinburgh playhouse – provincial in the extreme. Their playbill for the coming season consisted of tired old renderings of A Midsummer Night's Dream and indifferent plays scribed by Mr. Denholm. As actors, both he and Mrs. Bartleby struck Elspeth as less than compelling. Neither was of a particularly attractive bearing – Mr. Denholm was still just young enough to grace a stage, but slight and mousy and with a girny, whimpering voice, while Mrs. Bartleby was far too old and bulky to be playing the parts she was given.

"Yuh mus'n fret over them. They'll not be of much hindrance to you, Ellie," Nonie assured her at the end of the second performance. Constance Veronica Sturges – the Primrose of Tyrone, as the play-bills described her – would not be a hindrance herself either. She had been performing around Bridgetown for nearly a decade and had hardly become a sensation. In the candlelight of the Lyric, Nonie could look quite glamorous and fierce, but up-close, in daylight, the pockmarks of some childhood illness defaced her. On stage, she feigned a low, breathy voice that sounded neither Irish nor Colonial, but which adequately maintained the attention of the audience. Off stage, she veered between her natural Hibernian tones – especially after a rum or two – and attempting to sound, inexplicably, like a darkie servant girl.

"Neither of 'em have a following in the town. Denholm come here when nobody in London waste their shillins on him any more. Mrs. Bartleby, she from Jamaica, and afore then, Virginia. She say she was in music-hall, but I heerd she was a five-nickel dancer in saloon bars. Don' yuh pay either of 'em any mind."

Laughing at the deficiencies of their senior actors, Elspeth and Nonie quickly became co-conspirators against Mr. Philbrick's little regime. Bartleby and Philbrick, Nonie informed her, were secretly compromised – a circumstance which prejudiced the Manager's casting decisions.

"You have to hand it to Mrs. Philbrick and poor old Edmund Bartleby," said Christian. "Either they're touchingly immune to all gossip, or relieved to have their spouses off their hands. They're the only two people in all Barbados apparently unaware of what's going on."

Despite what it might mean for Elspeth's career, the fact that the relationship between the general manager and the leading lady was widely known and casually commented upon – even though both parties were married and their spouses close by – amazed and delighted Elspeth. The West Indies seemed to her at once quaintly old-fashioned and remarkably freethinking. On the one hand, there was all the silly pomp and circumstance of the old order; social gatherings on the island were like scenes from plays authored a hundred years ago, ridiculous in their etiquette. On the other hand she and her fellow thespians behaved like spirited children far from home, without parent or nanny, King or Government, to check them. There was a laxness about their morals – lambasted and deplored daily in the town's Gazette – that agreed with Elspeth's natural temperament.

In this nook of the newly emerging world, it seemed, a lowly player could live the risqué life she thought available only to aristocratic artists – the Lord Byrons and Mr. Shelleys of this world. The junior members of the cast joyfully imitated the style and panache of the great Romantics. Before her first week was out, Elspeth was learning how to dress, talk and act like a freethinking artisan. She was not so well read as she would have liked, but now, instead of spending days and nights walking over bogs and peat land, she could devote time to reading. Or better still, glean the gist of great texts from conversations with her colleagues.

The theatre itself, while grander than any house she had ever seen, let alone played in, still possessed something of the ambience of the penny gaff. The auditorium was of no great size, yet the company retained a group of equestrian actors and a menagerie of animals. In the least likely of dramas, a horse might be ridden down the narrow aisle to dance on stage. Trained dogs performed tricks between acts. Melodramas and pantomime stories had been delivered, in recent months, by actors standing on the backs of horses cantering around the stage. The playbill for the Lyric's next production – Rob Roy McGregor – proudly announced the spectacle of "Bailie Nicol Jarvie on Horseback!"

By the fourth day – although still in a kind of Limbo, the strength and health she felt building inside her having no outlet in her role as novice – Elspeth began to distinguish the colleagues of her own generation one from the other. The young ladies of the company hailed from all parts of the world: Nonie, from Ireland; Virginie from France. Isabella claimed her dark beauty was Spanish, though it was rumoured that she was a quadroon of Venezuelan farmers' blood mixed with African. Some had no memory of where they originated. Their conversation was shockingly direct and their ways of speaking and turns of phrase comical and artless. The young men lacked the dullness and baseness than the rustics back home, but weren't nearly so sickly and pernickety as the gentry whom Elspeth had encountered in Scotland. The sun had darkened the lads' and lasses' skin and brightened their eyes. The entire company, with all its attendants and spouses and aficionados, was tall, confident and deliciously disreputable. Elspeth could have kissed each and every one of them out of sheer gratitude for their existence – excepting, of course, Mr. Philbrick and Mrs. Bartleby.

Many people – even those born and bred in the West Indies – complained of the heat, but not Elspeth Baillie. The light fell on her skin like angels' kisses, the sun wrapped its warmth around her like a passionate lover's embrace. The climate entirely suited her constitution. She had never felt so healthy in all her life, and even the slight scrofulous wheeze that had pestered her since childhood vanished within days of disembarking from the Alba. Her hair grew faster and thicker, its colour in reality unchanged but, under the intense light of the Barbados sky, glowing with a vibrant chestnut sheen – a deep, dusty, cherry colour, like the cinnamon she saw in the slaves' and freemen's markets. She felt her neck growing longer, more slender. The damage of so many years of bending and crooking against driving rain and whistling winds on trudges between fairs and trysts over sodden heaths was quickly undone. For the first time in her life she could walk to her full height, broaden her shoulders, and strip away layers of shawls and coats and underskirts. She felt half her true weight and twice as quick and wondered if a sea breeze wouldn't one day lift her off her feet.

When Lord Coak eventually returned to town he heard about the comments Elspeth had made to Mrs. Bartleby about the Lyric's production, and of a growing division between the two women. "Now that's a storm I'd like to have witnessed," he smiled to Elspeth. It seemed he was not unduly concerned by his protégé's forwardness, although there might have been a tincture of reproach in his look. Elspeth felt she still could not read Coak as well as she could other people. She would not have much opportunity to rectify the matter, as she was destined to see even less of the planter in the coming months. A business expedition to Havana was pressing, to which city he would be sailing at the end of this visit.

"I had no idea you would be absent so much," she said, and heard a five year-old's whine in her own voice.

"I am the owner, Elspeth dear, of the Lyric. Not its manager. You will inhabit its soul much more than I ever could."

During his short stay, Elspeth moved back into the Overtons' servants' quarters, while Coak took a room, for a few days, in the house proper. She was brought again into the drawing rooms not only of the Overtons, but also of Belles, Seallys and Grahams – Barbados's high society. Coak showed her off like a new medal, his very own Daurama, White Witch Woman of the North. He spoke enthusiastically of her "native talent" and her unblemished gift. With not much more than a week or so behind her in the company of professional, sophisticated actors, Elspeth already wished to show she possessed more than "native talent".

She had had no time to properly increase her knowledge, having only watched a few rehearsals before whiling away the evenings in the prop room and Nonie's lodgings. Her new friends had taught her the trick of pretending expertise. The naif of only a fortnight ago was already being replaced by a confident young woman quoting "Prometheus Unbound" and "The Ancient Mariner" – though she knew nothing beyond those brief, memorised passages – and flirtatiously asserting her new-found, liberating atheism. In return, she was admired more openly for her prettiness, and complimented on her outspokenness. Colonial gentry apparently delighted in their artisans' nonconformism where their Scots counterparts abominated it. It was at one of these functions that Elspeth met George Lisle – the son of the rich planter who had come to inspect her on her first night on the island.

"Master Lisle has been on vacation in London," Mrs. Overton informed her, when the heir to the largest fortune on the island arrived, dressed unremarkably, a tousled and distracted bearing about him. "Normally, he can't tear himself away from the theatre – as you'll soon discover."

She had already heard his name; had gathered he was a favourite of the young actors and stagehands, who referred to him as a bosom buddy, regardless of their status in comparison to his. Nonie, Virginie and Isabella giggled at the mere mention of him. At first sight, she could not see why. Master Lisle was not particularly tall – unlike his father – nor refined in feature. Heavier set than she had expected of a man both high-born and a favourite of her girlfriends, he blended a little too easily into the set of thick-bodied colonials. He was also, she reckoned, a little older than she had been given to believe. Once introduced, though, she quickly felt at ease in his company.

"I hear you're quick with advice to the Lyric's luminaries, Miss Baillie."

"I merely made a passing remark."

"Make more of them!" he beamed widely, leaning in innocently as a brother or cousin might. "Too many fresh talents have buckled under the weight of the Denholms, Philbricks and Bartlebys."

As he said this, he smiled genially towards each of those doyens in turn, nudging Elspeth lightly, and she began to see why the company had taken so much to him: he lacked the stuffy formalities of his peers. Expressions flew fast across his face, unchecked by duplicity or calculation. George Lisle talked hard and enthusiastically, but he listened hard too: his minute reactions to her every word meant either he was genuinely engaged with what she was saying, or that he was a fine actor in his own right. "Perhaps you're just saying what you think it is I want to hear, Mr. Lisle. In a few moments you'll be over there with Mr. Philbrick saying something quite different."

"Of course."

"Then you're a fake."

"Nothing wrong in faking, if you're aware that's what you're doing. Look at these planters and administrators and shopholders. They're all fakes and don't even know it."

"But you're different?"

"I know how to keep on Philbrick's good side, so that I can run free around the theatre, but I'm only too aware of what bunkum it is to be a colonial planter's son. Live as long as I have, Elspeth, in a world as dreary as this – at the slightest flicker of intelligence and energy, I'm a mosquito on the scent of blood."

George seemed a genuinely open and pleasant man, with that

same whiff of candour and rascality she loved so much already in her colleagues. They chattered amiably in a corner of Mr. Belle's hall, long enough for Nonie, in passing, to raise an eyebrow, and Christian Bloom to give them both a knowing look. Lord Coak passed them from time to time but gave no indication of displeasure. Elspeth felt a flush of anger at this patent lack of interest. Was she to believe that her patron's audacious request in Greenock amounted to no more than it pretended to be – a test of dramatic ability and resolve? Having seen what he had seen, how could a middle-aged unmarried man not be nettled by the sight of her giggling in close intimacy of a younger man? Close on the heels of that spasm of anger followed a further, stronger one, of shame. Coak was what he seemed. And what need had she for the lustful gape of a soft-fleshed old coof?

Eventually Coak did look around at the pair of them, and George, as if reading her mind, remarked, "Don't be fooled by his businesslike air. At this very moment he is seeing you, in his mind's eye, naked."

She considered telling George that the businessman would not need much of an imagination to conjure up that sight; that he had already sat back in his armchair and studied every part of her meticulously. She might even have acted on the impulse – not in order to create a scandal, but for the sheer adventure of being bold with a young, rich, stranger – had not Coak broken way from his party to approach them.

"D'you think she will do well, George?"

"I've yet to see Miss Baillie in action; off-duty, she's mesmerising."

Elspeth watched Coak stare for a moment at Lisle's face. If there was jealousy lurking in that glance, she could not detect it. Perhaps he considered it in his interests to encourage a liaison between his apprentice and a young gent above her station. George's mind was working along the same lines as her own: "Albert believes he can create true talent the way he can refine sugar. No doubt he feels more processing needs to be done in your case."

"I'm not sure I want to be processed."

"You're raw cane to him. There are processes you must go through in order to meet his expectations."

"Do you have an example?"

"A bit of tragedy seldom does an actress harm."

"Suffer the slings and arrows of outragous fortune. Of an intimate kind, you mean?"

"For an actor, is there any other?"

"So I am supposed to love and lose like a comic heroine of the bard's?"

"My guess is your chosen victim will be the ultimate loser. But, yes. Coak is a sugar planter first – never forget. A period of pulverising, followed by some distilling, package the whole thing up, then he'll pour you like syrup onto his audiences. And you can count on me, Mistress, to be in the front row, eyes and mouth agape."

The Overtons' town house was in an area just south of Bridgetown called Garrison Savannah after the barracks situated between the mansion and the sea. Returning from the dampness of Nonie's lodgings Elspeth realised the beauty of the place. Her quarters looked out onto the back of the house, over gardens towards the sea beyond a broad stretch of open common land, home to bizarre wildlife. Vividly plumed birds strutted, reminding Elspeth of Joeys, the clowns of Scotland's fairs and festivals, as they tumbled and bowled along, legs parading disjointedly. The stunted little doves of this island looked like circus midgets. Yellow-breasted waders cackled like an act she had once seen where a man played the whole of "Scots Wha Hae" by tapping on his chin, the sound echoing from his toothless mouth. Tall trees bent in the breeze like strongmen straining under unimaginable weights. Misshapen squirrels scampered below her window. George, at breakfast the next day, supplied her with the names of things. They walked together in the garden, and he pointed out a tiny bird which Elspeth had feared was an enormous insect.

"Hummingbirds. You can hardly see their wings they beat them so fast. Look at their long beaks, for drinking nectar."

"They're beautiful," she said, and was aware of how quickly she had changed her opinion of the creature. The nectar, he informed her, came from petunias and prickly pear and snake-lilies. And the scampering little animal was not a distorted squirrel but a mongoose. The Flame Trees lit the morning like red and pink candles; an old fig sat at the back of the gardens like an ancient giant, weeping private grief into its beard.

George had to return to his own estate that afternoon, in the Parish of St. Thomas, not quite as remote as Coak's Northpoint. Now that he was home from his travels, however, he would see her regularly at the Lyric. "Nonie and Christian haven't taken you to the Ocean View yet? We shall rectify that on Monday evening." He bowed, breathed a kiss on her hand, and left. Coak himself had a meeting scheduled with shippers in the London Naval Club in town, so Elspeth had all Saturday afternoon and Sunday to continue settling in her new home.

Left to herself, she marvelled at the gliding and distant crying of birds wheeling over the ocean. She stared for hours at the bright orange and red breasts of smaller birds outside her window: glowing blue and purple crests, feathers that looked black in one light, deep green in another. The plants in the gardens grew in shades from subtle silvers and emeralds to roaring reds and smouldering violet. There were tiny petals and implausibly large leaves, bigger than her own body, fruits that bulged in odd shapes, succulents stabbing the air, stamens quivering in the warm breeze. From her new home, Elspeth could look out on all this activity, and fill her senses with colour and the dreamy scent of frangipani and coconut.

Lord Coak had negotiated, on her behalf, the use of two of the Overtons' servants. Dainty and Tuesday were as exotic to her as the flora and fauna outside. She had assumed that these shadowy people she had glimpsed by the careenage and serving drinks in lounges could only understand a series of simple orders, and that, otherwise, they confabulated in their own African idioms. She was astounded now to learn that they spoke a category of wild English. Moreover, she could understand them, and they comprehended every word of hers. She asked them the names of things as she noticed them, and began to learn a new vocabulary: aloe, seagrape, alamander, cochineal.

"Them's called upside-downs," Dainty told her. "See how de flowers hang?"

She went out with them to the garden, and touched and smelled all the flowers there. "Sea grape, ma'm. Taste a berry, it near ripe." Tuesday, the younger of the two bent down and tore a few leaves from a thick bushel. "Use it fuh wash yuh hair, make it soft soft and glow like a cane-fire by night."

"This be aloe. Put it on yuh skin, it like a babbie's kiss. Suds up well, too."

Ackees and ginneps, booby-birds and hummingbirds, mango and avocado: the names were as bizarre as the things they denoted. Dainty and Tuesday brought her selections of all the fruits that grew in the orchard, or wild on the savannah. Papaya, grapefruit and mango – the sweetest taste ever to have touched her lips. The alarming golden curved tuber the girls called plantain, which she had heard of as banana but had never seen. She peeled the skin as she was shown and put the bared flesh in her mouth declaring with a giggle that surely this must have been Eve's forbidden fruit, not the dull and boorish apple. The black girls laughed with her, but she knew they thought her as strange as she thought them.

Dainty, Elspeth reckoned, was about the same age as herself, Tuesday no more than fifteen. "Unusual name. Tuesday."

"The day I was borned, Ma'm."

And to Dainty: "I can see why you are called Dainty. But how did your mother know you would be petite?"

"I don' know what me mother call me. Mister Overton named me Dainty jus' a while back. 'Fore that I was Nursey. And 'fore that Toadie 'cause me used t' leap aroun' like a frog when I was a chile. You can call me somethin' new if you like."

"Dainty is fine."

On the Sunday after the party, Elspeth got to know a third servant – the most impressive of them all. The gardener, Henry, measured, she calculated, more than six and a half feet in height.

"I from Barbuda, Miss." He allowed her to follow behind while he pruned and raked, silent until he was asked a question. His back was like no human's she had seen before: muscles bulged under his shirt where she never thought even the strongest of men possessed muscles. His skin was so brightly black that she thought she might see her reflection in it, as one does in highly polished dark wood. She discovered that he had been bought by the Overtons and brought to this island when he was a boy. Were it not for his lack of colour, she thought, he would be the perfect model of a working man. Tall and strong, but gentle in speech. He was the father of several children whom Elspeth caught sight of from time to time. She could not tell his age as he displayed none of the natural signs of ageing: his skin was taut around his eyes, his hair black and he showed no sign of stoopage or stiffness. Yet one of his children was nearly full-grown, and Henry himself spoke like a man who had distilled some wisdom from many years of life. His presence was more substantial than that of most white men she knew, even amongst the burly, wealthy planters she had met since coming to the West Indies. With his air of authority, his strength, and the sense he gave out of being somehow absent, she could envisage him on stage as the Creature in Shelley's Frankenstein. She had not read Mary Shelley's book, but had seen reviews at the Lyric of a recent London production of the play, coinciding with a reprint of the book. The idea lodged itself deep inside Elspeth. Henry's distance, the strangeness of his appearance in conjunction with the pleasantness of his manner, reminded her of the sad, terrifying creation of Dr. Frankenstein.

Lord Coak, during the two days before his boat sailed for Cuba, called on her at her rooms, where they discussed theatre, Elspeth's great future in the Indies, and her eventual triumph in the whole of the Americas. He told her that he spent only a couple of months of each year on the island, the rest of his time being spent in Europe inspecting sugar refineries, negotiating shipments, and visiting the great theatres of France, Italy, and Germany. For the foreseeable future – for reasons to do with the sugar business – he would be more often visiting Havana.

"As a result, my dear, I will not be here for your first performance. You will not be angry at me?"

No, she would not. Though it was Coak's agency which had led her to this unexpected point in her life, his significance beyond financial support had already decreased. Nonie's, George's and her colleagues' influence were now more important to her; the opinions of the Philbricks, Denholms and Bartlebys unwelcome, but more crucial now than Coak's. "Think of me. It's all I ask."

"I do little else, my child."

✳   ✳   ✳   ✳

The Ocean View was a small hotel on the outskirts of town, run by an American couple from the city of New York. They had fashioned the establishment in classic New World style: simple wooden furniture within a plain, stern wooden structure perched on an outcrop of rock. Sitting on the view's balcony was like being on the prow of a new-built ship. The Börgmanns had "set the place up", they said, "for commercial opportunists, salesmen and speculators". It seemed to Elspeth that it housed only gamblers and drinkers.

Of the latter, the Lyric's players, when George Lisle was in town and spending, were the mainstay. The rooms above the balcony were used by the gamblers, Americans in the main who sat over endless hands of cards, their play interrupted occasionally by shouting, swearing or even out-and-out fisticuffs. The owners were never in the least dismayed by these outbursts. Mr. Börgmann could be seen on a morning calmly fixing broken furniture in the breeze of the hotel's porch; Mrs. Börgmann inside sweeping up glass, coins and even blood, singing some old German song to herself. The proprietors never raised an eyebrow at the potions mixed by Virginie, Isabella and George on their premises.

"You've never had a Dalby's Turbo! What kind of a tomb is this Scotland of yours?" Virginie handed Elspeth a muddy-coloured liquid. "Loathsome-looking, n'est ce pas? Believe me, there's naught better in the whole world."

Elspeth raised the cracked glass to her lips, the brew's caustic smell almost causing her to sneeze, and what looked like skelfs of wood making her wonder if she were the butt of a practical joke.

"Course it should be mixed with sarsaparilla, but this dump of an island is as free of sarsaparilla as it is of any other civilised thing."

"We make it with bark from the mauby tree," said George. "Drink up, and you'll see just how the eye can be deceived."

The first sip was shocking, due to the sharpness of the mauby sap, but quickly turning fresh on the palate, perfectly invigorating for a warm evening. Two sips more and Elspeth agreed it was one of the finest things she had ever tasted.

"What else has it?"

50

Virginie, proud to be reckoned the best mixer of Dalby's Turbo, listed the vital elements. "Tonight's particular mix, ma'am, includes fine Italian gin imported by our illustrious Lord Coak, a phial of pure bush rum lovingly and illegally distilled by the Belle Estate slave-gang and procured by Derrick here, a dousing of Mrs. Börgmann's own mauby, a little juice extracted from the cactus plant – and some few drops of the elixir of which the poet said, 'The poet's eye in his tipsy hour hath a magnifying power.'"

Elspeth had no idea who the poet in question was, or what the elixir was he was praising, but soon felt the promised effects in Virginie's Dalby's Turbo Calmative. The Caribbean breeze that wafted their balcony became gentler, cooler but still warm and nurturing, as if the dark velvet sky were exhaling perfumed breath. The tartness of the mauby electrified and enlivened her bones while relaxing her flesh and making her arms and legs buoyant, as though she were floating on the sea. The draught even seemed to improve her eyesight: as night closed softly around them, the features of Virginie and Isabella, Nonie and Christian, Mr. Denholm's under-study Derrick, and George, all darkened and, in contrast, their eyes brightened. She felt surrounded by stars, gleaming gazes and flashing glances, white teeth sparkling between ruby, kissable lips.

"We are pilgrims of the soul, don't you think George?" Isabella lounged over the balcony rail, black hair loose and trailing over her cheeks and neck. "We come from everywhere and, in our work, become everyone."

"And thus no one in particular," said Christian, his arm hung limply around Nonie's shoulder.

"Precisely! Don't Mohammedans believe that truth resides in nothingness?"

Elspeth had never heard such conversations before. Words skimmed freely like stones across water, and she watched them jump from Isabella to Derrick to George. It was a game she knew she could play: "I imagine," she ventured, "in the case of Mrs. Bartleby, whoever she is supposed to become, becomes her. She'd turn Cordelia into the Wife of Bath."

"Juliet the Procuress!"

"Jeanne d'Arc as played by La Celestina!"

It seemed whatever Elspeth said – whatever, as her mother would have said, "came up her hump" – was perfectly acceptable to these people. She felt knowledgeable; found she could pursue an argument, never thought of before, and end in unexpected places. If she could recall to mind only half a speech, or a fragment of a verse, miscalled an historical event or mistook one writer for another, no one cared. The words and thoughts themselves were enough, emancipated from the dull Scotch addiction to common sense and gravity. Only the style in which a thing was said was of any import. Language was all, if you were draped over a chair sipping on Dolby's Turbo.

"It is the followers of the Buddha, I think, who follow the path to nothingness," George gently informed the company. "Fools like Bartleby and Denholm are clay statues – on stage and off. Too rooted, heavy, nailed-down on their little plinths. For you – true artists – on nights like these you are the children of everythingness. Pure sensation. Your power is being of the world, not denying it."

Elspeth was the first to laugh. She didn't know why, only that George's seriousness struck her as funny. The others fell silent for a moment, looking at her, but she couldn't stop herself. At last Nonie joined in, then Derrick, and finally George, his laughter the most raucous, as he had been the cause of it.

"Thank the good Christ!" he cried, "for Elspeth Baillie, or I'd have carried on all night talking…"

"…Die Kacke!" cried Elspeth, easily imitating the American-accented German of Mr. Börgmann, and causing more laughter.

And yet Elspeth's intention had not been to inhibit their talk. Whether it was truly clever and learned or not made no difference to her. The experience was new, and free, and open to her. She could heedlessly follow the peculiarities of her mind and speak them out loud. If admiration or laughter followed, so much the better. In the lull that followed the laughing, she looked towards the dark horizon, at the other side of which she thought Scotland might lie. "At this very moment my sisters and cousins are singing ballads in some Lowland fair…"

"Not at this moment, quite. It's afternoon in the mother country."

"And a Mohammedan somewhere is praying on his mat…"

"While we fly on ours."

"…and that Buddha fellow circles the earth."

The mention of ballads inspired Nonie to sing an old Irish air, Christian humming and thumping his chair in accompaniment.

"I'm a roving young blade
I'm a piper by trade
And there's many the tunes I can play."

Virginie suggested a swim. They drank down the dreamy concoction in gulps and filed down wooden steps to a patch of sand in front of a treacle sea, Nonie and Christian singing in duet.

"So come fill up your glass
With brandy and wine
Whatever the cost, I will pay."

George led the way, tearing off jacket and boots. Derrick stripped down to his breeches, Nonie to her shift. Elspeth kicked her shoes far across the sand and ran, frightened, having never swum in the sea at night before, when it seemed like a deep crevice from which you might never emerge.

"So be easy and free
when you're drinking with me
I'm a man you don't meet every day!"

They splashed and yelled and squeaked. Derrick baptised them each in turn, immersing them wholly in water that felt thick like cream. When it came Elspeth's turn she sank deep under the warm blackness, the slow tide sticking her garments to her skin here, billowing them there. She could see up through the dark ocean, her friends undulating noiselessly above her.

"I baptise thee Elspeth, young Princess of the Lyric and Queen of the Song!" shouted Derrick as she splashed back up, catching her breath. They fought in the water together, hand-cupping the precious black liquid, hurling it from one to another. Nonie's hair covering her face, George's breeches contouring his broad thighs and – Elspeth was sure – swollen sex. Isabella, naked to the waist, turned around and around in a private trance that might have been Buddhist or Mohammedan, her brown breasts sailing. A distant moon turned their bodies to gold and the empty night sucked their shouts and laughter up into the sky.

* * * *

On the Tuesday night, after a day of watching the rehearsal she had now seen countless times, the same group set off towards the Ocean View to continue Monday's festivities. After only a single glass of Dalby's, however, Mrs. Börgmann brought her a note from Lord Coak, informing her that he was leaving the next day and would very much like her company at the Overtons' that evening.

He was waiting for her, not in the drawing room with Mr. and Mrs. Overton as she expected, but in the little anteroom next to her chamber in her servants' quarters. "I hope you don't mind me preventing your enjoyment of a companionable evening?"

There would be plenty more of those. Isabella's draught had relaxed her, and the walk through Garrison Savannah invigorated her. "It would be an ungracious girl who denied you a little time and company."

"I should tell you, Elspeth, that when I leave tomorrow, I will be gone for some time. Three months at least, perhaps more."

Elspeth responded with what she hoped was an acceptable mix of sorrow and consternation, only a little of both she actually felt. She had made friends here now, had gained confidence that she could make her own way, and would soon enough succeed well at the Lyric, even without Coak's presence. Still, he was her mentor and protector, and the prospect of losing him for so long a period made her feel a little vulnerable.

"I have spoken to Philbrick, and we have agreed that you should make your debut in two weeks' time."

"Two weeks! In what part?"

"We agreed that your first venture ought to be an interval performance, while the best role for you is being found. A short piece – perhaps a song, or a recitation. I think your Lady of the Lake would go down rather well."

Elspeth was delighted with the notion. She needn't learn any new lines, would have the stage to herself, and was sure a West Indian audience would be most affected by that ballad. Bring off a startling performance, excite a standing ovation, and her next appearance would surely be in a leading part. Without waiting to be asked – if he had any intention of doing so – she immediately began to rehearse for him.

"Huntsman, rest; thy chase is done,
Think not of the rising sun."

Isabella's tincture had chosen the verse for her. She felt suffused with a dreamy calm, but with no hint of sleepiness. She spoke the lines slower than usual, until that feeling she had had on stepping down from the boat onto her magical isle returned: either she was moving slower through the world, or the world had slowed around her. She turned her arms as if they were still in last night's black water, her body and head gliding, Scott's words floating on the air.

"Rest! thy chase is done,
While our slumbrous spells assail ye."

Coak smiled and followed closely every tiny movement of her hands, her fingers. She felt with him the way she did with an audience who were keeping pace with her; an audience whose single mind worked in unison with her own. She undressed. Not lewdly – the way she had glimpsed Glasgow hoors doing in vulgar city taverns – nor even delicately. But plain and prosaic, like a woman humming as she readies herself, alone, for bed. And in so doing, she actually felt alone, Coak's presence fading from her. She was an isolated woman, stepping out of skirts and drawers, shaking off shoes, for no one's enjoyment – not even her own. Her song sounded above her casual actions, as if sung by another; and Coak ebbed away like George's Buddha, fading happily into nothingness.

"Sleep! nor dream in yonder glen,
Here no bugles sound reveillé."

IV

With Coak gone, Elspeth found herself more and more in the company of George Lisle. He was a much admired – not least by himself – and risqué humorist. He liked to inform everyone that he was a disciple of the philosophy of Free Love. "Naturally, it's the theory which appeals, intellectually. Not necessarily the vulgar practice."

She was perfectly aware that Lisle's position allowed him to take mistresses, all the while conspiring with his father to marry well. But wouldn't the former of the two destinies – lover rather than wife – be a cannie adventure! Elspeth felt she had the skills required to play the scandalous *innamorata*.

Like any other young woman, she had dreamed of a handsome young man – a gentleman not unlike George – falling so deeply and irrevocably in love with her that he would horrify polite society, sacrifice his heritage, and take her publicly as a wife. But there was enough of the hardened travelling player in her to know that such romanticism was best left between proscenium arches. She could waste her life hoping for such a bold champion to happen along. A more realistic proposition was to settle for being mistress, and enter into an arrangement which would allow her to live independently while continuing unhindered with her career. If any children were to result from the liaison, she judged it preferable that they enjoyed a moneyed, rather than a legitimate, start in life. In Scotland, she had heard tales of supposed noblemen without a farthing to their name. And, even if George tired of her, she calculated he was not the type to throw her overboard altogether. When the time came – as come it must – when he forsook her, she considered it likely that he would continue both their friendship and his financial support. She even considered suggesting such a scheme to George himself. But it occurred to her that, should he reject her and the snub become known, it would have a detrimental effect on her standing, and be too harsh a blow to withstand personally. And what would Lord Coak make of such an arrangement? Four months her patron would be gone – not long enough for her and George to live out the three-act drama that was forming in her head. And doubtless, even from abroad, Coak was being kept up to date of goings-on at Bridgetown by Philbrick and others.

So, for the meantime, she let the friendship grow. George became more liberal in his attitude towards her: taking her hand in company, remarking openly on her figure and costume, kissing her delicately on the cheek. All this in the bare light in open society. On those nights when Isabella made up her Dalby's Turbo, the kissing became less subtle. On the mornings following those parties, events of the night before were a little hazy. Certainly, they all drank, played dice sometimes with the gamesters, swam, always talking and always cavorting. She could taste George's lips on her own, but sometimes, too, she thought, Derrick's, and even Christian's, though he and Nonie were devoted fiancés. As the sun trickled early into her room, before Tuesday or Dainty brought her her bowl-and-water, her drowsy head was strewn with pools of dark seawater, the tang of mauby, twinklings of stars, of Nonie's white and Isabella's brown breasts, suggestions of the boys' naked backs, and suspicions that she might well have surpassed them all in acts of public indecency. No one ever made mention of what they had got up to the night before, until they reconvened, by which time all details were lost or dismissed.

During waking hours she practised her poem in a room made specially available for her by Mr. Philbrick. At luncheon, and of an evening – sometimes instead of joining the others at the View – George took her to the Careenage, where they walked and talked, and sipped tea on the porches of grander hotels. She loved how the boats – from tiny skiffs to magnificent yachts and ocean-going ships – rocked on the water, masts and ropes chiming like Sunday bells. Just as he had taught her the names of plants and animals, George instructed her on shipping, pointing out across the harbour, distinguishing clippers from windjammers, sail from steam.

"The old three-master is a supply ship. Raises its sails thrice a year to return to Bristol. You ought to see it at full rig – a sight dying on our seas, sadly. It'll be replaced by the likes of that ugly great hulk there. A steamship, bringing wood and coal in from the forests and mines of America."

They sat together on the terrace of the Regency Hotel, the waiters bowing to her in her distinguished company.

"The clipper out beyond the quay? You won't see many more of those either, if there's any justice. A slave ship, ferrying its foul cargo from Senegal to Liverpool to here." George declared himself to be an Emancipist. "Though don't tell my father. That's a little surprise I'm saving up for when I'm master of my own fate."

He spoke to her about politics as if she were already tutored in the subject, and took for granted her interest in it. Wilberforce and the Houses of Parliament in London, the local contest between the aristocratic Pumpkin faction and the merchants of the Salmagundi alliance. For that fortnight in the summer of 1831 Elspeth dallied with her beau, planned her stage debut, dreaming of great achievements from Georgetown to Washington., while she learned about the evils of slavery, and tasted the delights of the beau monde.

Excitement was building for the imminent debut of the new young talent from the British stage. Playbills had been pasted up and the local newspapers carried half-page advertisements. The financiers of the Lyric were animated by her long-term plans. She brought to their attention new works which had been highly praised in Great Britain, by Sir Walter Scott and her own namesake Joanna Baillie. She caused great argument with the suggestion, casually mentioned during an interview with the *Gazette*, that the Lyric produce its own version of Mrs. Shelley's terrifying tale Doctor Frankenstein. She went so far, on the whim of the moment – the memory of her meeting with Henry still fresh in her mind – as to suggest that a Negro be cast in the role of the Creature. George and even Mr. Philbrick congratulated her on achieving more publicity in one fell swoop than the Lyric had received in its entire existence. The radicals were divided on the issue. Of her own circle, Virginie and Nonie argued passionately about it, while the traditionalists – including Mr. Bartleby and, to her alarm, her landlords Mr. and Mrs. Overton – were outraged at the very idea of a darkie performing on a civilised stage. Whatever the politics of her sally, Elspeth succeeded in making a name for herself throughout the island.

George convoyed her daily from the theatre to her lodging house, trying to shock her with jokes and remarks and off-colour observations. Elspeth laughed and remained staunchly unshocked. Together they made their way, she with her parasol and Mr. Lisle in his hat, across the Careenage, past the bright clean stone of Lord Nelson's statue, along Bay Street, the sea to their right stretching all the way to South America, where lay jungles and mountains and savage Indians who tore the beating heart from maidens to offer as sacrifices to the gods. And on towards Garrison where the comely couple would pass companies of soldiers on drill and the officers commanded the men to salute the lady.

"They can't realise I'm just an actress."

"It's your beauty they're saluting. They don't give tuppence for your status. Sensible chaps."

A short six months ago it was all so unimaginable. Elspeth Baillie, elegantly dressed and parasoled, hair gleaming like the setting sun, complexion bright, traversing a capital city on the arm of an affable, young heir to a fortune. She had sworn to herself that she would never write home. She would never again make contact with those dreary people of the drenched and muddy world she had been made to inhabit utterly against her nature. The only shame of it was that now she couldn't describe all the wonderful things that were happening to her dismissive father, her timorous mother, or her faithless friends, not one of whom had seen her off on her life's journey, nor even congratulated her on her stroke of extraordinary luck.

Her debut recital at the Lyric Theatre was scheduled for the eleventh of August. The announcement was made on a Wednesday, at the end of the run of the present season of plays. One last gala performance at the season's official close – traditionally a short play accompanied by sketches and comical interludes – was advertised to take place that weekend. Calderon de la Barca's *La Aurora en Copacabana*, severely edited and freshly translated by a young colonial scholar, John Colliemore, distilled the saga of the Conquistadors down to several moving scenes between Pizarro and an Inca Princess. That role was to be played by Mrs. Bartleby, though the father, in the shape of Christy Bloom, was twenty years her junior. Virginie and Derrick were to perform the finale, the death scene of Dona Sol and Hernani, from a piece that was pitting audiences against critics in Paris, while Nonie spoke a soliloquy from *The White Slave*. The gala ensured the biggest audience of the entire year, and it was at the second interval – after a performance of dancing dogs – that Elspeth Baillie would be presented to the people of Bridgetown.

Her final rehearsal was effected before an audience of fellow players, stagehands, writers, investors, and all their partners. She made few mistakes, found a rhythm suitable to the occasion and, all in all, discharged her duty well enough in difficult circumstances. Taking her bow, Mr. Denholm and Mrs. Bartleby offered her from their pews some little notes of advice, to which Elspeth paid no attention. Mr. Philbrick's anxiety on her behalf – that she would have to soften her Scots, move less busily around the stage, work on her projection – insulted her, while the vociferous encouragement of Nonie and Ginny, Bella and Christy buoyed her almost as much as George's obdurate trust in her powers.

George Lisle had turned up faithfully for each and every one of her rehearsals, offering his own nuggets of advice, but in such humble tones, as from a pupil to a maestro, that she listened attentively to him.

"I think you will do well enough now, Miss Baillie."

"Well enough?" cried George. "You'll hear gasps and sighs such as you, Philbrick, are a stranger to."

He ran up to the stage, took her hand and stood proudly by her side. "I predict instant success. If this woman is not completely and immediately the official darling of the entire colony, I'll eat my best hat, and then yours." He presented her with a variety of boxes, tied prettily with ribbons, one marked "Robe en style Pauline Bonaparte". Inside, a beautiful, diaphanous dress, double-layered in muslin and crinoline, the outer part hanging low at the neck, the inner, more translucent still despite its intricate laced pattern, would cling closer, and not much higher, to the décolleté. An exquisite little box contained silk slippers with silver stitching.

Virginie and Isabella were more excited by the raiment – so unusual now that bustles and pantalettes were the standard fashion, and so fragile that they must be breathtakingly expensive – than by Elspeth's performance. They managed, eventually, to tear themselves away from the boxes and say everything expected of them. Nonie clapped loud and long. Derrick and the rest of the boys cheered at the tops of their voices. Christian stood up on his seat and declared, "She won't leave a dry eye in the house!"

"Nor even a dry seat!" rejoined George.

"Especially if she wears that on stage!" whispered Virginie to Isabella.

The young Turks left the older members and repaired to the Ocean View, and after an innocent tea and rum, George walked Elspeth back to her quarters, strolling arm-in-arm, saying their halloes to all who passed, and then, when the rain came on unexpectedly, making a sudden dash, laughing and shouting.

Elspeth revelled in the new experience of warm rain, the drops soaking her hair, running down her neck and back like fingertips stroking her. She held her face up to the sky, marvelling that such puffy little clouds in a blue, blue sky could produce any kind of downpour. The rain showered her eyelids and lips – without a hint of the stinging cold that used to permeate her skin and make her insides shiver. She and George ran into her rooms and took off their outer layer of clothing, leaving George in his shirt and she in her shift. They laughed at the audacity of it, like children illicitly dressing up in their parents' clothes.

"No harm in it. The dressing rooms are like this all the time," said Elspeth.

"You must invite me round sometime."

"Back home we were always like this. Cattle sheds don't have changing rooms. Aunts, cousins, brothers, parents all together."

"But did they all feel quite so naked as I do under your glare?"

To warm their innards, George concocted a cheroot of tobacco and another leaf she had already seen, but never tasted, at the Lyric. Nonie had advised against it.

"She says bang enslaves the mind."

"Nonie's mind does a good enough job of enslaving itself. If I were to worry about the ill-effects of crops on public health, I would be more concerned by cotton than bang."

"Cotton!" Elspeth laughed. "I've never seen anyone drink or eat cotton to their detriment."

"Cotton does something much worse – enslaves the majority of humankind. One way or another."

The cigarette smoked, they shared a nightcap of rum, and finally fell together onto Elspeth's bed as the evening outside brightened after the rain.

Her hair was still wet and she was drenched through to her undergarments, though she could no longer discern what moisture belonged to the shower and what was her longing for George. In her dreams of how it would be to make love to a fine and sophisticated gentleman, she had imagined crisp, clean linen and a large bed, something approaching both of which she now had. But she had also pictured the scene to take place in darkness, yet here there was still a soft light flushing the room. The gentleman would have whispered to her in French – a language she knew nothing of, save for the odd word or phrase in speeches she had learned. He would undress her slowly in the velvety darkness, kiss her gently, woo her into submission. She would be wearing exactly the kind of garments George had just given her that day: delicate, sensuous fabrics, revealing more than was decent. She'd never got round to opening the boxes and changing into the exquisite clothes. The remainder of the reverie was lost in a blur of enchantment, but had very little in common with her rather more mundane experiences with ploughboys.

Now that she was with George she found to her surprise she had no desire to follow that dream. Nor, it appeared, did he. Thomas in the field handled her more subtly at his tree-trunk, had not gone at her in the frenzy that George suddenly displayed, and Elspeth, in the heat of the moment, was glad of it. The ploughboy hadn't gawked and spluttered quite as clumsily as this polished young gentleman. Those old notions of gentle caresses seemed to her suddenly a child's fantasy. She found herself wanting to utilise the arts she had developed for her patron and have a younger, lustier man gaze upon her. Her peach-coloured skin and supple body – more radiant and slender, she knew, since her transposition to the Indies – should be enjoyed by more than an old fop who had no interest in touching the fruit he gazed on.

No man apart from Albert Coak had pondered her gentle slopes and tidy lines, or appreciated the autumn leaf of her sex, or noticed how her hair twined round her neck and streamed down the delta of her back. He may have given no sign of wishing to approach her, but at least he had appreciated the view she offered. With George she had lost any vestige of shyness. It seemed to her that in that moment, in the mysterious light of another continent she was her body. No more and no less, and she took pleasure in exhibiting herself boldly, joyfully, pushing herself away from her lover so he could exploit the spectacle better. Her body itself, as if by itself, demanded to be seen, and she curled herself rudely round him, hearing his lust, grasping at every part of him, and being grasped in return. Her mind was aware only of their limbs and their combined movements – apart from involuntary lines and strophes learned in the heaths of Scotland flitting through her carnal desires. Flickering humming-birds in a thunderous sky.

"I have immortal longings in me."

And, perhaps because his gaze was so intense and grateful she found that she too wanted to gaze. To wonder at the porcelain skin of a well-kept and kempt young man. The angles of him, the dark curls around his head and haloing his sex. "I've always loved a standing ovation." They laughed in mutual gratitude and complicity; then became serious again, intent on the grave business between them. They locked eyes and saw reflected between them youthful devilry. Yet, annoyingly, her rational mind began to stir again. The room, the bed, the rain all impinged on her; her clothes, the sound of her own voice and accent, could not quite be silenced. As on stage, she would have to work harder, push the part she was playing to its limits, to inhabit it completely.

Thomas had used the worst kind of language towards her and though at the time she felt she ought to be offended, she now wanted to use those very words – and hear them in return. She hissed words in George's ear she hardly knew the meaning of herself and which an English-educated colonial could only guess at. She voiced expressions she'd heard the gamblers at the View use as they played their killer cards to force the hand of an opponent. Her calls of coggie, prick, pap, drove George to include, amongst more amorous murmurs, obscenities of his own. His blurts of quim and fuck excited her, but also returned her to the reality of their situation: low-born Scot debauching a superior landowner's son. As on the Alba when she considered which of all the possible Elspeths she must one day become, she was bewildered – happily so – at what kind of Elspeth she was now. Lusty lass of the soil? Bohemian free-thinker? The artful mistress or virgin bride? Her body seemed decided on lusty lass and the language she found them both using eliminated virginal maiden. She remembered poor Tom's pleas, as if they were lines in a script by a forgotten master, and turned them into urgent commands, ordering her social superior where to look, when to touch, when not to, what to say. George pulled at her shift, bit her hair; they kneeled on the bed, his body pressing her up against the wall behind.

At last their urgency began to blot out the room, the night outside the window, her sense of herself. He seemed to move around her in disconnected flashes: his eyes staring, penis below her then behind her, his hands clutching her, then himself, as if they both might break up, spin away from the centre of themselves.

Instead of laying her down he pushed her upwards, his head working its way down her body and sucking, not kissing. She knew from colleagues at the theatre it was common practice for well-born men in this Colony to be introduced to intimacy in the brothels of Bridgetown. George's display was clearly more than mere instinct. She felt envious of those scarlet women – of their knowledge and candour, and dearly wished to outperform them in her new lover's eyes. She thrust her flank out for him and, as she did, some distant part of her wondered if this was how a high-born man would abuse a commoner like her, and remembered her father's dire warning – she'd become nothing more than a weel-travelled hoor. Even if that was so, she didn't care. She would use this slim young gent, his skin and hair soaked with lust, as much as he used her.

"Open yourself for me," he said in a low tone, as if in the voice of some other; some being lost inside him. She did, and knew she had found another role to excel in – temptress, fallen woman. If this was the future her father had predicted – wantonness and immorality – then she felt no shame in the least. She returned George's look with a brazen stare of her own, savouring every sharp angle, the tightening of his buttocks, his livid sex, the drops of sweet sweat on gold skin and black hair, the pain of desire in his eyes. Her body took over completely once again, her movements like thoughts. Each had captured the other utterly, and in that captivity Elspeth wondered at this new version of herself.

She waited for George to leave before sunrise, readying herself for the inevitability of many clandestine farewells to come. She anticipated lonely mornings, sudden desertions, the hollowness of absence. There was nothing to be done about it. George was her illicit lover for the time being only. She let him slumber for as long as she thought safe, then kissed him awake. They lay apart for a moment, as if astonished to find themselves alone in bed with last night's words and actions buzzing around them, biting, like mosquitoes. George looked down at his own body, like a man looking at a stranger.

But he did not, as she expected, leap from her bed, pull on his clothes and run to the door, embracing her hastily before leaving – maybe forever. He lay on, hardly waking, nuzzling in to her.

"Shouldn't you be home before breakfast?"

"I should."

"Then better wake up. I don't want you banished from here quite so soon."

But when George refused to go home, she said, "If we're discovered, there'll be all manner of trouble."

"If you're worried for your own sake, then I'll leave…"

"What sake would that be? I'm an actress. I've no one to scandalise."

"And nor do I care a jot what anyone says."

"Not even your father?"

"Least of all."

Young gentlemen were no doubt permitted a limited number of mistakes. The dawn was calm and warm and soft, and she wanted nothing more than to keep George's body close to hers and gave up persuading him to go.

When morning proper came they woke to a sun shining heartily, the air crisp and clean and fresh, their bodies touching one another at ankle, thigh and shoulder. Still George did not rise from the bed, but lay there as if in a trance, beaming smiles at her, his fingers clasped around hers. The sun rose higher over the most perfect of days, with hardly a wisp of wind to blow the casuarinas and laburnum trees outside her window, or convince a bird to sing more than was necessary. The whole world seemed in a stupor, induced by the beauty and violence of their first night together. At last Elspeth mustered the willpower to stir, wrapped herself in her nightgown, and went to Daisy's and Tuesday's room in the basement.

"If anyone from the theatre calls, tell them I'm resting today."

Tuesday and Dainty tried to hide them but she caught their smiles as they turned their heads away. Should she be angry – scold them for their prying and presumption? They were only doing what she would have done in similar circumstances. They must have heard George and her last night. Not in detail, she hoped, just activity in the room above them. Even that made her shuffle in front of the two, now over-serious, faces. But Tuesday and Dainty weren't the Overtons, or even their English-educated handmaids. From what she had heard at the Ocean View, Africans were creatures of love and lust. They coupled continuously and according to Virginie so randomly it was almost inadvertent.

Elspeth had the idea – from where, she didn't know – that these foreign couplings were torpid, spiritless affairs. An act darkies were driven to perform, the very acceptability of it amongst their own kind robbing it of any danger and passion. Whatever they had heard the night before was just more strange behaviour from white people. She instructed them that she was not be disturbed all day, and that only a tray of fruit and a jug of water should be left outside her room later in the morning. The maids smiled more openly – as if she had made some confession to them, allowed them a degree of intimacy. And perhaps she had. Their stifled laughter reminded her of younger cousins back home, herself a short while ago, sniggering at the slightest suspicion of adult intimacy.

Back in her room, she dressed for the day. George rose and dressed, too. Both feigned composure, but dressed themselves quickly, backs half turned to each other.

"You've no regrets?"

The question took her by surprise, but she knew what he meant. That they should have made love was beyond question unregrettable. It was the manner in which they had done it that was causing them to worry. Now, literally in the light of day – a sharp all-disclosing tropical light – she panicked. She felt more naked than she had last night, shameful parts of her soul exposed that no hand could modestly cover. She felt her colour flame high and saw images of her previous self, only a few hours ago, flash before her eyes. How wanton! How crude she had been! Those fierce words she had spoken – no, shouted – like a wildcat! She had twisted and distorted herself so that he – a well-born gent, almost a stranger to her – could peer into her most personal corners. Now it appeared to her that their lovemaking was not only vulgar but that, instead of being elevated by a social superior, she had degraded his sensibility.

Then she became aware of the same vexation in his eyes. He had not asked the question in triumph, callously, but hesitantly, anxiously. "I was a little earthy with you last night."

He saw the crime as his, not hers! Having had his fun with a gullible actress, he was now concerned for her. The shame she had momentarily felt began to lift from her. Yet still, those acts that had seemed natural at the height of their passion belonged to a new class of encounter, and to a new inexplicable Elspeth, that she could not bring herself to speak of directly, or even refer to them. With some effort, she replied, "Perhaps I was not so ladylike myself."

George Lisle threw his head back and laughed. "You were not! By Christ you weren't!" He took her hand and cradled it, kneading out of her the last drops of embarrassment. Strange, how some parts of life cannot be spoken of, even thought of, but are easily undertaken, acted out. We think of ourselves as children of words, of actions that can be considered, or at least reflected upon, but there were great furrows of her life that could not be talked about openly.

Events so real to her but which, later, had to be tucked away, even from herself. The embarrassment began to grow again between the two of them, and the only way out of the predicament was through touching again. He kissed her and brought her tightly against him, until she was lost in his bulk, fumbled through waistcoat, linen and serge for the touch of him. Her body responded to the rustle of her own garments, the silks and satins and brocade that Lord Coak had gifted her.

Before their passions rose beyond control, they retired quickly to the window-seat and wondered at the change of hue daylight gave to their skin: her rose-pink and auburn of last night diluted in the sun to peach and amber; burgundy strands in his coal-black hair. The scents, sounds and movements of her tropical garden pervaded the room. His fingertips frisked for her through shift and drawers, birds delving and digging for flesh. Some feelings are to mortals given, with less of earth in them than heaven. She saw his shoulders and elbows and sex as palms and succulents that looked hard and unforgiving but which became pliant to the touch. She felt strong and straight, her skin renewed by the morning sun and fresh sea air. The steady, building heat of the day drew them towards the same ferocity and tenderness they had experienced the evening before.

They luxuriated in the yards of time they now had at their disposal – George, clearly, had no intention of going anywhere. Last night had seemed to her urgent; now they felt no hurry and she found more in him to look at, found new textures, new sounds, gentler words than before. They each whispered how beautiful the other was. They broke off from their urges to enjoy a simple caress of the face, a kiss on closed eyelids and lashes. Their initiation over, they could ease each other, lose their fear of what was permissible and what was not. Nothing was improper between them now. There was not a touch, a kiss, a posture, a word in this or any other language denied to them. No part of their combined bodies was out of bounds, or something one feared the other might shield or withhold.

As their second night approached, they sat again by the open window, though the air outside felt hotter than the room. The sun – a glow of such perfect crimson that even George admitted to never having seen such a beautiful sundown in all his days in the Tropics – began setting over the ocean. The only movement was the swiftly scudding clouds high in the darkening sky. From behind them came the odd flash of lightning; then thunder in its wake, low and distant. But whenever they relaxed, left off from touching and returned to the realm of words, Elspeth would worry again about the consequences of his staying with her so long.

"Don't ye have a hame t' gang to, my jo?"

The rustic talk was meant to cover her anxiety – after all, their love-vocabulary included the bawdiest of vulgar Scots. Words which young George Lisle was quick to learn. But immediately she had done so, she feared that, rather than impress him with her talented mimicry, she had shown her true, low-born self. George did not appear to notice. He simply shrugged and said, "They're used to me being out all night."

The look on her face was enough to betray an additional anxiety – but George assured her, between caresses, that his absences had not been with other women, but those nights carousing and gambling at the Ocean View. They ate the last of the fruit the maids had left for them, feeding one another papaya, mango and orange, sharing the escaping juices.

Then, quite literally out of the blue – there was not a rain cloud in the sky that they could see, only wisps of scarlet trailing high in the sky – it began to rain. After the intense, oppressive heat of the long day, the shower was like a blessing, as if the heavens were reassuring them that their sin – if sin it was – was being washed away. They leaned out of the window and let the water fall on their hair and cool their skin. The coconut and banana trees swayed and bowed outside in the grounds, and as the shower became heavier, the drops began to fall fast, straight as a die, a curtain of sparkling steel, dense as mail, severing them from the rest of the world. Elspeth prayed that the weather would imprison them, if not forever, then at least up to the last moment before her heralded entrée at the Lyric theatre. The wind rose, and fell, then built again. The sun had all but dropped into the ocean, blood-red and surrounded by a halo of black. George had never witnessed this particular pattern of natural events before.

"You have the profoundest effect upon the world, Ellie. To change me was a good trick – but to change the aspect of the sun itself!"

"Perhaps there's a real storm brewing."

"Then let it last for a century!"

It was unwise for George to take to the road, and they were fated to spend a second night together. The constant low grumbling of thunder grew steadily more ferocious. George strained to peer out the window, looking south along the coast.

"Perhaps the storm's on the other side of the island."

They dressed – enough for modesty – and Elspeth called out for one of the servants. Dainty told them that a storm was indeed raging, and not so very far from them. Housemaids of the Overtons had just returned from town, having seen the wildness of the sea playing havoc with ships at Carlisle Bay.

By nightfall, the rain had abated but the winds were worse. They went back to bed and he cradled her in his arms, looked deeply and long into her eyes, and told her he loved her. He said it with such sadness, as if he knew the loss implicit in his words. And she believed him; began to feel that perhaps, she too, was capable of real love for this man. She lay awake hours into the night listening to the trees being blown about, and her gentleman's soft, regular, breaths. She rehearsed in her head the Lady of the Lake for tomorrow's first performance, while stroking her lover's brow.

"Each purple peak, each flinty spire,
Was bathed in floods of living fire.
But not a setting beam could glow
Within the dark ravines below…"

This storm was no accident. Like the sailor sacrificed at her departure, here was a further sign of things to come. The sea whipped itself into a frenzy and Elspeth shivered with delight at the sweeping away of the past, and the advent of further pleasures and accolades to come.

V

She awoke to the shaking of the stone around her; opened her eyes
to see a turret of the great mansion drop outside her window, crum-
bling like a sugar column. It exploded somewhere unseen below a
moment later, a grey dense cloud rising in its wake. George jumped
up with a shout, stared in amazement first at the night outside – the
gale howling, timbers groaning – and then at her. The floor beneath
them rose up, as if a beast below were breaking the surface of the
sea, tossing a boat a fraction of its size out of its way.

He cried, "Jesus!" and Elspeth flinched at the blasphemy. Cursed
herself for their many sins that had brought hell's hand from out of
the depths.

George took hold of her and marched her – the two of them near
naked – through the bedroom door, down the shuddering stairs,
out into the fury of the night. He drove her on through the gardens. Where to, she couldn't imagine. Rain like she had never seen
before spewed from the sky. Long freezing spears hurled by some
demented spirit. The noise of the wind: stone cracking, wood buck-
ling. Figures darting here and there, silhouettes from other broken
wings of the house flying past, all in such confusion that Elspeth
could make no sense of anything. By the time they had put a little
distance between themselves and the house, half of it had been
torn away, brick and plaster dissolving in floodwaters. They waded
through slough and mud where the garden had been only hours
before.

George shouted angrily at her, "Get a move on!" As if the storm
were of her making. A trap to lead him to his death.

Then, abruptly, the storm stalled. Simply stopped, like a candle
blown out. Not a bird sang, nor a tree moved. The silhouettes faded
into the night, falling stones poised mid-air, and trees, half-felled,

swayed, as if wondering what force had bent them into this position. The world holding its breath, petrified at the sky's hatred. She saw then where George was leading her, and she tried to pull back. He hauled her towards Henry's feeble chattel-house. If the bulk and strength of the great stone mansion had not been enough to protect them, what chance would they have in the flimsy little hut of the gardener's?

"Wood bends with the wind. It doesn't collapse."

They were surrounded by massive trees blown over like skittles. Roots had torn up the earth, waving gutlessly in the air, over the deep wounds they had made in the gardens. She followed, pulled along by her stumbling protector. Henry opened his door and ran towards them, lumbering through water and wreckage. A dull red light began to gleam as if the heavens were opening a bloodshot eye to look on the catastrophe they were causing. The gardener wore no shirt and his breeches had been torn and rolled up at the calf, just like her image of him as Frankenstein's Creature. The brutal embodiment of the storm itself. She reviled his blackness; wished hopelessly for the calming wisdom of a Lord Coak, an Overton, a superior white man from a steadfast castle; an elder who would know how to deal with Nature's stupid temper.

Henry made straight for Elspeth and lifted her at the waist, held her above the water as though she were a mucky child. She hung on to George's hand, as he stumbled along beside them, pale and shocked. Henry strode more steadily, stronger than George, more used to physical exertion. The rain began again, and a wind gently whistled. The night's orange light gave Henry's and George's eyes a lost, ghostly look.

Inside Henry's house his wife and children – more of them than she had realised – were huddling on the bedstead, keeping their feet curled around them, above the waterline. The gardener sat Elspeth down on a high shelf that ran along one side of the house. To make more space for her he cleared, with one lunge of his massive arm, all the cooking utensils and gardening tools and knick-knacks, letting them fall into the water and float or sink along with the rest of the debris. He repositioned her and then turned away as though he had just put an old doll of his daughter's out of reach.

George tried to clamber up beside her, but fell back down with a little cry of pain. Henry came to his aid, and the two men spoke. She could not understand what they said. Not because she couldn't hear them – the hut was as quiet as the grave, the sky still inhaling – but her brain could not organise the sounds into any meaning. Even words, her old allies, failed her. Henry helped George up and sat him beside her, then bounced the shelf up and down to demonstrate its strength, proud that his workmanship was of value in calamitous circumstances.

"You be safe up here. That mantel take any weight and you a li'l elfy ting, Mistress."

Everything Henry did he did merely in the way of duty. His face betrayed no real emotion. He had gone out to round them up as a shepherd might gather in his landlord's sheep. The hard fact struck Elspeth like a falling stone. All of them – the smiling maids and servants, the skivvies at the theatres – they all giggled or nodded, assented to everything, because duty demanded it. His chores done, Henry turned back to his family, pulled two of the older children in towards him on the tabletop. His wife and younger daughters remained sitting on the bedstead, placid and staring into space, glancing at their visitors, clumped together in the soaked, muddied bedclothes.

The last thing Elspeth could remember was the sound of the wind getting its second terrifying breath, and thinking she would never sleep again. She laid her head on George's shoulder; he raised his hand to stroke her but could not reach out far enough. He gave another cry of pain. She lowered her head onto his lap and he stroked her hair with his other hand. Then, miraculously, sleep came after all. She drifted into the safety and calm of inner darkness, George whispering in the distance, "Be over soon. Rest now."

Now it was calm, the light peeking in the windows fresh and clear, sparkling like a rock pool in the early morning. She had regained partial wakefulness often enough during the night to know that the storm had built to at least one more riotous climax. She had dreamt that she was back on the Alba, the wind and rain pitching Henry's hut more than the Atlantic ocean had ever shaken her cabin. She would have chosen the terrors of the high seas any day to the reality of this morn – calm and untroubled as it deceitfully was.

The air was distilled and sweet; the world weightless, her body like a feather. The birds sang and the sea in the distance swished calm and regular. The echoes of last night's howling wind and crashing trees and stone and bricks now murmured only softly in her ears. George's judgement had proved correct – the chattel-house still stood steady. The water level had risen and pots and pans and loose articles had been tossed around. But the cast of human characters remained unchanged. Everyone was where they were when she had fallen asleep, all open-eyed, like a chorus required to hold their positions. Statues of loss and confusion. Henry and the two youths on the table, his wife and smaller children on the bed. The gardener woke a little after Elspeth and gently lifted the two boys he had been supporting, setting them down on the crowded bed with hardly a motion on their part. His legs, as he swung round to alight from the table, sank into the flood up to his thighs. He slushed through the water and the floating remains of his livelihood, and pulled the door open. The water from outside met the water within and created a little eddy around his bare legs. Looking out the open door, Elspeth saw the full extent of the damage.

The sea had leapt unaccountably from its bed. The sky had cracked and crumbled, and everything that ever was, was ripped up by its roots. The gods, she thought, are children who leave a shameful guddle behind their pranks and games. How on earth could such a supernatural mess be cleared by mere mortals? The day ahead would be different from the one she had been expecting – the day of her debut, the day she had been working towards and planning for months. She nursed the idea for a moment that things might be put back in order for her recital tonight, and nearly smiled at such a foolish hope.

Where does one start to tidy a clutter like that? Pick up that tree? Sort out the walls of the house from the roof? See if there is anyone buried under the rubble? Look for things left whole and undestroyed, pile them to one side? Wake up George now, or let him sleep?

None of these were matters for a woman like Elspeth to decide.

Her father had ever railed against her for being "haunless, daft and yissless". She had claimed, to him and inwardly to herself, that, when a true crisis came, she would rise to the challenge. Her daily ineffectiveness – striking sets and camp, loading carts – would be overcome and she would find within herself an heroic capacity. Well, here was a crisis beyond her worst expectations, and no heroism stirred.

What they must do, she and George, was find people to help them. Henry was strong, but not strong enough to do the work of twenty, forty men. How many would it take to rebuild this little corner of the world? Henry had his own house to put in order, and then his duty was to his own master at the mansion. His wife and children stared dumbly at him as if at any moment he would turn around and smile, lift all the chaos away with his huge arms, drain the water and clear the mud, turn the day into one like any other. They followed his every move – fishing out a passing joist, plucking it from the water, then throwing it back again. It chilled Elspeth's heart to think that even a functional and instinctive being like Henry was at a loss.

She had to get down from this shelf. George had to call on the resources of his father's house. People, servants, maids, slave-gangs who could get a good day's work done, construct somewhere for them to be this evening. The first task was to wake him and send him off to muster helpers, bring tea and food, set about putting things in order. She dreeped down from her shelf, slipping into the warm sludge, stretched and took a hold of George's hand. It was cold from the wet and wind. She looked back out through the door, getting a broader view than from atop the shelf. Her vision was unobstructed for miles. Nothing stood to impede the view. The ground was strewn as far as the eye could see with rafters, planks, tabletops, chair legs – like a Glasgow barroom after a brawl – bricks and stones, blue porch tiles, red roof beams, chimneys, felled palms and grapefruit trees, single plantains and coconuts, everything higgelty-piggelty. Sugar canes, snapped up and thrown from fields miles away, floated past the chattel shack, leaving a tang of sweetness in the air.

George was huddled into his coat, face towards her, calm and calming, as he had been throughout the worst of it, protecting his mistress chivalrously throughout the storm, finding this sanctuary for them to survive the night. She shook him.

"George," she said, soothingly. "Georgie."

His body juddered to her touch instead of rocking or waking. Henry watched her trying to rouse him, and made his way back through the deluge towards her. George slumped forward and she saw the splinter of mahogany protrude from his side.

"Had that in him last night. Didn't want to pull it out. Save him bleeding."

Elspeth nodded. The spear must have struck him on the way out of the house, or in the gardens where bits of the world flew about animated by the force of the storm. This complicated matters. In the midst of this catastrophe George's death felt matter-of-course to her: another little piece of an enormous mess that would somehow have to be dealt with. As she dragged her legs, entangled in her muddied robe, she felt sorry for him. What a price to pay for two nights of gentleman's pleasure! If only he had had the sense to go home, he would not now be sitting, cowped on a shelf, like a broken mannequin. Pleasure is a wanton curse. Drink it and ye'll find him out. She paddled towards the door, out into the fresh, bleached day.

Elspeth Baillie lost in her land of dreams. The water at her feet raced away at her step, and she walked forward with the sure step she had learned from years of tramping through peat-bogs and lowland marshes. The sun sparkled and the air was sharp and diamond-bright, but her head was slumped low again, her shoulders huddled, as if she were battling against the old bluster and sleet. She had nowhere to go; no one to go to. No father or mother. No Lord Coak or Nonie. No Dainty or Tuesday to be seen. No George Lisle.

She walked and she walked, thoughts tumbling like blown leaves: George naked, George dead, the wailing Creature, Henry her saviour. Lines from roles and songs and poems. Gin a body kiss a body, need a body cry? Past the chasm where the house she had slept in with her lover had stood only hours earlier. With effort, she raised her head and looked out from Savannah, scanned the horizon. Half of Bridgetown had vanished. People in the distance wandered as she did, in ones and twos, dazed and aimless. There was weeping in the breeze; there were gaps in the world, whole neighbourhoods vanquished. Between the Garrison and Trafalgar an immense hole, like the fascinating cavity of a pulled tooth. The Synagogue was gone. The barracks were crushed. Fort Charles no longer protected anything, its saluting soldiers swept away. The Lyric Theatre, and with it all her plans, had been picked up and hurled into the sea – the smug sea that lay before her, calm, smiling, unconcerned. She walked on, automatically heading back towards town. Like one that on a lonesome road, doth walk in fear and dread.

Her nerves and mind jangling with wild self-accusations: had she herself caused this dreadful trespass? Her obscene fornicating, her seduction and corruption of a finely educated young gentleman had resulted in his death, had brought on the greater obscenity of the storm. She passed a house, buckled on its knees. A door opened and out filed a line of black people. They passed her without a word. She let her head drop again and kept on walking, walking.

Slowly, like Scottish drizzle that appears from nowhere, the notion grew that George Lisle had loved her. Loved her more than she knew, than she had given him credit for. He had been speared and wounded, conducting her out of an exploding house, ushering her to safety instead of saving himself. He had cradled her as he lay dying, making no mention or complaint of his predicament. One day she will cry for him, her tears will flow and gush for years; she may never be dry-eyed again. But at this moment tears were of no use to either him or her; there was enough water to deal with.

Had she passed town? Or was the town not where it used to be? At forks in the road she took one or the other, without thought. Her mind was beyond all decision-making. Her body had once more taken charge. North. The only word in her mind. A memory that the Coak plantation lay somewhere North. A woman sat on a stone where a house, a street perhaps, may once have been. Her hair was soaked. Her fine robe soiled and ripped. Face powder streaked.

"North?" asked Elspeth.

The woman wasn't much older than her, but she looked like a

hag. A ghost come to haunt her. Her hair a holy mess, clothing disarrayed, one shin and one breast exposed in accusation. Raped by the wind, degraded, a reflection of Elspeth's conscience. The idea of "north" bemused her, and she turned and looked to her right, as if a faint memory of there once being something called north lay in that direction.

Discourse & Argument
A Disclosure On Captain R. Shaw
& the Path that led to his
Discoveries & Life's Work

Only vainglorious old scunners – with as much of interest to say
as a vomiting cur – log their tedious adventures & dreary thoughts.
& only those partial to pukings adjudge them profundities. Amid
the dross there are but a few Scientific & Progressive Men who have
committed – reluctantly as I do now – the History of their Practice to
paper.

Perhaps one day I will be granted a degree of leisureliness –
surely my Successes will allow me that! – to supplement these first
scribblings with greater detail. For the moment the barest facts will be
here recorded.

There is a War going on in the heavens & until it is triumphed
War will be waged on earth. 'Tis the only way of explaining the vile
state of things. I have been a soldier in that War – & a Tactician in
it. I am a Christian man – though religiosity in its present guise holds
little attaction for me – & I know in my bowels that the Almighty has
been in trouble for some decades & still is.

My Father & my Forefather recounted to me tales of our common
Progenitor – the first Shaw in this land – of his valour & struggle for
Justice. He was faithfull to his Celtic blood which is of the house of
Gaul. The Gallic & the Celtic are close related as is proved. They
are of the same Nation & therefore share the same circumstances &
Nature. I have respect for their attributes but am sensible too to their
Faults.

The Celtic is the most spiritual of all the Races. Churching &
psalming can be a weakness in him – put the Celt in a tight spot
& it's as likely he'll reach for his prayer book as for his blade. In
the credit column we must concede that he will take up arms in
defence of Good & Right & for the deliverance of his Soul. He is
not so bellicose as his Saxon cousin who in matters Political is his
Superior. Sometimes these natural allies have become confused in
the Battlefield. Such was the case with my Forebear who fought
one Tudor King in the cause of a Stewart one. A Jacobite he called

79

himself – but became Loyal to the King of England upon his removal to this Land once the cause he fought for was lost. It was Kingship itself that mattered – that state being a reflection of the Heavenly Order.

But a black beginning – as my father was fond of saying & indeed was himself the proof – makes a black end. They sent that first Shaw to this land in Punishment in the year seventeen sixteen & degraded him to the rank of slave. Robert – as was his Christian name – was made the Property of a fellow Scotch man – a Lowlander more civilised than the Highlander – who blamed him for his stance in the old War but was sympathetic to his Nature. This Planter – Bell by name – ensured that Robert served only the minimum of his Indenture & manumitted him after the passage of five years. Thereupon he bestowed on Robert ten acres of his own land in the parish of St. Andrew & the largest of his slave houses. Robert Shaw – as is inborn in our family – worked industriously & kept lealty to his Patron & became a faithfull servant of the Colonial Yeomanry or Militia.

By the time of his son – my great-Grandfather Jamie – our family property had increased to twenty acres & by the time of my Grandfather – Robert again – we kept a gang of Negroes. Robert Shaw II was promoted to the Rank of Captain in the Militia. His family were yet poor & no blame in that. This second Robert Shaw bequeathed his rank & acreage to my own Father who was not such a canny fellow in matters of agriculture. I was brought into this world in the year seventeen ninety-seven – while we fought the French rebels in the New World & our Militia was redoubled in strength.

My Father was a misguided unchancy beast but I believe that at bottom he was a Good Man. I say this as someone all would agree was treated most unjustly by him. His name was James & he was loved by all acquainted with him. Such love was the root of his weakness for he came to thirst for the friendship & good word of others. He saw no wrong in any man or woman & was beloved by his own Niggers – many of whom he manumitted before they were ready for such responsibility. He even gave them parts of his land – causing altercation & argument throughout the Colony. At his demise he had decreased rather than amplified our family holdings.

Whereas my Father was always for smiles & banter & the tussling of my hair my mother was strict. I am of a blend of bloods. My mother was of Norman descendancy – a haughtier people entirely. She was a lover of the Law – but more prone to material consolation than my father. She was never much of a Church-goer but solemn & righteous. My father used to joke that she needed no Kirk as she was her own bishop & priest & congregation.

She was strict with me – understanding that the Child is the apprenticeship for the Man. In my Father's company I mirthed & played more than was good for me but with her I remained stony of expression & conduct which earned me some compliments from her. As I grew up she despaired of me, detecting traits of my Father's character. I played with any other boy & was a leader of them all whether Christian or slave or of colour. My mother was of the opinion that I should ensure they retained a respectfull distance as one day I was to lead them in more than childish games.

Her husband took to drinking his own bush rum which caused as much disharmony between he & my mother as did his taking of a mistress. It occurs to me now that she was relieved to be rid of his rude attentions. To be free of him can be the only reason she did not cause more of an uproar than she did over Nancy – his fancy woman & slave.

It was well known that many men used these lesser mortals to expunge their baser desires but few were so open about the matter as my reckless father. James freely courted the woman in society. & a great black buxom blunderbuss of a woman was Nancy! Favoured – I'll grant – in the light of her eye & the whoop of her laugh & the shape of her succulent rear & paps even at nigh on forty. Before I learned of her unholy partnership with my father I had fair adored the besom. She turned the dreary house into a carnival & she japed & jested with me. So it is not her I blame for the calamity but James who preyed upon her guiltless inferiority. But his greatest sin – & one that smote me to the spirit – was yet to come.

He had a son of her. In one stroke he mixed blood that should not be mixed. He made an open harlot of poor Nancy & a rejected woman of my mother. & he cheated me of my ancestral rights. Had he sold the chile to a neighbour's plantation – in the antique &

accepted style – my mother & I would not have suffered as we did. But his need for the delusion of affection made him think he loved Nancy & her bastard son more than he did my mother or me.

This was the cause of my mother's demise & the prompting of my own rowdiness. I had just joined the Militia – the bastard Negro boy arrived in my fourteenth year – & I took my duties seriously. Yet within a year or two I was finding consolation in the cup & the jug. My mother for her part rather than rankle of affrontery had the gumption to drop dead. She did it one morning with her usual competence & lack of fuss dressed in her Sunday best right in the room where her body would be laid out.

Thereafter I took delight more in drinking & carousing with my fellows & saw my imbibing as a means of watering my mother's grave with ruefull tears. My Father could not complain of my Rudeness & Mischief as he himself was seldom sober in his advancing years.

He had come to be a critic of the Militia – fallen as he had into the sphere of influence of Nancy who it must be said was clever. Quoth he: "The Militia is nae more than the defender of the rich planters, Robbie."

He had taken to addressing me in the Scotch style & using other words of that land – two generations removed from him – about the same time as he had taken up with Nancy. It was part of his deterioration under the black whore. He reminisced of his own father & the earlier Robert the Jacobite. He dreamed of "guddling trouts" in broad rivers & traipsing through gloaming with lassies. There's no fool like an old fool, as my mother used to say and – though it shames me to scribe it – he wasted his talents on rum & injudicious talk & riding his Nancy like she were a thoroughbred mare.

As to his mistrust of the Aristocracy of this colony I shared his opinion in certain measure – they cared nothing for hardworking farmers & failed to discriminate between us & Negroes. "Your Yeomanry Robbie would spend its time better defending the people they were weaned with & not wasting their time guarding the fields of those who despise us." He was deep impressed with the philosophie of the babbling French. "There is not a man jack of us who would be welcome at the table of a Combermere or a Bell though the latter be our ain kin."

Ain kin! Never was a man so insensible to his "ain kin"! Had he not thrown over his own wife – as Christian & white as the Saviour's robe – in favour of a heathen African woman? My Father's new-found devotion to kinfolk was naught more than Romanticisation. As much as he employed words of the old country he prattled in the gibberish of the Dark Continent. Among his "guddling" & "Robbie" & his "muckles" & "pickles" he gaily spoke of "unna" which is the grunt Nancy used when she meant "you, sir" & he shouted out "Bashment!" & "Rassole!" so that no educated person could make head nor tail of him.

My Father misunderstood the Struggle of his day. The Nobility had for many years betrayed us – manumitting slaves & giving them more land than we had – thus devaluing our industry. We were squeezed from above & below & black fellows who had tasted the crack of the whip comported themselves & dressed as though they were our betters. In years to come I would understand how melancholy a sight it was to see an African dressed as a London dandy. My father could not comprehend my argument that an alliance with the poor dumb slave was a worser kind of moonshine than trusting in the Landowners.

I left my father's house at the age of seventeen meaning to return to it only when he had passed away & the land was mine. To pay him his due he did not injure me more by delaying much in perishing – only six years after the loss of my mother – when I was at nineteen years of age. Tippling at a rumshop frequented by the basest of fellows he got himself into a Discussion & the knife of a yeoman ended up in his pickled breast.

But returning to our acres for his burial I was dealt an even greater blow – one that altered my life for ever. My Father – I learned – had not bequeathed our land to me – his only son – but to his African mongrel bastard. He had made a cock-laird out of the pickaninnie & a familial cuckold of me.

The news was delivered to me as bold as you like by none other than Nancy herself. & at the funeral of my own father! She had the effrontery to be in tears & to put her arm around my shoulder & thought herself gallant in telling me it was her intention to act as a parent towards me.

A parent – Nancy! She continued that – although the deeds to my property were now in her misceginated bastard boy's hands – if I came home I could regard the house & acreage as mine own & even tell others that that was the case to absolve me from any shame. She declared that she was content to return to her old chattel-house & that the larger of the two domains would remain to all extents & outward view my own. Even now I have not the words to express the fury that enveloped me.

Naturally I did not let the matter rest there. I at once made my way to the great Plantation House of which my father was a tenant. The squire of that land – Mr. Yorke – had a great good deal of sympathy for my plight & felt certain that my legacy would be justly restored.

For many years there had raged a debate in our country as to how much land a Negro or man of colour – the ill-begotten results of farmers & their brainless concubines – could own – if any he could own at all – & to what degree he could protect that land. My Militia friends assured me that if Courts could not settle my case sensibly & that if Nancy & her bastard child should need to be killed, I should rely upon their help. But another Law had been passed that made the Killing of a Negro a crime.

Thus I had to place my trust in Mr. Yorke & the unscientific & sophistical ways of the Courts over the return of my propertie. Months – & eventually years – went by & I wasted time conferring with big-wigged & small-spirited solicitors & juriconsults who were satisfied that nothing could be done. A few scant acres of Irish Jacobite land – as English Magistrates in their wisdom perceived my inheritance – was of little interest. Moreover my unchancy father – it seemed – knew his jurisdiction better than he did his black strumpet's cunt. (Perhaps if I am granted liberal retirement I will polish this text. For the moment I will write as my hand directs.)

I met the mulatto who was the offspring of my Father one night while walking out from a Militia meeting. It shocked me to see him – for he was like an hourglass come to life. That bawling suckling had grown legs & arms & – though he could not have been more than twelve years of age – a grinning insult to me & reminder of years wasted – he strutted & swore already as his kind are wont to do til the end of their days. As is the temperament of his Race he waited until my comrades had gone some way off before approaching in order to inform me that he refuted his mother's promises & that I was not welcome in my own home nor ever again would be.

Nancy had informed me that should the Law find in my favour she would bow to it. Yet all the while she was slyly engaging solicitors of her own & of that kind who succumb to Wilberforce's lunatic way of thinking. Her brat had heard that I had talked with some comrades of applying the Law directly & Hanging him as he Deserved. It seems he was not content with this arrangement & told me so all the while waggling a blade at me.

I had seen – at Mr. Barclays plantation – sensible & civilised castigations that corrected unacceptable behaviour - & could I have done so I would have proscribed & enacted one now. Lashings & starvations & incarcerations have their place but I was never a man – nor ne'er became one – who deals punishment greater than is required. Mr. Barclay employed one particular lenient penalty – a preferred approach in the prime years of mastership – that impressed me. Could I have enacted it now – stopped up the muck spouting from the cretins mouth & replaced it with muck of my own – could I have seized him & prised open his bulbous lips & shited in his throat as I had seen done to good effect – I would have done so. But that is a task for two or more men.

I had a rifle on my shoulder but it was not loaded. There was nothing I could do. I did not run. I turned my back on the mongrel popgun – no brother of mine – black as he was as the Earl o' Hell.

For several days & nights I kept to my lodgings at Bridgetown, boiling in my own anger & shame, not even attending drill. Subsequently I was refused promotion to Captain though the title had run three generations in our family. I drank for various days & then ceased. Once the anger had gone a little out of me I read my Bible & some books & papers that had been loaned to me concerning the New Jerusalem. Amongst them was a tome of Scientific work by one Alexander Kinmont. A countryman of my ancestors, this great Philosopher understood the Biology of the races & it was a wonder to me to see in print many ideas of which I had experienced the reality.

In this new light I reconsidered my whole life – & saw that the land I had been cheated of was in any case worthless. Even if I were to spend the greater part of my time & mental energy on regaining what was mine it would never provide me with a satisfactory income – so degraded had it become under my Father's rule. Nor could such a life meet my restless Nature & intelligence.

Land had been the undoing of our Pedigree – making those that had it greedy & those without it debased. Custodianship of crop is not the only way to serve the Lord. I became sensitive to the divisions in this Colony that others could not & still cannot see.

Reading the Book of Kinmont I mark as the Birth and Baptism of my own Great Work. I enlisted myself in the twin camps of Gods footsoldiers – no greater rank do I claim – & Human Science. My labours beckon me. There is little time for reflection & composing when there is so much of Importance & Urgency to be done. The lessons taught me by Mr. Barclay will have to wait for another night. As will the Revelation granted unto me by an unsuspecting lady. Poor flibbertigibbet! How could she possibly comprehend that she has been used as a vessel to convey a message from powers beyond her ken! From the moment I cast eyes on her – half dead half blind & crazed she was – I knew the girl to be marked out – & paid special Attention to her.

VI

The glorious era of Bridgetown and the Lyceum had lasted scarcely a month. Everything had changed, but not quite enough. She had been a common kail-worm until the New World became her chrysalis. But before she could emerge with full-grown wings, ready to climb and soar, the pupa had been blown off the branch, halting her metamorphosis. A full year later she could only still wonder what kind of butterfly she was destined to become. Whether a swallowtail, or an admiral, or even a painted lady. Any would do, rather than remained imprisoned in her cocoon.

It was as if time were a mysterious fabric that could shrink or expand itself according to some unknown law. No matter how Elspeth, trapped inside, semi-formed, kicked and struggled against it, time thrust her forward, then yanked her back. In Northpoint the fabric was being stretched beyond endurance.

Of the journey from Bridgetown, she could remember little. Strangers as dazed as she had given her fare to eat – as to what kind, her memory failed – and water to drink. But she remembered, perfectly lucidly, reaching the estate of Lord Coak. There was a gate. A pathway curled back from it, like a childhood memory. An unclear expectation arose with each bend but, in the end, nothing was revealed. Just another unkempt track, leading to a plantation house like others she had seen in and around town.

Lord Coak's house was built of the brightest Barbadian coral stone, gleaming like a pearl against the wild woods that lapped against it. It looked like it had been thrown up, perfectly formed, by some movement in the earth's surface. A man was waiting on the porch, as though Elspeth had been expected. She walked towards him, roots bulging under her feet, thick foliage of grapefruit trees and akkie bushes forking out, scratching her face. The heat was intense and wet, like a botanical glasshouse. She imagined that if she stood still long enough the vegetation would burgeon before her eyes and bury both the house and the man. She stumbled as she approached him. He caught her, steadied her, then let go and walked away, disappearing inside the house. She managed to follow him in. Inside, large winged beetles lumbered from room to room as if looking for something they had mislaid. She found the stranger sitting in the largest chamber, in a broad band of sunlight, two glasses and a jar in front of him.

"Yuh must be Baillie."

"Pleased to meet you, sir."

Then an elderly black woman appeared, just in time to catch Elspeth before she fell.

It took her several weeks to recover from the arduousness of her journey and the shock of the storm. She was in a bed, in a spacious room, sparsely furnished. She knew that she had been visited regularly: her water was changed, her face washed. Faint memories of her head being held and a woman's voice encouraging her to drink. After some time – God knows how much – she became alert enough to identify the old black lady who had caught her on her arrival. Once she managed to sit up and throw her legs over the side of the bed, she saw out the window: a bluff rose up steeply and on its far side was a pleasant little cove.

"How long since I arrived here?"

"Be a while now."

"This is Lord Coak's estate, isn't it?"

"It is."

"I'm sorry. I've forgotten your name."

"Annie Oyo. Not that you're in need o' a second name. I answer to Annie."

At times, especially in the darkness, when the woodwork creaked or some sound crept in through her window, she felt again the hammering of the storm and had to find her chamber pot to vomit from fear and disgust. If a male voice from elsewhere in the house – perhaps the man who had been waiting for her at the porch, and of whom she had seen nothing since – reached her ears, her heart rose in joy, thinking it was George. Then she would fall into sweaty slumber again, seeing nothing but dark, shifting colours.

When she felt well enough to venture into the world beyond her chamber, she instructed Annie to dress her and take her to her master.

"Lord Coak has not returned yet, has he?"

Annie shook her head.

"Then I will speak to – forgive me, I have forgotten the name of the gentleman."

"Cap'n Shaw."

Annie helped her down the polished wooden stairs of a house perhaps smaller but nearly as impressive as the Overtons'. Walking for the first time since her arrival, she found she had developed a stabbing pain somewhere unidentifiable deep in her torso.

"You are feeling improved now, I hope?"

Shaw was so tall and thin he appeared to walk on stilts. She recognised him now as the man who had visited Lord Coak at the Overtons' the night of Elspeth's arrival in the Colony. He might have been made entirely out of wood: the stiff, jerky stride of his legs as he walked towards her and a face streaked with ginger hairs that seemed to be carved onto his cheeks combined to make him look like a puppet controlled by invisible strings. He was dressed for work: a white open-necked shirt and fustian breeks, both garments earth-soiled.

"You must forgive me for imposing on your kindness like this."

"You're welcome."

"Thank heaven his lordship made mention of me, otherwise you might have turned me out into the wild. I must have looked like a vagabond."

"I am unsusceptible to the facade of dress, Miss Baillie."

"When will Lord Albert be home?"

She had never referred to Coak by his first name before, not even with the title attached to it. But this "Captain" clearly had some position of authority here, so it was important that she show him she had a measure of influence.

"I don't expect him before a month."

"A month!"

Shaw sat and observed as she feared for a moment that she might faint again in front of him. "I promise I shall not trouble you as long as a month," she managed to say. "In a day or two I should be well enough to travel back to town – if some transport could be arranged for me."

"You shall be staying here, I fear, Miss."

He looked at her coolly. There was that hint of lust that most men tried and failed to hide, and Elspeth recognised Shaw's particular strain of it: more concealed from himself than from her and tinged with acrimony. "The city is in a state of chaos. There is disease, lootings, all manner of tribulations that would not befit a young woman. I have written to his lordship and informed him of your arrival here, but dispatches to Havana are slow. I must insist that you wait here until his return."

At the mention of the effects of the storm, Elspeth felt again the stabbing in her back or side – she could not tell exactly where.

The loss of George and the violence of the storm engulfed her as the days – so slow in a humid, remote place like this – went by until Lord Coak's return. The nights continued to pass in a kind of fever, as if the air was saturated with Virginie's potion. The heat throbbed in time to the pulse of the cicadas and frogs, the distant but interminable lapping of the waves. In the mornings, she barely noticed the sea, nor the constantly hot whipping wind. She spent much of her day confined to her room, but took walks whenever she felt strong and bold enough, and when there was air enough to make exertion possible. She thought she detected an uneasy atmosphere among her new neighbours, but paid it little mind. Northpoint was not to be her home for long.

What consumed her thoughts was this stabbing pain, as if the splinter that had speared George was now lodged in her. And though that felt fitting, it did not ease the physical pain. For weeks Elspeth looked inward rather than outward, listening to and concentrating on her own body, all her attention taken up with detecting any little change that might be taking place. She had not, so far as she knew, bled since before the storm, and the constrictions and aches she had suffered in her belly ever since, she began to realise, might have had a different source.

George and she reunited; her lover regenerating himself in her womb. Yet the idea seemed too remote, too unlikely. It hadn't occurred to her, on either of those two sudden, delectable nights, to take care of this possibility. A child could not possibly result from a woman like her and a man like him: a medical contradiction. She did not seek advice from any other quarter – though who she might turn to in this foreign place she could not imagine – but vaguely decided that, if indeed she were pregnant, and when her time came, she would have Lord Coak transfer her to Bridgetown or even London for her confinement. A baby would delay still further her return to the stage but, with proper lodgings in town and staff to assist her, it should not present an enduring problem. How Coak would react, if it turned out she was expecting a child, she had no notion.

She would have to wait – waiting being a skill she was beginning to learn – longer to find out. Uncertain and unconfirmed news of Lord Coak's expected arrival finally reached Northpoint in March 1832. Nobody came for Elspeth Baillie in all that time. Each day lasted a month, every week a year, as she waited, expecting some word from the Lyric. She implored Captain Shaw to let her visit Bridgetown, to find her old friends.

"That is not my place, Mistress Baillie," he insisted, though Elspeth felt that he considered it very much was. Lord Coak had written to him requesting that he look after their house-guest, and to dissuade her from returning to town until he himself had returned. He wrote to Elspeth herself in a similar vein. The Lyric had been utterly lost in the storm and his plans to reconstruct it would need some time to mature. There was no other theatre in Bridgetown to embrace her many talents. Indeed there was – he knew from regular dispatches he received in Havana – no theatrical life whatsoever in the aftermath of the calamity. He hinted at other reasons, too, for her to avoid travelling to town, then sweetened the warning with apologies for his absence, a fanfare of compliments, promises to return at the earliest date and exhortations to look after her own wellbeing: "A period of rest and restoration can only benefit you. We will return to our project as soon as is possible, and in a climate more fruitful for our ambitions."

He was right: she was still in turmoil – all the more so since suspecting she might be pregnant. Northpoint was not the worst place, she reflected, despite its remoteness and the ennui it produced in her, to regain some peace of mind. If indeed she was carrying George's child, there was nowhere better for her to be until she was certain. She never ventured far from the house, preferring to walk round it than away from it. In every direction she was obstructed. She could walk a little down the drive but, as the trees at either side grew thicker and the path became like a tunnel, she had to turn back. The hill behind the house was too tangled with overgrown thickets to allow walking; it was also alive with the tics and buzzes of insects and other life, some of which, for all she knew, might bite, and fatally. The canefields hindered exploration on the south-west side of the house, though she stood at their fringe sometimes and watched black men and women perform mysterious tasks, involving cutting long, gangly stalks of cane, shearing their leaves, and tying and carrying bundles of trimmed cane. They seemed to work all hours. At dawn and dusk their shadows repeated their mechanical motions.

Still, the place was pleasant and quiet enough. A return to the city could only illustrate too vividly what she had lost. Whatever remained of its streets would be empty of her old companions and their laughter; the hole where the Lyric once stood would contain only the echo of the applause she had anticipated; Garrison a vacuum without George Lisle's caresses and smiles. The worry that Lord Coak had implanted in her mind of darker threats, constrained her too. "I will explain on my return but there are other factors that would make it most inadvisable for you to enter the city." She approached Captain Shaw on the matter.

"Mr. Lisle. Senior. He's after your blood, as I hear it."

The shock of hearing George's name uttered for the first time since his death dismayed her for a moment.

"The Lisle clan lost not only their heir, George, with whom I gather you were acquainted, but also his younger sister, Clara."

"I had no idea," Elspeth breathed.

"Sir Reginald was caught on his estates during the storm, leaving his wife and daughter alone in their town residence to cope. He had believed that Master George would have been there to take charge of the situation but, unfortunately, the young man was not at home on the night in question."

She tried to feel for this Clara, but could not. Clara was only a name to her and one that, on the very few occasions he had uttered it, George had done so without, she remembered, much warmth.

"Sir Reginald has been attributing to all and sundry his family's tragedy to a strumpet. I use the wording I was given, Mistress."

The wooden Captain, Elspeth reckoned, agreed with Sir Reginald's opinion. But she was not the son's strumpet – even if she had set out to be. They had found some love together: real love, tender and bold. George had risked his name and fortune for her. He had protected her, and died by her side. And perhaps now he had given her his child. She was George's widow in all but name.

"Does he know where I am?"

"He knows all right. And so long as you're here, under our protection, you're safe."

"What could he do?"

"Powerful man like that? Have you deported, at the very least."

Despite the misfortunes that had recently occurred to her, Elspeth still could not conceive of a more terrible fate. Whatever she would become, she would become in this new world. To return to the old would be nothing but defeat.

When Lord Coak eventually arrived at Northpoint, she waited for him at the porch, just as Captain Shaw had waited for her. The little pudgy, bald man drawing up in a hired brougham was as welcome and grand a sight as Mark Antony surrounded by phalanxes of gladiators and blaring horns. She ran down to meet him, not waiting for him to alight, but jumping into the carriage and only just managing not to throw her arms around him and kiss him.

"Well, you've lost none of your energies, my dear."

"How long it's been!"

Here he was – her magician, the alchemist who could turn stone back into gold. She felt her skin tingle the way it had when she first came to this island. She could swear her hair was thickening again right before his eyes. Lord Coak was her sun – not that burning ball in the sky that hurt her eyes, that made her skin clammy and her clothes stain like she was a common farm girl. Over the next few days, Lord and guest walked together in the grounds, and she realised for the first time how extensive his plantation was. He explained to her that his was the only agricultural estate this far north in the island. From the top of the little bluff he showed her its boundaries, embraced between hills and ocean.

"The climatic and geological conditions give our sugar a particular quality that is highly praised by the distillers of rum. There is a sharp, fresh salty tang to it. Though I'm a claret man myself."

She had already seen, on the few outings she had braved in his absence, the gang of black workers who cultivated his lands and cut his cane. Now they passed her – men and women alike in pursuit of mysterious tasks – nodding vaguely in their direction. Even up close, they still seemed distant, as cattle do in fields adjacent to country lanes. Lord Coak mumbled something about them being part of his present worries. Many were leaving, or threatening to, now that they could work elsewhere. He spoke of "manumission" – a word Elspeth had never heard before and did not understand. The problem seemed to persist whether or not these people stayed or went:

"Either way, you get little out of them these days." He was not criticising them. Albert Coak was simply stating a fact and ruminating on the problems it caused him.

From that hill over the cove Coak pointed towards Florida and Havana, and beyond to the Pacific and San Francisco. In the company of a rich, cultured planter, this far-northern settlement seemed not quite so isolated, and Elspeth less forgotten. They made plans together, discussed new plays he had seen, and pored over the texts he had brought back. He spoke of his ambitions to resurrect his destroyed theatre. Such a project would take time. First to recuperate the investment he had lost, and then to begin rebuilding not only bricks and mortar, but a company of players and administrators equal to the talents of Elspeth Baillie.

But that was for the future. "All my plans depend on the success of a venture on which I have speculated everything. This colony is in dire need of mechanisation and I seem to be the only planter prepared to sit down with the future. But it will require some patience on your part."

Old man Lisle, Coak told her, was determined to avenge his losses. He was making it known that there would be a proper theatrical life now – in the forms of a Gentlemen's Arts Club and a Ladies' Society – bringing decent and moral plays from New York where, it so happened, he did much of his business. There would be no more performances of dubious morality. Exemplary and virtuous theatre was all the more necessary now that the twin disasters of the great storm and abolition were testing the steel of the province to its core. There was no place in the present metropolitan climate for the talents of the likes of Miss Elspeth Baillie. In the meantime, Coak proposed that she settle for a few months more at Northpoint: enjoy the clean breeze and restorative silence and sun.

"There is a plot of land, by the north wall of the house. I imagine you could fashion a little herb garden there for your own enjoyment, and for the general profit of the estate."

From the planter and from passing visitors and the pages of newspapers she learned a little about the goings-on in town. Mrs. Bartleby and Mr. Philbrick, it was rumoured, had absconded together to America, leaving spouses and children behind. Nonie and Christy had both survived the storm and had sailed for England together. Isabella had gone to Venezuela. Of Virginie she heard nothing. Derrick had taken employment in a hotel – in what capacity she didn't know. Although Coak was sceptical, she read articles about the reconstruction of Bridgetown and the building of grand residences more magnificent than those they replaced. She heard second-hand of the building of civic establishments, hotels de luxe, extravagant government palaces. The *Gazette* trumpeted the excellence of refurbished and newly fabricated theatrical venues, every one of them associated with Mr. Reginald Lisle.

In less than two weeks Albert Coak had gone again. Elspeth's belly had swollen during his stay and though she had hidden it as best she could in unfashionable cloaks and wraps, it amazed her that he hadn't noticed. She had worried that he might request a repeat performance of her Greenock audition. Nothing but business, however, seemed to occupy his mind.

He would be gone this time for a month or so. Only a week into it she lay on her bed in her meagrely furnished upstairs room, swathes of colours, like lugubrious Northern Lights, coating her dreams more thickly than ever, interrupted regularly by the terror of being speared and emptied out. With the first stirrings of dawn, a murkiness outside her window like a Scottish morning, she came to properly and cooried down into the warmth of her sheets. But the warmth turned quickly to a cold dampness. She screamed when she saw the mess of her bedclothes: brown liquid, like mauby, smelling even bitterer, soaked every inch. She was lying in a sea of black blood. Shouting for Annie, for Lord Coak, George, her mother, and gasping for breath, she scrambled manically in the mess looking for her baby.

She never spoke again about her baby. The terrible night of her miscarriage was almost worse than that of the storm. Annie had tried to calm her, but Elspeth just kept on shouting at her: "Find her! Find my baby. She's in here somewhere. We have to find her!"

Whether or not a little barely formed body had been found, she never discovered. She must have blacked out, for she had no memory of the event beyond the blood and her own screaming at Annie. But she knew there had been a change somewhere in her innards. Not an emptiness, but as if the baby – the girl, she was sure it was a girl – had burrowed further inside her.

She began to reinterpret the great events of her life in a different light. Lord Coak's spiriting her away; the death of the sailor as her ship broke from the old land; the storm that had reached its zenith on the very eve of her First Night. Waking in the pitch of night, far from city lights and sounds, Elspeth berated herself for not seeing from the beginning how it all pointed to disaster. Life had raised her up and struck her down, and all in little more than a single rotation of the earth around the sun.

The Coak Estate – for over a generation economically sound enough – had begun, along with most other plantations, to trade very successfully indeed. Though destructive in its immediate aftermath, the great storm was not wholly injurious in its consequences; it proved, even, to have beneficial aspects. The seasons became more favourable and the vegetation more active. Elspeth, as much through boredom as any active interest, noticed the air of industry everywhere around the estate. No matter when she looked out her window, or embarked on one of her short walks, there were men scurrying to and fro, carrying implements for digging or cutting or carrying. Women bore bundles of cane on their backs in the fields, and the crops themselves appeared to be undergoing one long single harvest. The health of the farm workers – she read in the *Gazette* – men and women still in slavery, and freemen and citizens in general, were all improving.

As her old hopes faded, other responsibilities filled up the spaces in her life. She began to order the house according to her liking. She laid the foundations, as Coak had suggested, for a herb garden, as well as a little policy of plants and shrubs at its eastern end. She instructed Annie Oyo and the few black servant girls in the kitchen to change the tedious pattern of meals, introducing chicken and other fowl, sugar-topped milk and rice puddings and other innovations. She reprimanded Coak, during his brief reappearances, and Shaw for having settled so long for slave food – an endless round of potatoes, sticky messes Annie called coocoo, tasteless boiled husks from the breadfruit tree.

The piecework and tatty-howking that was part and parcel of a troupe of family players in Scotland, she had thought had gone forever. Yet here she was – put back out to work. Naturally she was not expected to labour amongst the biting insects of the canefields, but, as house servants were needed to replace absent cutters and bearers, her domestic chores increased. To her surprise, she rather enjoyed them. She thought of herself as Miranda, mistress of her own little world. Merrily, merrily shall I live now, under the blossom that hangs on the bough. The petunias and blue lumbagos sang in crisp maiden's hues around her; match-me-nots sprang to attention at her touch, every bloom a different colour from its neighbour.

Coak spent weeks at a time in Bridgetown. In the few intervening days he was busy in his study writing, and mealtimes were taken up with agricultural matters with Shaw. Not long before the anniversary of the great storm, he found a little more time for her. He had received a box of plays, chapbooks and novels from London. He read aloud to her, and in French, the opening chapters of Victor-Marie Hugo's *Notre Dame de Paris*, translating a paragraph at a time. At night, she took a bundle of penny dreadfuls, recently published in London to bed. She learned lines from volumes of poems: Spenser's *Faery Queen*, and Keats's Odes. By the time of his next return, Elspeth had learned the entire part of *Hamlet*'s Ophelia,

"Up! be bold!
Vanquish fatigue by energy of mind!
For not on plumes, or canopied in state,
The soul wins fame!"

There was no commemoration of the previous year's storm in the summer of 1832. Elspeth herself lost track of time, unable to follow the seasons in this land. The sun seemed equally hot throughout the year, and rain could fall unexpectedly at any time. Each time it did, she suffered her own memorial for George. When, in the November of 1832, Coak returned for a longer stay, his meetings in private with Shaw took on a more urgent air and lasted longer, prevailing throughout all their shared meals. Elspeth listened and began to understand some of the debate: an upturn in production and an increase in prices had coincided with a problem of labour shortage. Many freedmen were taking advantage of the economic climate and the British parliament's anti-slavery legislation, to leave and start up their own small sugar fields or grow other crops elsewhere on the island. With full emancipation on the horizon, the estate – despite trading well – was facing a looming crisis. The need to implement mechanisation was pressing.

During these conversations Elspeth learned the histories of the two men with whom she now shared her life, such as it was. In the case of Captain Shaw she did not so much learn as was instructed. From time to time over a meal he would break off from conversation with the planter to illuminate a particular point for her, illustrating it with edifying examples from his own life and philosophy. Then, one night, having taken more brandy than usual, Lord Coak having retired to bed, Shaw decided the time was right to explain himself fully to her. He did so in the form of a lecture, like some script he had learned by heart. Indeed, as the night wore on, he produced a sheaf of handwritten notes and referred to them as he spoke. "There is a War going on in the heavens and until it is triumphed, War will be waged on earth."

He began his story four generations back, which forewarned Elspeth that this was going to be a long, perhaps a fatiguing, epic. Her attention waned often as the night wore on, but she caught, she hoped, the gist of the thing. His great-great-grandfather, she gathered, was the first Shaw in Barbados. While she baulked at the wooden man's priggishness, Elspeth found herself drawn in by his tale and his eccentric beliefs, though at times unnecessary details lost her again. But it was a story after all and Elspeth lived for stories. And words – not as racy or as much fun as her old friends', but extravagant in parts all the same.

"His name was Robert and he fought one Tudor King in the cause of a Stewart one." She knew something of this – Jacobites who had been Barbado'ed over a century ago. By the time of the Captain's great-grandfather the family property had increased considerably, though she missed exactly how that had come to pass. By the time of his grandfather – another Robert, confusing Elspeth – they kept a gang of slaves.

Shaw's father, it seemed, was a drinker and a womaniser. He looked at Elspeth intently at this revelation, judging her response. But the actress knew how to keep her expression inscrutable. Not that she was scandalised anyway. The liaisons of tenant-farmers were not so different in the old country, and the free-thinking that George and her Bohemians had prompted in her made Shaw senior's peccadilloes a mere trifle.

"He had a son of her," and Shaw leaned further in towards her so that she might understand the utmost gravity of that matter. She didn't really. Father and son became ever more estranged. The younger joined the militia, a family tradition that the elder had rejected.

At points he thought crucial in the narrative, Shaw stopped and drank, and stared at the wall as if he were considering where next to take his story. There was clearly no such decision to be made – Elspeth was all the more convinced he had learned the piece by rote. But during those breaks Elspeth lost the drift a little. She would catch a sentence or so – at one point wondering if he hadn't just said that he was not, in fact, a militia captain at all? When she picked up the general thread again, Shaw was waxing lyrical – or as lyrical as an oaken man can – about discoveries he had made in the Bible, and some tome of scientific work by a man called Alan or Alexander Kinmont. A Scotsman apparently who taught him great things about physiology, and perhaps physical science, or something, and Life in general. Precisely what the Captain – if he was, indeed a captain – learned of these matters, Elspeth was left to guess. Shaw drained his glass, stood, turned, and walked out on her without so much as a goodnight. There was not to be another history lesson for several months to come.

Whereas Shaw, despite that single night of outpourings, remained aloof to the point of common rudeness, as the second year at Northpoint wore on Lord Coak and Elspeth became increasingly a consolation to one another. He began, in the safety of the estate of which he was master, to confide in her. He did not make a declaration as Shaw had done, as though it were a last will and testament, but serialised his tale. And like occasional editions of a penny dreadful, Elspeth pieced together the story of her benefactor's life, the chapters separated not by publications, but by the narrator's silences, or longer absences.

Albert Coak, it transpired, was the eldest son of a successful merchant who, from early childhood, showed a weakness for frippery and diversion. His father had begun the family business in England, importing and refining sugar. Their West Indian home was initially a mere foothold in the Americas from where he hoped to advance his trade. He bought an ancient mill, still in good working order despite its age, together with this smallish but attractive enough and solid coral-stone plantation house at Northpoint and its extensive acreage, all sold by a bigger landlord who had found that corner of the island too salty, too windy, and too remote to merit his time and money.

"There he was mistaken. There's no doubt this land takes energy to work, but its produce is second to none on the island."

Coak would tell his story after dinner, a jugful of rum shared with the Captain, and when he was at ease. Often, he would repair to his room, hinting to Elspeth that her company would be welcome. Sometimes she would recite or read for him, and then ask him questions, urging him to continue his autobiography. He would lie across his bed, while she sat at the window, often covered only with a sheet. He began his reminisces haltingly, but then, lost in the memories, he would talk quietly and lucidly, staring up at the ceiling.

The fastidious father took the mild and gentle son with him to his newly purchased plantation, and left him there. Although Albert was young, his father felt that gaining a sense of independence early in life, as well as learning the business from scratch, would be advantageous. His mother was not so convinced but yielded to the superior knowledge of her husband in the matters of business, the West Indies, and boys. "You might say my dear, that I was 'barbadoed' like a common convict. A month before my fourteenth birthday."

Coak *père* returned to the island regularly for the next several years. A housekeeper and small house staff were added to the plantation gang, to look after the young man's needs, although he was instructed always to be the authority in the house.

Elspeth nearly wept at the thought of such a lonely boyhood. Abandoned in a remote, solitary spot without friends or family, simultaneously the most senior and most junior member of the household. The more she heard of his history the more her gratitude to Albert merged into compassion and even warmth. Those who tended to the boy – governess, cook and maid – were women. Under his command was a work-gang of slave men. Captain Shaw was hired in the first year of the boy's residence on the island to run the agricultural side of things and maintain order and discipline amongst the slaves. Inside the house, when his father was in England, his young lordship was the sole male presence, Shaw having his own residence by the gate of the plantation.

"He must have been a terrifying companion for such a tender-hearted boy," said Elspeth.

"Not at all. He worked hard, kept his distance, and was always respectful."

Whenever it was a necessity or when his father felt it would help with his apprenticeship in business, young Albert was taken into the city. "I sat through meetings, luncheons, political arguments in drawing rooms, and repellent discussions in the Nautical Club and the Assembly Club."

In the evenings he was introduced to life as it was enjoyed then at the London Naval Hotel. But Coak hesitated to recount to Elspeth this part of his life's history. He broke off from the story three nights before leaving for business and did not invite her back to his room until a week after his return, a full two months later. Then he explained that the London Naval was in fact a bordello. A whorehouse, run by one Mary Bella Lemon, the free coloured daughter of a Scottish engineer and a slave girl. Mary Bella and her nineteen girls became the nearest things to friends young Albert Coak ever had.

The speciality of the London Naval was the games and scenarios Mary Bella Lemon contrived. She dressed her harlots in the costumes of pirates, harems of the East Indies if their colour was right, African deities, Inca Queens and English governesses. They were taught songs and cameo sketches to perform, in accordance with their disguise, to whet the appetite, and open further the wallets of their wealthy clients. It was at Madame Lemon's side, and with the Empress Catherine, Jacoba and Salammbo, that Albert found his love of theatre.

"Of course I soon knew their real names, but they preferred their *nomes de guerre*. Empress Catherine. Salammbo. Anne Bonny. Lady Obeah. La Gaucha. I miss them all."

Elspeth saw in him the stripling lad he must have been. The older man's eyes still retained a shadow of shyness, of fear. Those same eyes in the shivering young frame of an obedient, polite, timid lad would account for the girls permitting him into their rest rooms and dressing chambers. There, he told her, they prepared for their clients, singing songs from Ireland and Guinea and from the backstreets of Bridgetown, often conflating them all into the same chorus. His eyes, as they stared up at the ceiling, glittered in the candlelight as they moistened while he told her how those good women had tried to spare him the sight of his father – inebriated and in the act of fornication – by taking the boy-child away and entertaining him in their quarters.

"They played games with me. A thing my mother never did. Pass the parcel which they intrigued to always finish in my hands, with a sweet wrapped up inside, or a note promising a kiss."

They also introduced him to rum and to the opium pipe, and further promises: to acquaint him with the art of love when he was ready.

During the months when his father was in England, the lad had one of the plantation men drive him into town so that he could be with his new-found friends. Elspeth felt it indecorous to ask if indeed he himself became an initiate of Mary Bella's voluptuaries, but Coak broached the matter himself. "My father's drunken misuse of these lovely and affectionate creatures was detestable. I wanted to make up for him, restore honour to our family name. And anyway, they were my friends. I was quite satisfied by simply being in their company."

A pleasure – Elspeth found out only after another lengthy absence of the narrator – he continued for many years, until he was no longer a boy, but a young man with business influence in the town, and a stake in the London Naval itself. He swore he still never became one of the women's clients. He continued to take pleasure in listening to them sing and talk, watching them dress and undress and dress again.

Now Elspeth understood: her benefactor, this man who kept his distance, cowered in corners while she walked naked around him, had never been ready for initiation. She stroked his hand while he spoke, like a mother consoling a sad son.

"Did it survive the storm – this palace of pleasures?"

"Gone long before. Other, rather more repugnant institutions took its place. No doubt they thrive in the present conditions."

"So you lost your friends?"

"Catherine died. Jacoba ran away and Anne left. Salammbo took seriously ill. Mary Bella grew old. The newer girls who replaced them complained about my presence. So too did a few paying clients, including that buffoon Lisle, who was as bad as my father in his conduct with those defenceless girls."

Elspeth imagined these strutting gentlemen, glowering at Albert, too old now to be a favourite nephew, sitting among a group of semi-naked women, drinking tea while they took off their French maids' stockings or applied Egyptian kohl to their eyes, affixed tassels and veils and straps. She felt a pride in her work as a performer and reader to this abused, lonely man and felt more grateful than ever to him for having chosen her. And she had something to offer in return – the reincarnation of those exotic girls at the London Naval Hotel.

Elspeth and Albert – as he wished her to call him now – maintained separate bedrooms, although both doors, each assured the other, were always open. Regularly, he would come to her, and she would dress in costumes inherited from Mary Bella Lemon's girls and recite some lines of verse. Once or twice he fell asleep on her bed, but would wake in the middle of the night and return to his own room.

By day, he worked hard, then at night spoke to her of the investigations he had been undertaking in Cuba and the American States and his vision of himself as a pioneer of cane cultivation and sugar processing in his own little corner of the world. He had already engaged engineers in Scotland and Holland to draw up plans for a manufactory which could refine sugar at Northpoint. The problem, as ever, was labour. A larger and more efficient plantation, processing and refining its own matacuisse, needed a stable workforce. Since last year's Emancipation Act he could depend on no cutter, carter, burner, or even housemaid, staying with him.

"I believe I have the answer to my problem, and therefore to yours too, Elspeth. An entirely new workforce, brought in especially for our needs. God willing, we will have you on the stage again soon."

On Shaw's advice he had been making enquiries via associates in Germany, England and the Low Countries for dependable and loyal workers, if not indentured at least employed for a period of five years – long enough to get his project going, though perhaps not enough to see it through. "But I have hopes that decent working folk from less favoured lands in Europe will put roots down here and stay loyal."

Captain Shaw at these discussions was predisposed to North Britons. An entire and intact group of labourers – men and women, preferably already married – to populate the estate. It was Elspeth who pointed out, delicately and subtly, assuming that Shaw would disapprove of women involving themselves in commerce and agriculture, that the most pressing difficulty they were experiencing was keeping the menfolk they already had in their employ. A number of white men, experienced and apprenticed in their various crafts, had so far shown loyalty to the plantation, or, at the very least, had failed to find better employment elsewhere.

And so it was that Elspeth Baillie suggested that they import women only. Then set about matching them to the best of the white cane-cutters and labourers the estate could engage.

The Captain made fun of her proposition but Elspeth coolly argued her strategy, speculating that a plantation with a heavenly host of young, fresh, untainted white women must surely become a magnet, a Valhalla for strong, equally young, ambitious men. Some days after those first discussions, Shaw himself returned to the matter. The idea had obviously taken hold.

"I was merely following your line of thought, Captain," Elspeth persisted. "There are a number of men, we could both list them by name" – although in truth she could not – "who have proved their worth and their allegiance. I imagine any offspring of theirs with decent hard-working ladies would be an investment."

"Next you'll suggest that we bring members of your own family."

"One actress amongst us, I am sure you'll agree, is plenty."

A month later Lord Coak sailed to England, with the express objective of finding a group of women willing to emigrate to Barbados. The two men spoke of the mission as though it were of their own devising. Elspeth smiled and recited to herself: "They'll take suggestion as a cat laps milk."

Coak wrote two weeks later, detailing a conversation he had had with a cotton merchant in London who had only recently relocated groups of male labourers to the town of Paisley, but was unable at present to accommodate any of their womenfolk. His carding halls were already full of spinners and pieceners and apprentices. The men were currently building vast machine-rooms but it would be a full decade before the industrialist would be ready to staff them. This owner was a man of humanitarian principles who had no wish to see another generation of women being made to adapt from rural to urban existence. A healthy outdoors life on a Colonial plantation would resolve the problems of the two merchants and the underemployed women at one stroke. Another month later, Coak wrote again, this time from Greenock, urging Shaw and Elspeth to make ready lodgings, rooms and chattel-houses for a group of some twenty-four women.

The coincidence of Greenock surely meant that the Fates were turning again in Elspeth favour, and she enthusiastically set about preparing for the arrival of the women. She and the factor had six months' grace to put everything in order. Working harmoniously and energetically together, they oversaw the refurbishment of disused chattel-houses, allocated rooms and drew up lists of duties together, Elspeth tolerating without complaint the mulish ways of the uncouth Factor. Busy all day and exhausted at night, she put her longing to return to the stage, and her recent despair of ever doing so, to the back of her mind. Her interlude as a convalescent was coming to an end: a year, perhaps less, to welcome the lassies and see them settled, and once again she would take to the stages of the New World. The stabbing at her womb persisted, as though some furious embryo were punishing her for her failure to set it free. Her murky dreams too continued to haunt her. But she had grown accustomed to all of that, even welcoming the pain in her stomach as if a reminder of George and his child, both lost but never forgotten.

Mother, Father,

I sit alone on this late-summer morn at the table of our house, perhaps for the last time, though I cannot bear to think of it so. The sun is not yet risen and the burn gushes speedily behind our cottage. If I could I would temper its rush, and hold back forever this dawn.

My brothers left before I was awake and took off to the furthest fields. You, my beloved mother and father, lie so close to me, behind the curtain that, had I the temerity, I could pull back and touch you both.

I must leave before the sun breaks. I have seen for the last time the light on my home and on your beautiful, loving countenances. You wake, yet you do not come to me. You feign sleep. I know you do so with good intent. What could we possibly say to one another on this melancholy morn?

That which must happen cannot now be stopped. Already in the distance I hear footsteps. My childhood companions putting the first of many thousands of miles behind them. Girls, daughters, sisters and nieces. How will this town be without us? There has been so much silence between us all, these last months. You have averted your eyes whene'er I looked pleadingly into them. You, strongest and dearest of fathers, who taught me to write and to think, to ask questions and understand God's mind, now you give me no words, no answers.

I pray that your education of me will be ample to sustain me through the hard choices that no doubt lie in wait of me in my new land.

Let me say in writing what I could not pronounce in speech. I do not blame you. You have given your lives to me. Everything I am I learned from you both. I will endeavour always to follow your teachings and your fine example. I will write as you have taught me. Perhaps distance will dispel the silence between us, and once I am gone you will find the explanations for our exile that you could not speak to my person.

I will not let go of the hope that I will return, though you have never encouraged the prospect of it. Every prayer I utter will be to that end. Why should the God to whom we have dedicated our lives sunder us now?

I hear you weep, mother, and am glad of it. The next time I will hear your tears I shall be holding you in my arms and the weeping will be cries of joy at my return.

Stay well, I beg you. Care closely for one another, as we girls shall care and guard ourselves. Stay well so that I might see you again, though I will be less a maiden and you both old.

Diana

VII

Early on an overcast morning at the end of August, not quite four years after her own crossing, Elspeth stood on the bluff and looked out over the ocean, eager to catch the glimpse of a passing ship.

The women would of course disembark at Carlisle Bay, but she hoped that the absence of a decent trade wind might force the ship to tack close by the eastern coast of the island. It was bright the day she herself had first caught sight of this island, and windless like this morning, so that Captain Douglas had sailed close in to land, possibly within sight of North Point, though the place was unknown to her then. About mid-morning a ship did appear on the horizon. A large, slow-moving three-masted clipper of a type she had seen many times before docked near Bridgetown slipping subtly past the Lyric. Less elegant than the schooner she had come on, the ship sat heavily in the water, freighted to the gunwales, so that it looked like it was already scuttled and sinking into the horizon. She waved though she knew she could not be seen from such a distance. Then she returned to the house to see off the cane-wagons which would bring the women and girls tomorrow.

It would not be a pleasant journey for them. There was only one carriage at the Coak Estate fit for a body to travel in but it could not contain so many people. The road from Bridgetown was rough and the poor ladies would be tossed around on the planks of the three carts with a jolting that not even the Atlantic could have inflicted on them. Elspeth would make up for the inconvenience by preparing a hearty welcome. An elderly cutter who had been with Lord Coak since the earliest days could still remember a tune or two on an old patched bagpipe, and he would play them in – a jovial march to rid them of their aches and pains. A roster had been drawn up to allow each of the girls to wash in a tent especially mounted at the back of the house. A generous meal was prepared for them by Annie and Dainty – the only one of Mr. Overton's servants to survive the storm of '31 and the infections that came in its wake. Elspeth, hearing her old housegirl's name in passing, had asked Albert to bring her to Northpoint, which he did within the month. She had been delighted to see Dainty again – a real person from those golden days in Bridgetown. She'd run to her when the black girl stepped in from the kitchen with Annie. Dainty had not run to her, but simply smiled. She had, however, brought her old mistress a present: the dress that George had bought her for her debut.

"I foun' it on Tuesday's back, but it too small fuh her. Anyway, she dyin' o' the pestilen'."

"Did you find the tunic and slippers that go with it?"

"Didn' see no slipper, mu'm."

The wagons trundled up through the trees towards the house – William McNeill playing an air he claimed to have written himself, entitled Mr. Patterson's Voyage to Darien. Elspeth came out to see the girls leaning out perilously from their open-ended carts. Their hair glinted gold and auburn in the sun and their first words, caught by the wind, took wing and danced around her ears.

"Hallo!"

"There's the wumman!"

"Lookit the fancy hoose!"

Their plain burr spoke of home and honest guilelessness, words and shouts sang of lapping of lochs and the smir over rowan woods; they echoed the songs of her mother, and the laughter of her sisters. Not until that moment had she felt a single pang of homesickness. She remembered Shaw's father – no matter how much the Captain reviled him, Elspeth could not help but like him. Still, yearning for that old dreich home was a nonsense. Nothing could befall her in this land that would be worse than the dreary trudge of her old life. But for a heartbeat, as the trio of sugar-wagons rattled up the drive, as if fresh from a mild Lowland morning, she remembered shade and peat fires and the shelter of home.

The wagons girned to a halt on the stony path, and the hallos and shouts stopped dead with them. Elspeth counted twenty women, and checked her tally twice over. The weary cautious travellers stared back at her. And she recalled something else: it's as weel t' gang as tae get there. Her father had always said so, along with other dire warnings about knowing your place and never getting above yourself. The women's hunched shoulders and furtive glances reminded her why she had so gleefully waved goodbye to the land of her birth when the Alba slipped into the Atlantic.

The girls ranged in colouring from oaty to ruddy, their locks pale as the bark of birches and dark as rowan leaves at the turn of winter. Freed from the wagon they stood there eyeing the ground and shuffling. Until the last of them descended, a woman a little taller than the rest, wearing a clean linen gown, the only arrival bedecked with millinery, a simple bonnet that gave her a religious air. She made her way to the head of the queue forming haphazardly in front of Elspeth, and turned to address the women.

"None of you drowned in the ocean, but perhaps your manners did. Let us introduce ourselves. You say your name, and 'Thank you, Mistress Baillie'." She turned and gave Elspeth a little bow. "Diana Moore, Ma'm, at your service. Please excuse us – we have had a long journey and perhaps are not at our most mannered."

Elspeth had not considered how the women ought to address her. She had no proper position in this house; was merely a guest like them, albeit dwelling at the owner's personal request and expense. "I have not long made the journey myself and remember how it empties the mind."

Diane Moore introduced the women one by one.

"Mary Fairweather. Seventeen years. Plenty of experience of the fields… Eliza Morton. Twenty-three years old. Has had some experience of service in the Laird's scullery, but also practised in agricultural work. A curtsy, I think, Eliza?"

Eliza, a sharp-featured woman with bright, peering eyes, curtsied grudgingly and moved quickly aside.

Diana listed all the names, like a litany of saints. Twenty girls in total. Mary Fairweather and Eliza Morton followed by Mary Riach and Mary Murray. Mary and Margaret Lloyd. Martha Glover. Sarah Alexander. Jean MacNeill. Jean Homes. Bessy Riddoch. Moira Campbell. Jean and Mary Malcolm. Mary Miller. Susan Millar.

Rhona Douglas. Elizabeth Johnstone. Martha Turner. And Diana Moore herself.

"Aren't there four short?" Elspeth asked Diana.

"One may yet arrive, ma'm. Another was inconvenienced before we set sail from Scotland. Misses Lorna Johnstone and Elspet McLean sadly took ill en route."

"Poor mites."

"They are enjoying at this moment a welcome even greater than this, ma'm, if that were possible."

Elspeth led the twenty successful pioneers into the house, as a thunder shower threatened. The table was set and fresh mauby made. Elspeth busied herself between the kitchen with Annie and Dainty and serving the nervous incomers in the dining room. Some of them opened up a little, having had a wash and a refreshment. Elspeth glad for the bustle and chatter they caused in this hinterland that had been so deathly quiet. The girls lowered their eyes whenever she came near, save for Diana and Mary Miller, being older and evidently having earned some authority over the others during the sailing. They volunteered to help Elspeth and the maids. After they had eaten, all were dutifully respectful of Elspeth's rendering of Scots songs, and the "Out damn spot" soliloquy of Lady Macbeth. Some, as the night wore on, shed a tear or two for families or sweethearts thousands of miles away. One girl – the Fairweather lass who, scrubbed clean, shone moon-like and meek – became bold enough to sing.

"I'm wearing away, Jean,
Like snow when it's thaw, Jean,
I'm wearing away tae the land o' the Leal.
There's nae sorrow there, Jean,
Neither cauld nor care, Jean
The day's always fair, in the land o' the Leal."

Elspeth smiled encouragingly at the rude rendition and squeezed a tear from her eye in solidarity with the sentimental girls as they mournfully chorused "Lochaber no more!"

Diana and Mary confided in Elspeth the strengths and weaknesses of the contingent – those who were likely to slack, and those who would work hard; the delicate lasses prone to sickness, and the hearty and thrawn ones; the girls likely to have an eye for their male associates, and the God-fearing decent women.

"Few can read or write, alas, Miss Elspeth. I have been using the excuse of letters to teach them. I hope I may find time to continue to do so."

"You most certainly shall, Diana."

When night came down, and the girls began to tire, Diana, following Annie Oyo holding aloft a blazing torch, led the group out through the trees and shrubs to their new homes. Elspeth stood on the porch and surveyed her now complete community. Some skipped behind their leaders, peering into the darkness of their strange new world; others hung their heads, walking towards long prison sentences.

At the far end of her herb garden – now neatly organised into flowerbeds, vegetable patches and herb plots – sat the long-serving workers of Coak. The Endmondson family, who rented a narrow rig of land from Lord Coak on the southern side of the estate, sat a-staring from the shadows, to show their loyalty on this grand day. The white labourers, in their hodden grey, faces scratched and dusty from work, stood silently, smoking with Shaw. There was a brawny black man – a more gnarled version of Henry. Five or six younger negro men – day-workers – and a gaggle of children stood in the shade of the bluff. The whole group was muted, veiled in the smoke of cheroots and pipes.

Early in the morning, Captain Shaw made his formal address to his new recruits.

"There is a war going on in the heavens, and we are its reflection on earth. We are the footsoldiers – yea, even poor uneducated women – not only of God but, perhaps more importantly, of Progress. For Progress is the Lord's gleaming sword, lighting the darkness."

The women hung their heads. More, Elsepth thought, to conceal their bafflement at what their overseer was talking about than in humility. Sweet Sarah Alexander stared hard at him as if she might get the hang of it from his carved features. Mary Fairweather's tresses shone through the dowdy cloud of fustian jackets, dingy dresses and oaty skins, her plain face made plainer by the Captain's flowery words.

"'Get thee out of thy country, and from thy kindred, and from thy father's house, unto a land that I will shew thee. And I will make of thee a great nation.'" No matter how much vigour Shaw gave his words they fell like dead birds from the branch. Only Diana seemed to be moved by his speech, giving him her full attention, nodding subtly at every pause. "You have been chosen, each and every one of you. Have pride in what you bring to this New World. The Scot is the most dependable of the Races."

"Aye," Elspeth heard Susan Millar mutter to Bessy Riddoch, "tae talk shite."

"You are staunch, but not obstinate; adept without being wily. With God's grace and good planning, you will find here men of other races appropriate to your own natures: Saxon and Nordic, who will compensate for your deficiencies and together with whom we shall build a new nation."

"Christ, Susie, we're in for a servicin'."

"I'll hae Elspet's and Lorna's too. I wouldna have them die for nought."

"You will work hard," Shaw continued through the sniggers at the back of the group, "but I promise you a fine future. Where the battle is being lost in the old world we will restore the advantage..."

Shaw droned on for nearly an hour until the assembled company were dead on their feet.

"Cane cuttin' canny be ony worse than this."

But there was indeed worse to come. Captain Shaw lined up his new recruits and inspected each in turn. He asked them their age, interrogated them on their working lives to date, then pawed at their arms and thighs, checking muscle, then teeth, and finally holding a burning torch close to the women's eyes. Mary Murray, the girl who was already squinting in the light of the sun, cried out when the flame touched her lashes.

"Watch out wi' your caundle, Captain," Susan called out.

"Ach, let him be," another shouted. "If e'er a lassie needed a glint in her ee."

Shaw assigned each girl to either a domestic or agricultural duty or a combination of the two. No discussion was permitted and he did not for a moment reconsider after he had made a decision. These were verdicts to last the full length of the women's lives. Elspeth shuddered at the Captain's gruffness, but there could be no doubt he knew his business.

Mary Miller was appointed head housekeeper; Diana Moore was responsible for crockery and cutlery, and commissioned to supervise all the women outwith the house. None of the domestic staff would have the luxury of working in the big house all year round. All would be needed at harvest – a rotation of three in different parts of the estate in any given month. Elspeth had informed Shaw of Diana's plan to teach the girls writing by helping them with letters home. Although the time he allotted to letter-writing was not generous, the Captain agreed to have their dispatches sent home from Bridgetown.

The girls worked for only a few hours on their first day, before returning to their shacks to wash and eat. Elspeth came down from her room and accompanied them, making sure none of them got lost.

She was not the best person to be their guide. Elspeth had never visited the workers' shacks, segregated from the house by lines of jacaranda trees and several huge figs. Diana Moore, after only one day at Northpoint, knew the route better than she did. On coming through the trees into the clearing south of the cove and west of the house, Elspeth was amazed at what she saw. A cluster of tiny brick buildings, dun-coloured and cold-looking, sat squat and glum under in the evening light. Each chattel-house consisted of only one room, no chimneys or windows, just four grey stone walls and a stone roof, a simple wooden door. Their new homes contrasted starkly with the liveliness of the girls as they walked, unperturbed, to the hovels they would spend every other night of their lives.

Susan, Bessy, Rhona Douglas and Eliza Morton walked in a group around Dainty.

"D'ye see in colour, Dainty?"

"Course I do."

"Can I touch your hair? You can touch mine."

"I've touched mo' white ladies' hair then ever I wanted to."

"Is it just as spikey down there, Dainty?"

"Wheesht, Bessy. You're richt bonnie, Dainty. Did ye ken that?"

"I can' mek yuh out, what yuh aksin'?"

"Whit?"

Captain Shaw had a good eye for which lass would settle well with which man, and permitted some minutes dallying during the working day to allow them to become acquainted each with the other. Conversely, whenever he saw an association being struck up between two parties wholly inimical to each other, he intervened, and saw to it that their shifts and duties did not coincide. Slowly, some good liaisons were founded. But not without a little heart-break and one or two catastrophes along the way. The process, to Diana's sorrow, was hindered by the absence of a minister – and the distressingly little time spent on matters religious generally.

It was Diana who had the idea of communal evening eating. Allowing simple labourers and maids into the big house for reasons other than cleaning or mending was at first preposterous to Captain Shaw, and not much less so to Elspeth herself. Diana insisted that it would allow the Captain to address his workforce on a daily basis.

"And wouldn't it give our girls a chance to talk civilly with the better class of hinds and orramen, allow them to meet respectably and pursue compatibilities? All under supervision, in full view of the community."

Such gatherings would also allow for vigilance over those romantic alliances that could only end in disaster. The factor was not completely convinced of her arguments, but Elspeth saw the sense in Diana's idea, and the evening teas that were to last for a generation were begun within the month. Every night, all those not deployed in duties elsewhere, sat around a large square table, specially made by Robert Butcher and his men, from the birch trees Albert's father had apparently planted seventy years before behind the wild little forest running along the northern coast. Elspeth sat at one end of the sturdy table; Shaw at the other. Annie and Dainty, with the help of the Scots scullery lasses, prepared a meal of eddoes, coo-coo mash, chicken when there was enough to go round, and mauby.

The Captain timed the meal, ensuring it lasted no more than forty-five minutes.

Shaw used the events for the purpose Diana had suggested. He perceived who was fiery of spirit and would settle better with a meeker partner. He predicted – in terms that gave Diana cause to blush – which men were likely to be productive of seed, and which women physically capable of bearing and weaning numerous offspring. He lectured Diana on the merits of matching males of Germanic origin with women who had some Gaelic in their past. The efficient and the spiritual would make for a peaceful marriage, and balanced progeny. So too, those men of English stock would fare better with women whose names suggested a more northerly east-coast ancestry – both were reliable but would complement each other in matters of fidelity, and in times of difficulty.

"The Scots Lowlander is prone to sulkiness. The Englishman is least affected by such tempers. He'll compensate for her trace of Irish."

"But what if the parties find no attraction in each other?"

"Don't vex me, Miss Moore, with the whims of your romantic poets. Never in your ladies' lives has the age-old process of selecting an economically advantageous husband not been imposed upon them."

"And if they are wholly adverse to each other?"

"You and I, Diana, are *in loco parentis*. If we do our work well, we will choose a better spouse for your friends than they could themselves. A winning smile and mirthful wit and – let me speak plainly – a bosom made for the squeezing and a ripe apple for a tail-piece do not necessarily make for happy and enduring associations. Bear with it, and you will see how we shall all enjoy the fruits of our work."

Elspeth observed, impressed, as Diana bore the extra work levied on her by Captain Shaw. Beyond her daily duties in house and field, she was tutor, scribe, and now matchmaker. After a matter of months she changed from reluctant matron into a bustling dynamic woman; it fatigued Elspeth just watching her. Her energies were still fuelled by a staunch Presbyterian ethic that felt to Elspeth like a language she once spoke but had now all but forgotten. Diana acted in accordance with the rule of the estate and within the law of God as she saw it, safe in the knowledge that God would take her into His fold – but not before returning her first to the land of her birth, her constant prayer.

Diana took to tying her hair back so tightly that it stretched her eyes narrow and tautened the skin around the temples. She made efforts to appear freshly washed and laundered every day, skirts rustling crisply in even the hottest of afternoons. She had trained herself to be better spoken than her true education had allowed, borrowing phrases and pronunciations from Elspeth and Coak. She was held by the other women in the kind of respect due to the daughter of a landed family, or the manse, though her stock was as humble as any of theirs.

When, in just under a year, the first baby arrived – a son, to Jean Homes and Obadiah Wilson, an elderly drayman who had worked one season a year at Northpoint for two decades – it was Diana who was called upon to perform the duties of midwife. Her grandmother, she told Elspeth, had been howdie-wife to the Parish of Roseneath, and Diana had heard many stories of birthings; had even assisted as a young girl, so she knew all about hot water and screams and the cutting of cords. She applied herself to this new role as assiduously as she did to all her other duties, requesting Shaw to bring books and advice back from his trips to town. When the Homes boy, before even a name could be allotted to him, took fever and sickened, she nursed him too. And when he died, Diana was appointed the chief mourner and officiator of funeral prayers.

"I cannot do that, Captain." Diana was the only woman who Shaw allowed to upbraid him – though he permitted good-hearted joking from Susan and Bess. Shaw, however, was not often upbraided successfully. "There's not a minister I'd have within two miles of Northpoint, mistress. Half of them are bishop-kissers, and the other half screeching half-caste fire-worshippers. There's a Presbyterian fellow down in the Parish of St. Thomas, but he's drunk most of the time."

He convinced her that it was in keeping with proper reforms and covenants that the people themselves intercede with their Maker at such times. So an hour was given to a ceremony before dinner,

Obadiah carrying the child in a cloth to the cemetery behind the old mill, where Shaw read from the Bible, Diana leading the congregation's response and striking up Psalm one hundred and thirty – "Out of the Depths I cry to Thee O Lord."

Elspeth was impressed and humbled by Diana. The woman was a true stoic: not the blood and mess of childbirth, nor the daily moans and complaints, nor the shortcomings of Coak and Shaw's rule, discouraged or quietened her. "A proper Scots lass," she was fond of telling everyone, "rolls up her sleeves and gets on with the job. We don't stand on ceremony or expect praise for doing what is required of us." She was tender with women in any kind of pain, be it physical, emotional or spiritual, but cajoled them into remembering there is little to commend complaining. God in His wisdom can be relied upon to confer suffering and solace in equal measure. "Our duty is to follow and accept."

Diana and the captain would not have been taken – even by themselves – as natural associates: he, crude of expression and toilette, uncongenial in his relations, while Diana set much store by mannerliness and sympathy. Yet she agreed with much of what he did and said. He was, like her father, a practical man, and learned above his station. Such erudition could only have been attained by dint of effort at some personal cost. Self-education was another good Scots trait in Diana's mind, so Shaw – despite his strange colonial accent and unpolished ways – had something of the old tradition in him. He was as loyal as a clansman, and she detected perspicacity in his philosophies and his reading of men's souls. Diana, also, had observed keen differences between people from diverse backgrounds; she was as convinced as he was that no good came of mixing apples with pears.

One night, in circumstances similar to the evening when he had inducted Elspeth in the facts of his life and the contents of his thoughts, Shaw, with Elspeth on his left and Diana on his right, brought out a jug of rum and the sheaf of parchments, handling it as though it were a Holy Book, and continued the story he had left off many months ago. These evenings were to be repeated over the weeks that followed, as he expounded on the lessons he had learned from his experiences and how they could be applied to everyday situations: a philosophy finally put to good use in building this new colony-within-the-colony. Diana, Elspeth deduced, was the true chosen disciple of his schooling.

"I found myself paying-work for a while on the estate of the admirable Mister Barclay," he said. "A great planter who had deeper interests than simply sugar and crop." This Barclay, it seemed, had made a deal of money from trading in slaves when that profession was still permitted. But his great innovation was to create on the island of Barbuda what he termed a Propagation Manufactory. At that point, Shaw broke off for the evening, favouring staring into his cup to speaking. When next the three were assembled he started again, but at a different point.

He told the story of how he came to meet Lord Albert Coak and became his trusted factor and partner. "I had long since relinquished ambitions to own a plantation or business of my own. I know now that I was destined to a greater cause."

As he talked of the younger Albert, Elspeth's mind wandered. She preferred listening, inside her head, to his lordship's story than to the Captain's. Salammbo, putting kohl on her eyes. Lady Obeah and her incantations. In her mind each one of them had become associated with her friends from the Lyric. Virginie as Empress Catherine; Nonie the Obeah witch-lady; Isabella, La Guacha. As Anne Bonny she saw herself. Just as she had done when she dreamed her way across the Atlantic on her elegant schooner infused with rum. Not a word of this, naturally, did she reveal to Diana. That lady would not have understood the beauty and the bravery of those fine, fallen women.

When she awoke from her reverie, Shaw had his finger in the air and was looking sternly at Diana: "Over many years Mr. Barclay had come to learn which African tribes worked harder, which were stronger, and which more compliant."

Diana felt it necessary, and summoned the courage, to ask the Captain if the African, of whatever nation, was not a creation of the Almighty just as we ourselves are. Shaw nodded slowly, as though the hinges of his wooden neck were in need of oil. He did not, he assured the good lady, despise the negro. "The meek shall inherit the Earth. I take the words of the Good Book as they are written undiluted. But the African's time has not yet come. His ascension will undoubtedly take place in the Last Age. Some time off yet, I trust. Meanwhile, we have work to do."

Elspeth saw that Diana was fashed, as she put it herself but not to Elspeth, by Shaw. He was her superior and paymaster, he put his trust in her and, although he was stringent, he was scrupulous. On the other hand he had doctrines that troubled her and manners she tolerated in nobody else. Elspeth picked this up from Diana's expressions and her habit of squirming in her seat when she was perturbed. But also from snippets of overheard conversations between the women when they were in the house, or thought she couldn't hear when she was working her little herb garden. Diana had plenty of souls to whom she could unburden herself. Elspeth made no attempt to become another. For one thing she had a position in this community to maintain – all the more delicately, given its ambivalent condition. She was merely here first, though the closest to Lord Coak himself – and for another, she did not wish to become too close to these neighbours as some day soon she would be leaving.

As time went by she watched as Diana found another confidant. Robert Butcher, like the captain, had Scots blood in his paternal line, but Calvinist Swedish on his mother's side. He was a colonial in patterns of speech and in attitude and had been a stalwart of Northpoint Plantation for many years, returning season after season until finally settling here. He was as religious as Diana. Ten years her senior, Robert was ideally suited to be a friend and comrade to her. More and more, as time passed, it was to Robert that Diana would confide her troubles. Especially when she had to deliver a child conceived out of wedlock – a service she was not sure was a permitted Christian act – or when she had to watch helplessly as a baby wilted and died.

Barbados
Winter 1839

Our dearest families.

Well over a year we have been here and still we have not heard from you. Communication between this world and yours is so very slow. Yet his lordship has sailed twice across the Atlantic in the same time. We know you will have responded and have not forgotten us.

We are still all well. Times have been hard for the manufacturers of sugar in recent years. It is doubtful any of us will make our fortunes here. We each of us have a hundred expenses we never dreamed of. We are obliged to buy our bedsteads at a cost of 20 dollars. There is not a bit of furniture in our chattel-houses, which is how they call our pretty little homes. We have no coinage ourselves, naturally, but Captain Shaw is happy to exchange our expenses for work, a system of months and years indenture per item.

Lord Coak's Estate is very remote and, though beautiful between hills, woods and sea, lacks some fundamental amenities. Not least, there is no Kirk (of any denomination – though my own father would prefer even an Episcoplian chapel, so long as the worshipper's mind is clean, than none whatsoever), nor minister to attend our spiritual needs. I have appealed and remonstrated often with our factor here to take steps to correct the situation, but he insists there are not enough men learned in Divinity even for the big towns on the island. Thankfully, we have our Bibles.

Please answer our letters soon. There are many questions I have to ask you. Of your own lives, certainly, but also some counsel on the work Captain Shaw has me undertake, and on new dilemmas all of us have to face.

We pray God you are well, and thinking on us.

Diana Moore.

On behalf of

Sarah and Mary Alexander. Mary and Margaret Lloyd. Jean and Mary Malcolm. Bessy Riddoch. Susan Millar. Moira Campbell. Mary Fairweather. Rhona Douglas. Mary Miller. (All others have either written independently, or send their warmest regards.)

VIII

A little over two years after the girls' arrival, there was a local disturbance. The Emancipation Act had been passed in 1833, but it took some time for its repercussions to be felt in the north. Rumours spread by itinerant labourers of skirmishes in Bridgetown, Oistins and plantations far to the south were barely noted by the inhabitants of Northpoint. In February 1836 – the hottest month the new recruits had yet experienced in the West Indies – the troubles came closer to home. A group of ex-slaves, believing that they were free now legally to go wherever and do whatever they wished, upped tools and belongings, and headed for the hills of the Scotland district, as the north-west of the island was known.

Mary Fairweather had sworn she had seen, while working in the field, a band of shadows pass across the hilltop to the east of them.

"Marooners!" cried Mary Miller, excited.

"We'll tak them up some meal and put-by," Bessy Riddoch suggested.

Nathanial Wycombe, a cutter with a house made of three old slave-huts bridged together with runners and boards, painted up like a miniature plantation house – and deputy in all but name to the Captain – reckoned they could only be runaways.

"They're free men now, Mister Wycombe," Bessy protested, "makin' their way in the world."

"They're savages and layabouts. If you give 'em victuals, you'd have a harder time getting rid of rats or crows."

But Bessy, with Mary Miller and Mary Fairweather and Susan, went ahead secretly with their plans to take bowls of coocoo and eddoe mash up to the men, whose bonfires they had seen in the middle of the night lighting up the sky.

"Whit if they attack us?" Susan suddenly asked in the kitchen while they mashed the food.

Dainty and Annie Oyo winked to one another. "I heerd they alreadys cut the throat o' two white folk," Annie said.

"Eddy eddy white mice, put 'em de pot and cook 'em like rice!" laughed Dainty.

"Dainty, is it no' a wonder a'body's able to onerstan' onything ye say."

Mary Fairweather squealed in fright. "What if they kidnap us?"

"Christ, woman, ye're a hell of a hopeful."

The idea of helping a group of runaway blacks was less an act of kindness than an adventure to break the boredom of working life. Mary Fairweather, however, remained the most tremulous of the gang.

"If Captain Shaw gets wind ae it, we'll a' be shunned."

Ostracism – from meals and from socialising in the fields – was Shaw's favoured punishment for the women. On the committing of a transgression he would sentence the offender to a day's, a week's or even a month's shunning, depending on the seriousness of the misdemeanour. Nobody could talk to the penitent at any time of day, nor help her with work or domestic chores. She had to eat in her own hut and remain silent throughout her sentence. The punishment of men took the form of confiscation of rum, snuff and cheroots, and the occasional smack across the lug.

"A week wi' oot hearing you wifies' blether'd be a blessin'."

It took a full month to hunt the runaways down. News reached Northpoint of a settlement in the hills, where men and women danced – in some accounts, naked – and lived like the children of Adam and Eve on the abundant fruits of the West Indian wildlands. When Shaw went off for a day or two in search of the miscreants – amazing how people could hide themselves for so long in such a tiny island! – some of the girls, usually headed up by Bess or Mary Miller, took to walking outside the plantation limits, in the hope of catching a glimpse of the gypsy rebels. Thus started the custom of escaping the confines of the estate indulged in by several of the women. Elspeth often spied their lights through the fig trees, the glimmer heading off down the drive at ungodly hours. Stories soon circulated of the adventures they met out there. Of travellers, wild animals, impromptu parties by the roadside with itinerant workers, and even freed coloureds. What became of the runaways, nothing was ever reported.

Albert had compensated Elspeth for the long interruption in her career by making sure she was still dressed in the most elegant of Paris fashions and that her boudoir was prettily adorned. Still only twenty-six years old in 1837 but, with the help of her attire, and the weight of a great love and a lost child, she walked the plantation with an air of deserved gravitas. Her gleaming, lustrous hair she kept tied behind her head and, when out in the grounds overseeing some task or other, she wore a straw hat that shaded her face and neck. Her body was still strong and straight. In her own mind, long gone was the girl who flirted and giggled with friends from the theatre, the seductress of young noblemen. Her expression became every day more serious, and her arms and legs sturdier than those required of an actress.

On his visits home, Elspeth shared her room with Albert for half the night. He never touched her, but she basked in his unrelenting gaze. The slightest, most common activities were enough to entrance him: washing her face, changing her shoes, eating at dinner. His treatment of her – as a child might stare in wonder at clouds, or an exotic beast – was enough to sustain her through his long absences.

Mailing her from Havana, London and Panama, he encouraged her to recite and sing in the evenings to the house staff. Within a brace of years she had established the custom of monthly concerts in which any woman brave enough to do so would perform properly rehearsed party pieces for the assembled company. Albert, three years after the coming of the women, returned home with the backcloths of the old Lyric Theatre which he had discovered in an auction house at Speightstown. Seeing those stars and crystals and a still-gleaming moon, despite some staining and water damage, Elspeth suffered a confusion of emotions. Albert felt for her, and wondered if he should have left the cloths to rot.

"My dear child, I should have thought that they would upset you. Forgive me. I still haven't the means to further our plans for a theatre – even if Lisle would allow it. The manufactory is taking longer, and using up more of my resources than I expected."

She knew he wasn't lying: for the past year there had been a steady stream of surveyors, government officials, advisers, running through the estate. Foundations for a vast new building had been laid, on the site of a disused canefield somewhere near the copse at the estate's border. She had heard enough of Albert's conversations with Shaw over dinner to know that his fortune was stretched to the limit.

"Losing you would be a blow, Elspeth. But I'll understand if you decide to take what little I can offer and begin your craft again elsewhere. I have good contacts in London and Edinburgh."

For a spell, the dilemma tormented her. To take to the stage again, perform in front of an audience, was a dream suddenly refreshed by those majestic old cloths that had been designed to be the backdrop of her grand debut. She agreed to give Albert an answer before he left again, this time to Milan. To clear her mind for the momentous decision, she set aside her plays and books, avoided Diana and Mary Miller, and walked the grounds, considering. Her route was always the same: coming down from the little porch, she strolled as far as the large fig tree in front of the house, turned back, walked down the west side of the house, up to the fencing of the first cane-fields, then back through her herb garden and the little copse of policy woodland, and thereby to the porch again. At every side there was an obstacle. The bluff cut her off from the cove, which the women, during the little time they had off work, used to paddle and sit and chatter. Behind the fig trees were the chattel-houses where Elspeth did not feel welcome. Right of them lay the thicket of wild woodland, whose shadows and obscure noises frightened her. Everywhere else, there was nothing but canefields. Sometimes she would walk a little down the drive, but the canopy created by jacarandas and cabbage palms oppressed her.

On the day before she was due to give Albert her decision, she found herself a little further down the driveway than she had ventured before. It was noon-time, and Mary Miller and Sarah Alexander were going to the gates to receive provisions from the Edmondson farm: a weekly purchase of live chickens, potatoes, eddoes and milk.

"I seldom come down here. I don't know why, now that I am here. It's rather lovely."

The trees at either side shaded them from the burning sun, and whipped up a little breeze between themselves. Rays of sun danced among them, so that light and shade were in perfect harmony. Their three voices took on a different timbre: the enclosure muted and softened them, creating an atmosphere of intimacy.

"This is my favourite neuk," Sarah said.

"Mine too," agreed Mary. "It minds me o' the woods down by Ochter Burn. Though it's mair tidy like."

Elspeth listened to their chatter about farm-folk and ministers, ploughboys and market days, as if Mary and Sarah had only come away for a day's excursion from their homes. She enjoyed hearing the gossipy talk of her old country, but it was akin to eavesdropping on a conversation taking place behind a barn wall or a cottage door – her own most crucial experiences took place here in the West Indies, not the Scottish Lowlands. The three women turned a bend in the road, and she saw for the first time the remains of an old building on a rise above the tops of the trees.

"That's where the laird's erectin' his manufactory," said Mary.

"But what's the old building?" Elspeth asked.

Mary shrugged and said it looked like an old mill, of the ancient, round type you sometimes saw east of their old parish at Roseneath. The heap of stones looked to Elspeth less like a decayed building and more like the result of some natural calamity. The stones were of a grey she had not seen on the island before and sat as though they had been petrified mid-tumble, or had pushed their way up out of the ground, poised to burst into dreadful life. She shivered at the sight, but carried on walking, the path leaning off to the left, down towards the gate. Mary and Sarah were laughing at some of the tales of the workmen – older slaves and freedmen in the main – who had been brought up from Oistins and Speightstown to work on the new factory, when Elspeth for the first time in six years caught a glimpse of the Northpoint Plantation Estate gates.

She had no memory of them. A simple, askew, set of rusted iron grilles set into sinking pillars, they could be gates to anywhere, in Scotland as much as the West Indies, yet the sight of them had a shocking effect on Elspeth. Her two companions had walked a little ahead, unaware of the trauma being wreaked upon their mistress. She could not catch her breath, felt her skin turn to ice, and her blood scorch. She thought she might be sick or fall over, just as she had done the night she first entered the big house. Behind the gates was visible only the smallest strip of open countryside: a few yards of roadway, a slight rise of pastureland behind, and a few stunted trees. To Mary and Sarah it was a bonny enough view: a patch of the world within reach, but where the rules and endless work of Northpoint no longer applied. To Elspeth, it loomed like a barren, malicious desert. The gates, road, field and tree moved in front of her, first hurtling towards her, then pulling back, the length of road stretching taut enough to snap. She turned away from the sight and her legs, though shaking and barely able to hold her, managed a few steps of flight. Hoisting her hem, she stumbled up the road as clumsily as she had on her first entrance. Soon, she broke into a run, Mary's and Sarah's voices calling behind her but lost in a rush of imagined wind streaming through the open gates.

By the time she had reached the big house, she had regained, outwardly, her composure, though her heart punched loudly and erratically in her chest, and her vision was blurred. Mary came dashing up the path behind her, but Elspeth ignored her, kept going until she had entered the house and found the safety of the stairs.

At that night's evening meal she gave Albert the conclusion he had hoped for. For the time being at least, she would stay at Northpoint.

"I think that is the right decision, Ellie. You've time and youth enough yet on your side. Together we'll make Northpoint the great success only you and I and the Captain could achieve. After that, anything is possible."

Two years at the utmost, he swore. Perhaps another one or two to erect their playhouse. She would be nearing thirty by then she calculated. But they agreed that not a single day would pass in that time that she wouldn't rehearse, read, discover new work, and discuss the arts with the greatest tutor she knew – Albert himself. She would breathe life into a Lady Macbeth and – yes, whyever not! – a Lady of the Lake that would have them tremble in their seats.

She excused herself early and sat by the window of her room. What need did she have of the impoverished theatre world of Bridgetown? Without Nonie, Derrick, Isabella. Without the Ocean View, which Shaw had told her had melted into the sea as if it were made of candy-sticks. Without George. Didn't she have a captive public here? And one more dependably appreciative would be hard to find. In a new place she would have to begin all over again, perhaps even in the chorus, competing with younger women. She was beyond that now. A woman of real experience and position. The frolics of another Nonie, the rivalry with another Virginie – it would be demeaning to return to that. Albert assured her that her star had not faded, that her time would come. A new palace would be built for her Miranda and her Ophelia; perhaps even here, at Northpoint itself. Once the manufactory was operating, Coak's plantation would become the centre of economic activity and, on its heels, a Colonial Athens of the North. The Lady of the Lake, Cleopatra, Medea would not travel to their audience, but the audience to them!

In the year of the women's arrival, the estate had had barely fifteen black labourers serving out their indenture, and only a handful of permanent whites. By 1838, the presence of new, young, European blood, together with the spreading fame of Captain Shaw's methods and philosophies, was attracting men from plantations across the island. But still, experienced cutters and craftsmen were too easily tempted to move on whenever they saw a better opportunity.

At harvest and sowing – three of each a year on the Coak Estate – every uncultivated piece of land was taken up by makeshift houses. In the intervening months the land was emptied again. Shacks were easily dismantled and carried on the back to other plantations. Since emancipation, islanders had become like turtles, moving slowly under the weight of their shells, from pasture to pasture. If Coak's dream of a great factory and Shaw's of a flourishing, settled community were ever to be realised, it was essential that they provide year-round work and put down stronger roots, deeper foundations, for their people.

Elspeth played her part by overseeing the enhancing and

improving of the old slave houses. She and her women set to work on cleaning up the stonework, clearing the weeds, putting down stone flooring and installing furniture. Shaw allowed the experiment to go ahead on the understanding that this was an investment the women themselves were making to the estate, and any expenses incurred were to be met by them. They had no actual money, naturally, but there was a notional wage rate, and owings were noted down in a book to be repaid at a later date, once their increasingly extended indenture had been served. No one was permitted to seek work elsewhere while indebted to Lord Coak.

Even those men who had found a partner were tempted away by work elsewhere. Already, after four years, some who had fathered children cared little about leaving them and their mothers behind, making faint promises of return. Diana continued to insist that not being bound by a God-fearing marriage ceremony made this behaviour only too easy. Shaw, though not a man of religious orthodoxy, eventually concurred. The only option was to bring a minister up from Bridgetown – a journey few clerics were anxious to make, and fewer still were acceptable to the factor.

Reverend Galloway attempted to make the journey in a polished gig, but the roads were in such a dire state that it gave up the ghost at Blackman's Gully, obliging the minister to continue on foot, arriving short-tempered and outraged. "This estate," he proclaimed the minute he set foot inside the gates, "has fallen by the wayside." He told them that terrible things were heard in town of the morality – or lack of it – in this outpost. "We hear of concubinage, fornication, illegitimacy, and an aversion to hearing the word of God spoken."

"We are so far from town, Minister, and have so much work to do," confessed Diana.

"Nothing should inhibit a good Christian from making the journey to church, at the very least for the important rites of marriage, birth and burial."

"We still say our prayers, and our Captain here reads from the Bible whenever such a circumstance arrives. And so do I."

Her argument only incensed the good Reverend more. "As for your Captain, I very much doubt he has been schooled in the proper readings of the Good Book. In your own case, do you truly believe that a woman may represent God at such homespun rituals?"

The man had arrived angry and became angrier as the day wore on. He could hardly believe his ears when Elspeth proposed he perform a general wedding rite to legally bind in the eyes of God those who were already cohabiting.

"You wish me to give my blessing to your desecrations? I think not, Mistress."

It seemed the minister had come all this way merely to condemn and convict the lost flock to the fires of damnation. But Elspeth, used to the ways of recriminating clerics from her days with travelling players – when many such men attempted to drive them from town – had a strategy for just such a contingency. Settling the minister before a plate of fried chicken and eddoes and a large jugful of ale, she called Diana into a secret meeting in her chambers.

"Reverend Galloway may find it beneath him to marry all those in want of it, but I think he shall wed at least one deserving couple. Who do you think would volunteer?"

Diana shook her head sadly and replied that she had not observed much hunger for the sacraments amongst her sisters.

"What about Jean Morton?"

"Not ideal."

"Has she not been living harmoniously with one of the men new to us?"

"Ben McGeoch. A Roman Papist, ma'm, and not one to keep it hid."

"Bessy Riddoch has two babes by her companion."

"Two different companions, tragically."

"Susan Millar?"

"She partakes of no spirituality."

They could not between them come up with one couple who could be safely presented before Mr. Galloway. Those who had already borne children could hardly be portrayed as good Christians and Diana would not consent to lie – even by omission – before a man of God. But for her plan to succeed, Elspeth needed at least one marriageable couple.

"That leaves you, Diana."

Diana stared at her mistress in astonishment. "And who is it you think I should wed? Shall I step outside and seize the first uncouth cutter I see?"

"Come, come Diana. Everyone knows you and Robert Butcher are in love!"

"In love! We are acquainted neighbours! We pray together and console one another."

"What more should respectable wedded partners do? Well perhaps something – but even that, I wonder, is not so far hidden beneath your piety. Mr. Butcher would make a fine husband I think. Consider your position in our little family here, Diana. The rest of us look to you, and look up to you – it would be a fine example to us all."

"Surely it is you, ma'm, we would follow in such matters."

Elspeth laughed and returned Diana's question: "And to which uncouth cutter would you have me propose?"

"I mean his lordship, of course."

Elspeth flapped away the question. "His lordship is not at home. And the more likely proposal I'd accept would be adoption."

"To care for and guide you – what more would a respectable woman need from a marriage?"

Elspeth swept out of the kitchen, aware that she looked like her old childish self walking out peevishly on her mother. On the porch, she calmed herself, took stock and decided on a plan. She saw to it that the minister was served further rations of food and ale, and a flask of rum, then went in search of Robert Butcher. As she suspected, that gentleman needed less urging.

One hour later, Diana, at turns glowering at Elspeth and beaming at Robert, stood by her fiancé – hastily splashed and combed – in front of Reverend Galloway, sweetened by a second jug of ale, and mollified now that he had an acceptable professional task to perform. The ceremony was officiated in the kitchen. When the godly man inquired why so humble a location had been chosen for the greatest of the Lord's sacraments, Elspeth replied that the recipients of that rite were the humblest of His creations and a kitchen was an apt setting. Galloway nodded solemnly and, while he prepared himself spiritually for the ceremony, Elspeth went out and spoke to the men and women who, treating the occasion as a holiday, were roaming around the herb gardens and bluff. Emissaries were sent out to chattel-houses and canefields to bring the flock – furtively, behind the cover of the trees – to the shepherd. Elspeth, delighted with her ingenuity, gave bluster to Sir Walter Scott's words:

"Whoop, Jack! kiss Gillian the quicker
Till she bloom like a rose, and a fig for the minister!"

Earnest again in the kitchens, Mistress Baillie bade the Reverend stand with his back to the door, to benefit from the freshness of the draught. Those girls and men who had agreed to partake in the ruse placed themselves in the camouflage of the figs and overgrowth of the bluff between house and cove. In that way, they could see the minister without him seeing them. Those who had already coupled stood together; a few women stood between two men. Mothers held their sons and daughters aloft.

Galloway intoned his lines like a hambone actor at the heart-rending finale of a poorly-written melodrama, insisting first on testing Diana and Robert on Calvin's catechism: "What is man's chief felicity?"

With much nudging and mumbling Diana succeeded in getting Robert through the examination. "I believe in de holy ghos', holy chur', cammunion o' Sents and de rising again o' we body, life everlasting."

Then, like Antony addressing the Romans, the minister projected to the audience of five – the fiancés themselves, Elspeth, with Mary Miller and Errol Braithewaite acting as guarantors. How much more drama he would have given his oration had he known that the true number of betrothed numbered nearly forty.

"Dearly beloved brethren! We are here gathered together in the sight of God and in the face of His congregation to knit and join these parties in the honourable estate of matrimony, which was authorised …"

On he went, repaying in full measure his rations and rum by selecting the longest text possible for such an occasion. "… sembably it is the wife's duty to please and obey her husband in all things that be godly and honest, for she is in subjection …"

Elspeth flinched at every movement in the trees, every squeak and giggle, beyond the open door. The old fool of a minister liked to embellish his rituals with much pacing and changing position, so by the end of the long afternoon he was directly facing the open door. Her heart leapt every time she saw a limb protrude from behind a tree, or an arm stretched up in a yawn, a child scampering from its hideout and being pulled back in with muted laughter. Galloway, mercifully, was much too transfixed by the power of the Word to observe any of these give-aways. "Whosoever polluteth and defileth the Temple of God, him God will destroy!"

At last, Robert and Diana were invited to join hands, which she did poignantly, and he gratefully, and the ceremony was brought to an end. Whereupon the rest of the hidden community appeared as if from nowhere from under boughs and behind hillocks. The minister naturally expressed his surprise at this sudden congregation, likening it to the appearance of the lepers before Christ. Elspeth assured him that the solemnity of his words and the beauty of his voice had brought God-thirsty people to him, and that seemed to dispel any suspicions he might have had. In this way the rite of holy matrimony was administered to all generally – albeit, quite literally, behind the minister's back.

As a group lined the driveway to wave cheerio to their saviour, Bessy Riddoch smiled broadly and called out:

"The minister kissed the fiddler's wife,
An' couldna preach for thinkin' o' it!"

Families for many generations to come considered their betrothals covered in full by the procedure enacted in the year 1838.

His lordship himself was not in the country that day, but on his return, having been informed of the general wedding service, he came armed with bouquets of dried wild heather from Scotland, and suggested to Elspeth that they include themselves in the sacrament. Although he himself had not been actually present, she had – if God's law could penetrate thickets and transcend the hoodwinking of His minister, then it could permeate the clean, open air of an ocean and bind patron and protégée as well.

He made his offer so lightly. Like a frolic, or another game of dressing up. It was impossible to rebuff, to let him down. She smiled, coloured her cheeks as only an actress can wilfully do, and curtsied. "Why my Lord! A mere milkmaid such as I?"

He pressed his offer, laughing, insisting she take the posy from him. She recited lines from her father's "The Shepherd Lass o' Aberlour": "Though ne'er I'll be mistress o' the good Laird's lot / but forby I'll be empress o' his cot!" Still acting, she feigned weeping, declaring she could never live up to such awesome responsibility. He looked at her with deep sadness, and she saw in him the lad at the London Naval, consumed with love for his Anne Bonnies and Salammbos. She was stung by pity for him, and by guilt at her own selfishness. The only favour this man had asked her – in return for freeing her, caring for her, paying for her, keeping her in dresses and books, giving her the run and running of his house – and she was about to reject him.

And for what benefit? She could not leave this place. She would never find a husband amongst ploughmen and carters, and anyway, she would always have George, her first, truest and only husband. The spirit of his child glowing forever within her.

Another role then. Lady Coak. Mistress of Northpoint, matriarch to New Caledonia. That night, she recited for her bridegroom:
"A damsel with a dulcimer
In a vision once I saw;
It was an Abyssinian maid
And on her dulcimer she played,
Singing of Mount Abora.
Could I revive within me
Her symphony and song ..."

The next day Lord Coak informed one and all that, henceforth, Miss Baillie would now be addressed as Lady Elspeth, and the plantation – in honour of all the loyal women who had settled there, and had begun to stock his estate with future generations – was to be renamed Roseneath Estate. Francis O'Neill fashioned a signpost for the gate, misspelling the name "Roseneythe".

Elspeth had the Lyric's old backcloth repaired to its former glory. Calling upon the seamstress skills of her colleagues, they began the lengthy business of repairing the fire and water damage and, in time, whole sections of embroidered stars, crystals and snowflakes were returned to their original exquisite state. It was finally hung at the back of the main hall at the beginning of 1839, taking a full three days and all the spare time of the brawniest men and the talents of the deftest seamstresses to put in place. A further curtain was hung in front of it, so that the community could take its meals in more sombre surroundings. The curtain was only revealed during the regular concert nights and tea-meetings.

From time to time, Elspeth would take a candle at night and slip between the two skins, so that she could be alone with the beautiful backdrop that never saw her perform. After all this time, and all that had befallen her, she could not shake off the feeling that some kind of slow change was taking place inside her. The Storm of '31 had merely shaken things around, like a river disturbed by a thrown rock, disrupting the natural flow of things. Her promised life and true husband had been propelled elsewhere; her girl-child washed up in the womb of another. Over the years, as the Scots girls produced more and more children, Elspeth kept a keen eye on the progress of the mothers, and quickly, after the birthing of a female, inspected it for any telltale characteristics of George Lisle.

Dearest father and mother,

Five years since my departure and still not a word! What sin have
we committed? Or is that you feel the sin is yours – that you sent
your flock away – and now you cannot face us? Even if I were to
concur with that way of thinking, I am sure by now we have all paid
penance enough. Why won't any of you speak?

Let me turn to less sensitive matters, and continue my journal
of life here, which I can only hope you are receiving and have
read. We are well. Lady Elspeth continues unabated with her
theatrical ambitions, producing abridged versions of William
Shakespere's tales and those of Mr. Scott on a stage erected in the
drawing room of the house. She has great plans for Roseneythe –
as it might as well be spelled now, for so it is written everywhere
else – to become a gathering place for drama of the highest quality
on the island. Captain Shaw, our hard but fair-minded taskmaster,
is not altogether persuaded of the plan. Undaunted, Miss Baillie
aims to make thespians of us all, elucidate us in her arts and put
us on her stage. I fear there is not the supply of talent amongst us
that she will require, although the Fairweather girls are passable
performers.

The estate is doing well, by all accounts, and although all of us are
still much indebted, we are assured by the captain, that our owings
will soon be paid off.

My husband is well; hardworking and gentle. In so far as I can be
in a foreign land, I am happy enough. Rob and I live simply, working
and praying together. He is the finest man outside of Scotland, and
next to yourself, father, in kindness, simplicity and decency.

Although you would find our ways here unorthodox, I believe
Roseneythe is at last a properly Christian community. More than half
of the ladies you knew as lasses are married with quines of their own.
Sarah, Bessie, Jean all have families around them now.

I am still in so much need of your guidance, Father and Mother!
My Rob does his best by me, but there are complexities here beyond
both he and I. I will not commit these thoughts to paper, however,
until I am sure you are receiving these letters and intend to reply. We

are troubled that something has become of you all, otherwise, why is it you do not respond?

Hoping in God's name that this letter finds you well, I remain, as in duty bound, your obedient daughter,

Diana Moore

IX

It wasn't Bessy or Susan, or Mary Miller, or even Jean Malcolm – a good-natured, sentimental girl who tried Captain Shaw's patience on account of her laziness and foolishness – but Rhona Douglas who provoked the first great scandal.

Back in old Roseneath, those who knew Rhona thought her an excitable, muddle-headed lassie, forever chattering and incapable of keeping still. Perhaps it was a response to her home life, where she had lived with her mother and grandmother. There had been an air of gloom in that cottage. Passing it, even on a Saturday night, not a sound was heard. Grannie, minnie and daughter could be glimpsed sitting round the hearth, heads bowed in prayer and over the sewing from which they scraped a living. Rhona, when she was set free, on Church mornings and market days to sell her drab shawls and hodden dresses, made up for the silence by talking twenty to the dozen. She spoke about nothing in particular. Small talk about stitching and mending, about pictures she had seen in the flames of her peat fire, an allusion or two to Bible stories, and half-cocked versions of gossip she had heard from other market girls.

Rhona was plain in the truest sense of the word. She was not unattractive: her hair had a nice brown sheen to it; her eyes were clear if speckled; the lass was plain to the point of fading into the blank hills of Roseneath. She was fair like a day without too much rain.

Rhona had arrived at the Coak Plantation as silent as if she were still sewing with her minnie and grannie. The blether and jabber of market days never returned to her in her new world. Most of the women had gone through an initial period of clamming up, as they got used to the heat of the island. They all wilted a little, lungs so full of broiling air they could hardly breathe let alone speak.

They became listless; their bones felt as if they had been replaced by sludge, and their flesh turned to porridge. One by one, however, they accustomed themselves to the heat. But no amount of time, no loose-fitting shift or straw hat could acclimatise Rhona Douglas to the sun and humidity.

Jean Malcolm's sloth was stubborn and willed, which stoked the factor's ire. Rhona's, by contrast, he hardly even noticed. She got through less work than any of the girls, but the effort she put into it seemed greater. Her skin reddened a little like all the others' but not to the point of losing its natural transparency. In the vibrant light of the West Indies her complexion still managed to fade into the background: the glare of hibiscus and petunia blotted her out. Yet Rhona Douglas it was who gave birth to the first black baby.

There had been other unnatural births, but the offspring had either been stillborn, or languished within days, before rumours of their colour had been divulged or confirmed. Mary Lloyd, whose eyesight had been afflicted since the day she stepped into the Barbadian sun, was given the benefit of the doubt: she had thought it was Tomas Gaustadt, the suitor she had stood next to at Mr. Galloway's service, that she'd lain with, though that gentleman had denied it. Mary Malcolm – never so unindustrious as her sister, Jean – had blamed some corrupting influence of the sun and the air in this godforsaken land for the contamination of her child. Such reasoning received nods of understanding from all around: hadn't they all experienced unnatural effects of the climate? Hair fried by the heat, crackling into negro curls; skin burnished and flaking so that they hardly recognised themselves; and – though spoken of less openly – a magnification of their baser urges.

It was generally felt that Captain Shaw was right about the impossibility of white and black successfully multiplying. A survivor offspring of such a coupling could only be a freak of nature. If it could happen at all, it would be as hail or snow falling in the tropics, or the moon eclipsing the sun: deviations from the norm that carried frightening omens. Diana, in her delicate and roundabout manner, had instructed that intimacy between a Negro and a European was not possible for a normal man or woman. "There are terrible tales of those who, losing sight of their God and their pride, fell into misguided unions. The poor girls were torn terribly – for our dimensions are quite unsuited – and, if they didn't die, were unable to bear children by natural means, and every moment of the remainder of their lives tortured by pain."

"Did ony o' them no' say it was worth it, but?"

"This is no subject for entertainment, Susan. Please be more respectful in such matters. If I may continue – the poor black man, whether inveigled into the sin or imposing himself on the victim, finds too that his virility has been throttled and likewise ends up barren."

Diana was proud of the way she could tackle these delicate issues openly – her experience as a midwife and as a scribe, committing to paper details of a very personal nature, had inured her to silly embarrassments. There being no doctor for miles around, and none prepared to travel so far north, Diana assumed the professional, detached voice of a physician. "On the rare occasion that a child has been produced from such a calamity, it generally dies quickly."

After the birth of Rhona's child, however – a noisy, hefty boy, fleshy as a pineapple – Diana's theories faltered. Voices were raised for the immediate expulsion of Rhona Douglas and her bastard. They should be driven out in the middle of the night and left to fend for themselves in the byways amongst brigands, runaways and the dark folk she had elected over her own race. Others called for mother and child to be separated: the boy given to a plantation to be reared, Rhona shunned for all time. Some women felt for Rhona but agreed that such behaviour needed to be nipped in the bud. Jean Homes and Moira Campbell stood firm in their convictions, erect in the pride of ladies who had lived faultlessly. Even Mary Malcolm, who narrowly escaped Rhona's fate, her bairn being stillborn, joined in with the condemners. Captain Shaw listened to these and other solutions, arbitrating which was most suitable.

Susan Millar and Bessy Riddoch argued, for the first time ever, at least in public, over the affair. Bess supported the factor's party, keen to make an example of Rhona, Susan taking a more charitable stance on the issue. Mary Fairweather and Mary Miller led the counter-attack on Rhona's behalf. Throughout the weeks of argument and schism, Rhona Douglas uttered not a single word in her own defence.

Dainty took the side of the pardoners, Annie Oyo the more punitive stance, though the views of neither were sought. Some of the men came down on the side of charity, including Robert Butcher, Diana's husband.

Elspeth felt keenly the disadvantage of her title and position: Diana and Mary urged her to intervene, to make a judgement on the issue. She was petitioned by all parties to join their particular side of the debate. Shaw never addressed her specifically on the question, quite content with his own experience and prudence in such breaches, but made it clear that her endorsement of his position was only to be expected. With Lord Coak in New York, Elspeth's loyalty at this time was rightly to him.

"An announcement from you," pleaded Mary Miller, "might just see the lassie safe."

Retreating to her rooms as often and for as long as she could without too much remark being made of her absence, she implored the ghost of George Lisle to help her. What would he – Emancipist and Liberal on the one hand, heir to a sugar fortune and pragmatist on the other – have done? Failing to detect any reply from his spirit, other than a faint gurgling in her bowels, she turned to the heroines whose words she knew by heart. What would Cleopatra advise? The only line that would come to her was "Be it known that we, the greatest, are misthought for things that others do, and when we fall, we answer others' merits in our name, and are therefore to be pitied."

She searched through books that Albert had given her, but whatever she found seemed only to worsen her dilemma: how dreadful it is when the right judge judges wrong!

What you cannot enforce, do not command. After two days' thought, she found a moment when Diana and Mary were together in the kitchens, and Captain Shaw standing at the door, supping a mid-morning mauby.

"I bear Rhona no ill will, and can't find reason to do more than rebuke the lass. But it must be admitted that she was in contradiction of our rules. I think compassion at this time might benefit us all."

She herself thought the speech pretty enough, but it satisfied no one. Shaw nodded, as if taking note of her position.

As the next days went by, she felt he must have taken her counsel aboard, for no action was taken yet against Rhona. Shaw let Diana nurse child and mother, encouraging the former's appetite and suck, applying balms to the latter. Shaw continued to rail about the dangers of Rhona's behaviour, but said nothing of banishment, separation, or shunnings. He reminded them all that, if they truly wished to construct their New Caledonia, fornication with lowly beings must be seen as the deepest infringement. But for the time being at least, he restricted himself to words.

After a fortnight, Rhona was having ever more difficulty feeding her child; the energy required for producing milk beyond such a lethargic woman. The boy waned. Diana, discussing the situation over evening meals, surmised that the milk of neither black nor white woman could help his hybrid soul. What had started out as a healthy life, dulled and sagged. The boy died before the month was out.

On the night of his death, Diana nursed him and soothed Rhona. Strangely, the very child that the mother had hardly the strength to hold while he was alive, took on a sudden powerful attraction for her, dead. Rhona Douglas snatched his body from Diana, squeezed it to her breast, and lamented over it. The midwife and apothecary, slowly, speaking words of condolence and succour, managed to prise the little cadaver back, and went out into the night, to rid Roseneythe of the poor, lost soul. The following week, Rhona appeared back in the fields, as ashen, silent and ineffective as she had been since the day she arrived.

At the last harvest of 1841 Lord Coak gave his permission for a triple celebration. There was an abundant crop that year and, more importantly for the future, the building of the sugar manufactory had been completed, though its extensive machinery had still to be installed. But the main cause for merriment was the commemoration of Lady Elspeth's ten years on the plantation. A gala concert was organised at which, all who could, played, recited, sang or danced. Elspeth offered a shortened Lady of the Lake to make room for an extra piece: All hail, great master! Albert responded by reciting himself – for the first and only time in public – with a complementary text from *The Tempest*. I have done nothing but in care of thee.

Elspeth was thirty-one years old and, though a certain maturity had settled on her features, it served only to enhance her comeliness. She had kept out of the sun as much as possible to preserve her skin from turning dark or as red as the Scots women's complexions. But, ten years! Ten years that seemed shorter than the ten months that found her in Greenock, and left her storm tossed in Northpoint.

She made an inventory of the successes and failures of her life to date: a vocation wiped out by the whims of weather, the loss of her true love, exile. But also, survival and marriage to a gentleman who had made a lady and a matriarch of her. The prospects of rebuilding the Lyric had hardly been mentioned for three whole years, and when they were, her role in it was unclear. She still could not venture more than halfway down the drive, or two hundred yards in any direction from the porch without being seized by panic. The stabbing wound in her side returned only infrequently now, and the nightmare of being punctured and gouged had all but desisted. She more often submitted to slumber under the dark but soft drifting shades and the mysterious, but welcoming, shadows. She had maintained her position in this new family with decorum, and was treated with respect – saving the likes of Bessy's and Susan's impolite manners – by all. Fate, she decided, had not so much abandoned as lost interest in her.

She still felt, from time to time, movement in her belly. Some twelve girls had been born and, though she continued to inspect each new arrival, the hope that she would find something of her old self and George in the produce of another woman's womb became a madness she hid even from herself.

The concert finished in the wee hours and, the next day, everyone had been granted a late start by Captain Shaw. Elspeth, who had not slept after sun-up for several years, was up before everyone and walked round her herb garden enjoying the freshness of the morning. She loved to watch the West Indian sun pop up out of the sea, like a black boy shimmying a palm. Returning, she came across the only other soul awake – one of the Edmondson boys. She hardly knew the family. Mr. Edmondson had been a slave of Albert's before emancipation, and he and his family, living somewhere just beyond the cane fields, were always pleasant and respectful. She had seen the boy grow up, without ever discovering his name. Stumbling upon him this morning, she was shocked to feel her skin tingle and the hairs on her body unexpectedly bristle.

He was handsome, with large eyes, broad shoulders and narrow hips. There was something gentle about him, despite the harsh work and long hours he endured. From time to time she had occasion to speak directly with him and he was polite without being submissive. Shaw, she knew, had no time for him, nor any of the Edmondson family. "In the old days I would have sold him," he had told her. "The braggart has a mutinous look to him."

He was milking the small flock of black-belly sheep, which Elspeth herself had been rearing to provide cheese and meat for the estate. She smiled at him and he returned her greeting in kind. The morning getting hotter, Elspeth brought out a jug of water with arrowroot for him.

"T'ank yuh mu'm."

"You're very welcome. It must be hot work running around so after sheep."

"It is so."

"You don't like the work?"

"I do. They fine animals, an' I know each one differen' from the other."

As they talked, Elspeth couldn't help but watch a single bead of sweat that had formed under his hairline, and wondered if coloureds' sweat was actually darker than whites'. Perhaps like bracky water in a peaty, autumn burn. The drop sat on his smooth skin, perfectly in the middle of his brow, as if he were an Indian wearing an ebony gem. She reached into her sleeve and found her handkerchief. The boy, as if knowing what was on her mind, watched openly.

"You have a stain here."

He didn't lean towards her as she dabbed at his forehead, nor pulled back. He looked on as she took the handkerchief away and inspected the little stain his sweat had made on it. She smiled, and they went back to drinking their water, the Edmondson boy cupping a little in his hand for one of the lambs to lap.

His skin looked to her at once soft and resilient, and his character was one of simple acceptance. Elspeth leaned towards him and gently kissed his cheek. So plump and soft, the fascination and beauty of his skin lay not in its colour but its youthfulness. The lad smiled happily at her, but remained seated on his felled tree-trunk, the little sheep looking up at her. She moved to kiss his mouth, but the boy leaned gently aside and, still smiling, left.

Had he hit her, the blow would have been less painful. She would have preferred that he'd cried out for his father or Captain Shaw, rather than walk away unperturbed, imperious in his silence.

"Come back here!"

He turned and stopped, but there was no hesitation about him. Nor any hint of embarrassment.

"Obliged t' yuh fuh the water."

Elspeth sat alone on the trunk he had vacated. Had anyone passed by, they would have seen nothing amiss. The smile for the boy lay frozen on her face, and not even a shaking hand betrayed the tumult and nausea that raged inside her.

She was still young enough – not many would have guessed that she had just passed thirty. Her hair was still thick and dark, and her figure trim, but the sheen had gone from her tresses and skin. She was aware of hunching her shoulders a little – the way she used to, bending into the driving rain of her nearly-forgotten early life. To the boy, however, she was an old maid.

It was loneliness, yoked to the burden of authority and responsibility, that had caused her aberration with the black boy. Throughout the whole Douglas case she had heard Shaw and Diana expound that the desire which attracted different races one to another was a seed planted by the devil, as unnatural as a stallion studding a cow. She herself had long believed the same. Nonie and Isabella had told stories, heard third-hand, about women who had lain with black men: the results differed depending on the hour and how much Dalby's Turbo they had drunk. Either it was a glory surpassing all earthly expectations, or a brutish affair. The results of it could be anything from a girl's immediate conversion to the world of the negro – some, it was said, even leaving for Africa at once on trade ships – or a life of regret, pain and dissatisfaction. As for Shaw's and Diana's dire warnings of the offspring of such unions, she knew them to be his lies and her ignorance. Bridgetown was full of half-caste children. If a planter could produce a healthy child with a black maid, then a Scots plough-girl could do the same with a darkie cutter. The only true divisions were social – and she should have considered that before acting so impetuously with the boy.

It was not her colour that repelled him. It was her age. And, she intuited, her position in their shared society. Nothing in his reaction suggested that he was afraid of her; rather he disliked the impression she must have given of presumption. She was the lady planter, he a lowly peasant. Her desires were dictates, his of less significance. The boy's shrug was like Henry's disinterested rescue: he could have saved George and her, or not. The only reason he did was because it was part of his duties. It was not a duty of the Edmondson boy to reciprocate his mistress's cooings.

And anyway she was too old for him. Her life, it seemed, was like the growth of the fig tree before her, its branches extending, ageing imperceptibly, until they reached the ground and disappeared.

A month later, the boy left both the estate's employ and his family home. Shaw didn't ask why – he was pleased enough to be rid of him, and the boy himself made no accusations as she had feared, but left quietly. His father sent along a younger brother to replace the older, making no mention of the reason for the substitution. Elspeth overheard Eliza Morton saying that she saw the boy leaving. "Stravaigin' doon the pathway he was, a wee sack slung o'er his back, like Dick Whittington. I cried efter him, 'Ye leavin' us, Francie?' but he jus' kept on along the way."

Francie. Elspeth only discovered his name in retrospect.

A meeting was held in the autumn of 1844 to discuss the issue of letters. Not a word had been heard from Scotland for eight years. Not everyone attended: Martha Glover, Elizabeth Johnstone and Jean Homes had nobody left at home to hear from. Others, like

Bessy and Susan, had no wish to make contact with their waster fathers, put-upon mothers and already forgotten siblings, but they came along anyway, always keen for a little socialising.

For the rest the pain of their families' silence was keenly felt – and in waves, experienced, strangely, by all of them at the same times. The first years were the worst. They had expected a flood of letters – half-illiterate scribbled notes, pages dictated to a minister or clever sibling. Receiving no word of reply was like having gone deaf.

"I feel as if I've deed an naebody's came to my funeral," Jean Malcolm opened the proceedings.

When it was first explained to them that communication between continents was at best slow, at worst, dead-slow-and-stop, they had steeled themselves and waited patiently. The heavy work, setting up homes, new liaisons with menfolk and the offspring that resulted from them – it all dampened their need to hear from home. But on special occasions – the first baby born at Northpoint, the first child death, Reverand Galloway's marriage ceremony, the laying of the foundations of the manufactory – they all took up their pens again or rushed to Diana, and were dismayed all over again at the lack of reply.

"These are strange times in the old world and the new," said Captain Shaw at the gathering. "People move at a moment's notice from one farm to another, or from the country to the town. It's worse there than here."

"They cannae a' flitted!"

"Lady Elspeth gets letters often enough from the Laird!"

Elspeth saw the injustice, but also understood the difference between a lord of the realm dispatching personal communications alongside important business documents from offices and ships, and farmers' notes inaccurately addressed and delivered to haphazard quaysides. She said nothing, but decided to urge Albert on his next visit to make direct contact with old Roseneath and search for the women's letters.

"Your letters are taken to Carlisle Bay," Shaw was explaining, "and sent by the soonest boat to Greenock – a service for which, mind, the estate does not charge yuh."

"Ach, ye'll find a way, Captain, soon enough," Mary Miller shouted.

The factor ignored her: "As for your kin collecting the papers from the port, I cannot be held responsible. It's a good distance from there to your parish. Perhaps there is no one to make the journey."

"My faither visits regular!" protested one woman.

"Ma brither was posted in Greenock!"

"That was some time ago, Jean Homes. Perhaps his posting has changed."

"This failure to keep us in touch with our families must lie at the feet of the estate, captain. On behalf of us all I plead with you to correct the deficiency." Diana was not usually the one to challenge Shaw, but both she and Mary Miller had been changed women of late. Mary had produced a child a year for the last four years. Mary and Errol Braithwaite were the first couple wed by Diana Moore in a ceremony memorised from Reverand Galloway at her own marriage. Mary's firstborn, Nan, named for her maternal grandmother, appeared less than six months later. A boisterous child now, Nan was the light of Mary's and Errol's lives: a snowy-skinned, lively, laughing girl, her natural naughtiness got her into trouble with everyone around her, and they all shook their fingers at her without being able to hide the delight in their eyes.

After nearly five years of trying, Diana too found that God had granted her a child of her own. She had all but surrendered hope, submitting to His decision that she serve the children of others rather than bear one herself. But Robert Butcher had proved, for an older and staunchly religious man, keen on the duty to multiply – an enthusiasm that had shocked Diana in the early years of their marriage. Pregnancy turned the serious scribe and efficient midwife into a blushing bride, less harsh with her words, sometimes even verging on the skittish. She swelled up more than any of the other woman – a comical sight, her height not much more now than her breadth – but continued with her duties, attending birthings and conducting her own make-do-and-mend baptisms and churching of mothers. She nursed sickly children, and watched, tormented, as some of them died. She applied remedies – of her own concoction, and others learned from Annie and Dainty and even the Captain, who was very knowledgeable in the botany of the island – to the ill, and sorrowfully sped on their way to their Maker babes whose lives would not have been worth the living, or whose deaths, unaided, would have been too much to bear. But with her own babe in her belly the world seemed a brighter, more hopeful place.

She remained the factor's closest confidante amongst the women – while she and Nathanial Wycombe, the nearest thing to a "friend" the oaken captain had, were mutual adversaries – but, in her new condition, found it easier to confront him on a more equal footing.

"It's hardly within my powers, Diana Moore, to correct the ineptitudes of your families, let alone take responsibility for the colonial mailing services."

The women were irked by his manner, but could hardly fault his logic. In any case, the attention of many of them was taken up by squabbling, playing or crying children who found the meeting tedious.

"However, I have some encouraging news regarding this issue," Shaw went on, taking a letter from Lord Coak from his pocket. His lordship at that time was spending weeks in a row at Bridgetown, engaged in conferences with the House of Assembly and the Governor's office, discussing his new manufactory.

"A new railway is planned to connect the west of Scotland with both London and the coast. Lord Coak is actively involved and putting his weight, and some money, behind the early realisation of the laying of track. Such a development will revolutionise post-carrying. There are even plans – which again, Roseneythe Estate is actively fostering – to build a railway here in Barbados. Hold your patience, ladies, and soon the old Caledonia and the new will be like neighbouring parishes."

Taking courage from the success amongst the women for her marriage rites based on Reverend Galloway's service, Diana proceeded to elaborate a further ceremony for baptisms. Once she had midwifed the mother and presented the child to its father – if he were still on the estate – she recited, to the assembled community, prayers and readings taken from the Bible, a few old prayer books, and memory.

"The Saviour will work in the hearts of His Elect... Prevail against Satan. Obtain the Victory." To which everyone responded, "So be it!"

But for funerals there were no words. When the first of their own number passed away – Elizabeth Johnstone, giving birth to little Victoria, then Jean Malcolm of some slow wasting disease, howling her way distressingly to the grave – Diana led the mourners to the graves dug by their husbands, but said nothing. She had been to funerals in Scotland, but could recall only a black, blank silence. If any words were ever spoken, Diana could not remember them. Nor could she find any appropriate prayers in her books and, although there were pertinent verses in the Bible, she felt that silence was all she was capable of. When a child died, she was left utterly wordless.

Several babes had been born – to Mary Lloyd and Jean Malcolm among others – with debilitating symptoms. Small, weak, and either silent as the grave or in a constant scream, the children looked misshapen and discoloured. Not all the ailing babes were the result of transgression. Some were as fair as a ginger-lily petal; some ghastly pale, like the rotting flesh of flying fish washed up on the cove. The more openly expressed view of these tragedies was that they were the vicious effect of the sun and climate.

Diana's instinct was to nurse and fortify them all. But the Captain counselled otherwise. He knew more of life in the tropics, and had become a widely acclaimed expert on heredity. "Protracting these lives in vain is an act of cruelty, Diana Moore. To infant and mother alike."

The women – even those who had reproduced successfully – began to worry that they were not adaptable to the rearing of offspring in this hot world. Especially in the case of sons, whose mortality was especially high. Miscarriages and stillbirths – as if the infants were aborting themselves rather than be born in the wrong place. Babes who screamed their way into life, and just as quickly wailed themselves into oblivion. Daughters and sons who reached six months or a year, or even four, seemingly healthily and happily, suddenly gave up the ghost, giving no explanation for their departure.

In private, stricken with grief and fear, many whispered the influence of Annie Oyo or Dainty. At the height of their distress, some accused them outright of being witches. Or they blamed black labourers for poisoning their future competitors. All secretly wondered if God was not punishing them for leaving their natural homeland behind.

After much thought and prayer, Diana accepted the wisdom of Captain Shaw. She continued to struggle with her conscience: would the good Lord create a spark of life in a being detestable to Him? The factor reminded her, "We live in a fallen world, Diana. It is our duty to make judgements and take steps to return us to God's original intentions."

Children who were only slightly afflicted Diana ministered with ointments prepared from hollyhock and physick nut, sometimes with success. When a woman confessed to fornication with a black fieldhand, she dispensed a brew of fringigo and papaya and tree of life which together had an abortifacient effect, rather than see the patient give birth to a monster. The medicine either rid the belly of the regrettable issue or the infant was born dead. Often, God in His mercy allowed the woman He was punishing to eject the child unassisted by Diana, for which she was always grateful.

The corpses of these little unfortunates were disposed of quickly and without fuss. The child was taken from the mother's side at night, and spirited away. No one knew where, and no one asked. Diana would enter, say a prayer with the household, judge her moment, and wrap the corpse in a sheet. Only occasionally did a woman protest, but was silenced by her family. The midwife would slip out and disappear with her bundle into the night. The idea arose that Diana placed the poor mites in baskets which she set on the sea to carry them home.

All the while Diana herself prayed for a normal partition for her own child, and dreamed of a boy or a girl – she did not care which – returning with her to old Roseneath. She imagined her aged mother's eyes shining with love for her grandchild and her father dangling the bairn on his knee. These were the dreams that sustained her through her demanding partnership with Captain Shaw, and gave her the strength to endure many sad days.

In 1845, nearly fifteen years after Elspeth's removal from Garrison to Northpoint, Moira Campbell's second child passed suddenly away. The eighteen surviving women, plus some ten or twelve of their daughters old enough to attend, stood the following morning in silence at the top of the bluff to pray for the laddie's soul. The boy's father – Bernhard, a solid placid man – took the loss badly. He had produced to date three strapping daughters but not yet a single son. The child, Christened Georg, spelled in the father's Germanic way, was as peaceful and sweet as Bernhard himself. Brown-haired and green-eyed, he should have grown into just the kind of able, biddable man Roseneythe sorely needed.

The evening repast that night was a sombre affair. The pregnant Diana read longer from the Bible than usual, recalling God's command to Abraham to sacrifice his only son. Even Shaw was visibly moved and had kind words for the devastated Moira and Bernhard. He let the entire workforce sit on longer than their allotted forty-five minutes' eating time, signalling to Robert Butcher to bring out a flagon of rum, so they could all drown their sorrows.

The Captain stayed on drinking unusually late, in the company of Robert Butcher, Malcolm Baxter and Nathanial Wycombe. Robert retired when Diana finished her chores. Nathanial and Malcolm went off with a flagon of rum in search of Bernhard, reported to be wandering down by the cove. Still Shaw sat on, letting the candles and lamps gutter out around him.

Elspeth remained awake in the upstairs library, reading and talking to Mary and Diana about the day's sad events. The clock had already struck ten when Mary came in to bid her goodnight. "The captain is still below stairs, Ma'm."

"Is he drunk?"

"I've ne'er seen him fu', so I wouldna know. I dinna think so. Still, I'm feart o' spierin' him to leave."

"I'll go down, Mary. Thank you."

By the time she had closed her book, doused the lamps and went downstairs, Shaw had gone. Only recently, however, for she could still smell him in the musty air of the night. She had been aware of his smell at Roseneythe for as long as she could remember: an unexpected sweetness. Like any plantation-dweller, he smelled of sugar cane, but coupled with a balmy flavour, like children's candy, that might originate in the treacly cheroots he sucked on. Neither pleasant nor objectionable, it was Shaw's unmistakable mark, and served as a warning signal of his approach.

She followed this sugary trail out onto the porch. There he stood in the middle of the herb garden smoking a last cheroot and staring up into the sky, its contents of stars and moon buried under thick cloud. The night throbbed with insects, heat and frogs, like an aching head. The factor was only ten years her elder, but Elspeth had to remind herself of the fact – the authority of his demeanour and the thick veins that gnarled his neck and arms always put her in mind of the ancient fig trees around the estate. He had thickened out a little since she first saw him – that skeletal puppet that had bellowed at her now had the hide of an old horse.

"Poor Bernhard. Do you think he will recover from the blow?"

"He's not too old. Time yet to father another son."

"Can one son replace another?"

The Captain looked into the darkness of front of him. "Better a replacement than no son at all."

He walked a little towards the drive, and Elspeth, realising how little she knew of this man, followed.

"Did you ever have a child yourself, Captain?"

He shook his head slowly and answered as though giving his opinion on an agricultural matter. "I made a covenant many years ago to dedicate myself solely to my work. I was once a lustier man than the one you see before you. I hope the thought doesn't offend you."

She laughed – the notion of a lusty Captain Shaw was comical and yes, perhaps a little offensive – but also at the idea that anyone could suspect her of primness. "If once there was a lustier man here, Mr. Shaw, then there was also once a more forthright woman."

He nodded his assent, as if he had always known the fact.

"There was a time, sir, when I was known in this island for my bluntness. Perhaps too much."

They began walking towards the drive where his quarters lay, the Captain, thanks to the rum, speaking openly and relaxed.

"So I've heard."

"Though naturally I am ashamed of it."

She was not ashamed. She felt not the slightest tinge of remorse for anything she had done or said in those glorious days. She found herself giggling in front of this severe man – as though she were the girlish debutante of old – and being rewarded with a rare smile. They walked on down the driveway towards his home. She had often seen him at the end of the day walking in the direction of the gates, or marching up between the twin lines of trees in the morning, but had never discovered where his house actually stood. If they kept on walking, she would have to turn back – the bend before the last stretch of drive to the gates was her limit.

"Were they very dreadful, these stories of me?" Why was she doing this? It had never occurred to her to trifle with the Captain. He was much too austere, and too injured. Moreover, she knew he had little time for her. Perhaps it was a need for release from the day's tension and sorrow that triggered a devil-may-care mood within her. He, too, was in a lighter temper. She walked jauntily, as though she were at George's side again and the trees at either side of them ranks of soldiers saluting them.

"Such matters don't trouble me the way they do others."

"The tomfoolery of silly young actresses?"

Were it not for the baggy plainness of his work clothes, the captain would not have seemed quite such the peasant countryman. He would never be handsome, but he might scrub up respectably enough. She smiled at the thought – what airs and graces she had acquired since becoming a Lady! The upstart libertine of the Lyric was an act she had calculated to play; the colonial planter's lady had grown in her without her noticing it. "Thank heaven for you and Diana, captain. You keep us all on the straight and narrow. But I know you are a little scandalised by the easy virtue of the artisan class?"

She was playing her old self again, revelling in piquant conversation. She felt a spring in her step for the first time in an age. But Shaw was incapable of social gaiety. "I have important work here," was all he could say. His brow furrowed to emphasise the gravity of his words, but he forced a smile, creasing the skin between beard and mouth. In that costly gesture, she detected something she hadn't noticed before: complicity. Shaw regarded Elspeth as one of his own followers! Another Diana; a Nathanial Wycombe, even. How long had the distant, evasive Captain considered her a friend? They had worked together effectively enough in the past, it was true. But as enforced colleagues. What was it the taciturn, gnarled factor felt he had in common with a supercilious actress, the usurper of his patron's time and attention?

Bitterness. A hidden distress. The feeling of being blown somewhere you were never meant to be. Was that it? Shaw talked on as they strayed further from the lights of the house behind them, deeper into the driveway. The darkness, making the path unrecognisable, made it safer: there was nothing round the next bend; not the gates, not the road behind them, just more black night, as though the dark had hollowed out a cavity in the world for them. The blitheness she had felt just moments ago left her. Shaw and her alone in the midnight; two iron nuggets of equal magnetic field; each hammered by uninvited hands into new and unnatural shapes. A feeling of recklessness overcame her – like it used to in front of coarse audiences; against the oak tree with Thomas; the morning she kissed the perspiration off Francie Edmonson's brow. Lines and passages from plays filled her ears. And, Demetrius, the more you beat me, I will fawn upon you. In the gloom – thickening with every step – she lost sight of the path below her feet and the man walking next to her. Instead she saw a picture of herself, lying down, without warning, on the path before his feet. Use me as your spaniel, spurn me, strike me, neglect me, lose me. The feeling was akin to the abandon she had experienced with George – perhaps more powerful: the need to strip away layers of herself that had accumulated silently over a decade and more. The veneer of false pedigree, the film of unlooked-for and unwarranted dignity. She felt tree-roots and stones stabbing painfully into her back; caught her breath at the notion of her pulling up her skirts, feeling the dust and grime on her thighs, dirt on her breasts. She was overwhelmed with a craving to show herself to a man who cared nothing for her,

have him lay his wooden weight on her. The simplicity and directness of it! No preludes or preambles. No parading or reciting. The
freedom that was once gifted her with the help of Dalby's calmative and the sea. She had been withered by the ghostly caresses of
an old man's eyes; the cleanliness of fingers that refused to touch
her. Rejected by the lowliest of black boys, deserted by her dead
lover. She needed the fierce feel of skin and hair, the ache of rocks
beneath her, branches scouring her. She caught her breath, and
could not fill her lungs again.

How could she be mother to such perverse desires? "What worser
place can I beg in your love – than to be used as you use your dog?"
She became aware, through the raw fog in her mind, that Shaw
must have asked her a question, for he stood gazing expectantly at
her. As she leaned in towards him she saw the astonishment in his
eyes. He let her kiss him and push her body into his. He put his arm
on her shoulder and turned her around. For a moment she thought
he was about to escort her back to her house. Instead, he led her
into the trees. Without a word, he helped her over clumps of shrub
and boulders and she, assuming he was searching for a clearing,
looked avidly around too. She might be walking to her doom. He
would have her, and expose her for the debauch that she was. If
that were to be her fate, so be it. When her life was being properly
lived, chance grabbed her at unexpected moments and altered her.
His sickly-sweet smell, sharper now than ever before, the grip of
his fingers, and the ocean that surged under her dress, were all that
drove her on at this moment.

He did not take her deeper into the wood, but steered her towards
his house. The closing of the door behind her was like a breath
snuffing out the flame of her lust. She had wanted to be nowhere,
with no one, just her body in the wilderness, unfastened from her
life. Now, in the room where he lit the lamps, there was too much
of this man. His writing desk – a solid rich mahogany, gleaming
inappropriately in the mean room, on which were neatly set out
bundles of papers, quills, a Bible. The chair was home-made, and
the couch on which he sat and beckoned her to him was a hard,
homespun pallet. There were pages from Scripture pinned to his

wall, alongside other writings, all in his own hand. Sheets of paper with the names of Roseneythe's women and men, and a tally of their owings and their offspring. Hanging on a peg on the door was his militia suit which she had seen him wear, hunting down the maroons.

She sat beside him, but keeping her distance, the hot urges she had felt only a moment ago completely supplanted by a cold dread. Not of him directly – he looked too taut and heavy to make any lunge at her – but at herself; at the degradation she was capable of. She could see by his loose-fitting trews that he was erect, and the sight revolted her, and seemed to revolt him too, for he strained his head upwards as though trying to uncouple his upper from his lower half. He took out a cheroot and began to smoke.

Shaw could only have chosen to live so meanly: Albert would surely have lodged him better had he so wished. Sitting there, in silence, she knew she had never sunk so low in all her life. From the gaiety of the theatre and the finery and wit of George, she had fallen to the level of seducing a Christian man in his slave-hut. The glittering prospects of her days in Bridgetown had been reduced to a vulgar fumbling in the woods: she was the girl again, with her back to a tree after a show at a mean penny-gaff. Another woman would weep, she thought. But her eyes remained dry. Tears would come later, once she was safely home and confessing to George, her true husband, and their waiting child, who must be looking down now at her disgrace.

"I forgot myself."

He nodded. His grey eyes blank, as though he, too, had forgotten who he was. A man as grey as a loch at dusk, and as sad as the memory of it.

"Do you ever think of going home?" he asked.

Home. The word sounded different on his lips. Not the nostalgia of women riven from their hearths; no echo of soft spring and leafy dell. Something harder, more distant, but more real. She knew what he meant, and yes, every aching moment of her life, all she had ever wanted was home.

Elspeth prayed that no one knew of her infrequent lapses. Those few shameful liaisons that happened out of the blue over the next few years, and which were banished from her mind no sooner than they had occurred.

How could she possibly have explained – even to herself – that, at these junctures of her life, she simply could not think clearly; found herself in the midst of ill-advised actions, without ever having decided to embark upon them? The women around her could not know of her need for the touch of a man's fingers, not just the brush of his eyes. None – certainly not Diana or Mary Miller, not even the intemperate Susan or the drunkard Margaret Lloyd – could have understood what happened between Elspeth and Shaw.

On that first of their meetings, they sat apart from each other all night until, with the first blur of dawn, he escorted her to the house. They exchanged not a word as she hurried ahead of him, the light bringing the gates and the outside world back into existence and chasing her back to the big house. They bid each other a hasty, formal farewell at the porch. In the days and months that followed, he acted as if nothing had changed between them, treating her in the same formal manner he always had.

When finally they fell together onto his pallet bunk – nigh on two years after that first encounter – she was, as before, in a fevered and detached state. George had made love with a joy and inspiration; even the farmboy of her youth tackled and worked at her with a greater doggedness than Shaw. Yet, despite his deficiencies in energy, she found an unexpected gentleness in his touch. His milky sugar-scent anaesthetised her. At first she had tried imagining she was with George, but the mental transition was too great. George's skin had been soft, nearly hairless, and responded with a pulsing or goose-fleshing at her every touch; Shaw's hide was taut and hirsute, his movements edgy. But his gradual entering of her – so tentative as though he feared he might break her – rendered her dazed and drowsy.

Three or four more times they fell together – exactly how many she couldn't say, as each encounter was immediately obliterated from her memory. The drowsiness that overcame her when she was with the factor was only a magnification of the torpor she fell into generally. She continued to organise the concerts, oversee the work of Mary Miller, Annie and Dainty, dance for Albert on the fewer and fewer occasions that he came home – but all of it she felt she was doing in a mild trance.

For her neighbours in Roseneythe these were exciting times, full of work, weddings, births. Dramas now happened only in other people's lives: Diana losing her babe; Mary's girl, Nan, growing faster and more noisily than the rest of her generation; Martha Glover's death. The building of the Manufactory. Like the spectacles she now found she had to use to read the smaller text in books, the world was clear, but separated from her.

On the other hand, the dream of colours and shifting shapes that had seldom left her sleeping mind in all those years, seemed closer, intimate. She began to recognise the shapes as people, crossing to and fro, and the soft red glow as fire, or light. A memory of early childhood perhaps. Or a childhood promised but never lived. Elspeth, keeping the dream alive in her head when she woke, letting the colours drift and flow around her as she went about her mundane tasks, wondered if she had the power to remember events that had never actually happened.

In the same year as Elspeth's first fall into the arms of Shaw, Diana Moore was accused of murder. Martha Glover publicly claimed the midwife had stolen her baby from her side, and killed it.

Martha had problems from the earliest stages of her pregnancy and Diana had nursed her, as she had always done with all the women, successfully bringing her to full term. The night of the delivery, however, had been excruciating for the mother-to-be, resulting in her passing out as Diana cut the umbilical cord of her little boy. When Martha awoke both Diana and her baby had vanished.

No one else was present at the time, so it was Diana's word against Martha's, and the two descriptions of the evening were in every respect dissimilar. Martha admitted she had fainted, but only for the briefest of moments, and claimed that she had heard the healthy cries of her infant boy. Diana maintained that complications had set in early; that Martha – an elderly first-time mother, at forty-two – had drifted in and out of consciousness for several hours. She had woken briefly only when the child was being pulled from her, and was quite insensible again immediately after. The sad fact – and one which a woman who had waited so long for a child understandably could not endure – was that the boy was born malformed and lifeless.

Diana never said it directly, but everyone understood from the language she used that the child was also tarnished. Martha vigorously denied the rumour – but could not, or would not, name the father. She was an unlikely one, to be fair, to tumble with a darkie, but then, equally, she was desperate for a child, and perhaps her standards had dropped accordingly.

"Bring me the boy's body and I'll show you he was not only fair, but strong and healthy, too!" cried Martha to anyone who would listen. Elspeth, Mary and Nan Miller, as well as the less powerful women, all felt for her. But they trusted Diana's expertise – not to mention her piety. Mistress Moore was of a kind that shuddered at even the hint of a little white lie. And the idea of digging a child's body up was distasteful. When Diana refused to reveal the whereabouts of the child's remains, many took it as proof that she sent them out on the water in the direction of Scotland – another little Moses in a sailing crib.

Martha persevered for months, demanding that Captain Shaw take some action. Along with Susan Millar and Bessy Riddoch, Martha was one of the few women who had managed to strike up relations with the distant factor. She was friendly, too, with his deputy, Nathanial Wycombe, so alone amongst the women she had some purchase to pursue her case. For a week or two, all Roseneythe held its breath, waiting for Shaw's reaction.

"The mannie's in a swither," Bessy Riddoch said. "On the one haun' he has to bide by his complouter Moore, whae does hauf his work for him but whose sermonising he cannae thole. On the ither, Martha's a proper freen', and a freen' o' his Billie Wycombe."

At last, and to the relief of most, the factor came out quickly and strongly on Diana's side. She was, he proclaimed, the most decent, pious and dependable of ladies. She had worked loyally and steadfastly for over a decade, and her propriety and righteousness were not to be questioned. He defended her right – a right granted by his own authority – to inform mothers of the disposal of remains as she saw fit in each circumstance. Given Martha Glover's evident anguish at the loss of her child, Diana had acted properly, and out of a humane desire not to cause the lady any further upset. He reminded them all of the difficulty of producing and nurturing a successful species, made in their own image, under inhospitable and peculiar climactic conditions. Those who wanted the best for themselves and their families must bide by the rules he and Diana set.

In between the cheerless transgressions with Shaw were rich years for Roseneythe, but silent ones for Elspeth. She looked into herself, trying to pull the fading memories back from a void inside her. The shape and motion of the Alba; the dressing-rooms of The Lyric; the countenance of her darling George Lisle. She could no longer imagine the face of the daughter she was meant to have, and began to lose faith in the hope that that child would ever emerge even from another woman's belly.

Roseneythe Estate
1845

Father. Mother.

Perhaps this news will move you to speak.

I had hoped to write with good news, a first grandchild. However the good Lord has decreed I am not adequate for such reward.

Silence.

Mother, is that still all you offer me? Am I an evil woman, Father? Why do you hold your tongue?

The Lord raiseth me up and casteth me down. He tore the life out of my womb with such infliction of pain that I hoped the searing would continue to my heart. I feel now I could rip it out of my breast with my bare hands.

My child would have been an honourable boy – fruit of a good man. No taint of the lust and stupidity and degradation the majority of our number have shown here. But I held no ceremony for him. I took him this morning, before the sun began its daily scorching of us, and planted him with the outcast bairns. If he was so unacceptable in the eyes of God, then so he shall be in the eyes of the world. Captain Shaw came with me – we alone know the location of our local Purgatory. He is the only one who understands the torture I suffer. I begin to feel the fury he has for our Redeemer.

What do you say to that, Father? Your devout daughter tempted to howl curses at the heavens.

I shall never go home now. I have no wish to. You do not want me there though I do not want to be here. I will continue with the profession I have assumed here. From this day onwards I will do my duty as you taught me – you, parents who refuse to speak to their only daughter, who shun me as Christ Himself now does. I will do as I am instructed by my superiors. That is what I have been schooled that the Lord expects of me. Let us put Him to the test.

I am surrounded by silence – within me and without. How is it you cannot answer your only daughter when she calls out in anguish to you? Do you care so little?

Diana Moore

Recommencement of Captain R. Shaw's Disclosure

I left off my journal some years ago overtaken by the sudden &
momentous work at the Coak Estate at Northpoint. The record of
my Project here is fully reported & available for those who wish to
study my method. Were it not for my successes – & some inevitable
setbacks – I might have found time to elaborate on these rough notes
of my more Personal life. As it is I have only a few hours to bring up
to date the story that I began nearly two decades ago.

I found myself paying-work for a while on the estate of the
admirable Mister Barclay. This planter had interests beside those of
sugar & crop. He had made a deal of money from trading in slaves
when such a profession was still permitted. He had invested in the
island of Barbuda in the management of stud farms for the breeding
of slaves. He knew how much of Whydah could be mixed with
Congolese to produce a tall strong worker who yet was not rebellious
& did not eat too much.

Through study & practice I now know all there is to know about
the African. I know that the Wolof & Mandingo are to be avoided
– that they have knowledge that is not Natural & should not spring
from behind dead eyes. The Congolese – despite a bearing blacker
than all other Africans – are strong – indifferent to fatigue – tranquil
& born to serve. They take no heed of our world so that all is
balanced in theirs. Their distaff are full-breasted & breed readily. The
best produce will be the offspring of a Whydah bitch & Cormantine
bull. The other way around & you result a strong & healthy cub –
but prone to be sullen.

I say again – I do not despise the Negro. The meek shall inherit
the Earth. I take the words of the Good Book as they are written
undiluted. By mixing his blood we have robbed the African of his
innate weakness which looks to us like idiocy. It only does so because
the Negro's time has not yet come – nor will it for many a generation
& perhaps never now that we have toyed & interfered with him.
Kinmont saw in the passivity of the darkie no less than our Saviour's
own mildness & the least of His creations who shall be suffered unto
Him. The Negro's ascension will undoubtedly take place in the Last

Age – some time off yet I trust. Least until I have terminated with this damned Disclosure.

I heard that a young man in the northern Parish of St. Lucy was struggling to maintain his plantation. I had long since relinquished ambitions to own a plantation or business of my own – dedicating myself now to a greater cause. An Estate under the management of an unapprised young newcomer – he was reported to be no more than a lad – was the perfect place for me to practice my art & recent profession. I journeyed to the Parish to meet this man – or, in actual fact, boy. My life has been tarnished since squeezing out of my mothers thighs, by runts & shrunken striplings. I do not believe that I have ever encountered such a confused & lost Soul. It was clear that my very presence frightened the girlish little milksop – a pederast I took him of – a fucker of pups' arses – a pintle-licker – & an English pouffe. He was introduced to me by his father – who on the contrare was a manly gentleman – as Mister Albert Cox. Once the father had agreed my conditions & secured my services I built a house for myself on the Plantation. Only in one particular did the older man veer from the path of Truth – though he was still frank.

"From this day on Master Shaw you shall call my son Lord Coak."

"I cannot see how I can sir," quoth I, "unless it be the legitimate Truth."

"Well it is & it isn't," said he. "This is a New World, Shaw, where what went before is of little use to us. Perchance my son is not a Lord in England but peradventure he may still be one in the Colonies. He will get his work done faster & better with that Title hanging from his hat. So I think will you."

"I am not sure Mister Cox – if that not be too lowly a denomination for you – that I am convinced by your argument."

"I have money, Shaw. Enough of it and made by my own wits to have less need of a sobriquet. But you, man – have you never been denied something you knew in your heart was yours by right?" I need hardly put in writing here what I answered to that!

"I have done my investigations on you, Shaw, & taken up your references. It has come to my attention that – were the world in the right order – you ought by now to be a Captain in the Colonial Militia. Then a Captain you are here – & my son a Lord."

Then he added an afterthought that I considered most wise & proved to me the man's intelligence. "For what," quo he, "is a lie but the truth in masquerade?"

At once I saw the sense of his reasoning but I must confess that for nigh forty year since each time I uttered the word "lord" to that perverted English fop it stuck deep & hard in my craw.

It so happened that only weeks after my inauguration at the estate of Lord Coak – in the year eighteen hundred & fifteen – that our injudicious Assembly passed the slave registry bill – a demand that all Owners notify the government of the number – age – sex – & duties of their stock – to ensure that none were still engaging in the now illegal business of buying & selling slaves. The poor Negroes & indentured coloureds – being low in education & misinformed by Mischievous elements – mistook the purpose of this act & thought that they had been set free.

When Freedom was long in coming – though – as we are witnessing now – they have no gift for Freedom – they supposed that they had been cheated of their emancipation. A riot broke out on various Plantations – for the most part in the southern regions where I had worked with Mr. Barclay. Indeed I had met the coloured Francklyn who was one of the organisers of the insurrection & have seen at close quarters the slave Bussa.

I played my active part in the quelling of the bloodthirsty Mutiny & in the Emergency. I was permitted to re-enlist as a Militia soldier. The quelling of the slaves took no more than a few days but long enough for these half-made men living unnaturally in a foreign land to make some great destruction. After the successful subjection of the mutineers there followed several months of tracking down & testifying against the perpetrators of the crimes that were committed. I myself indicted over eighty men & some twelve women & testified at the hearings of nearly fifty. I attended as many of the Hangings as I could – not because I derived any pleasure from such woefull scenes – but because it is important that we are honest & direct in our actions & in the consequences of our actions. At each hearing I pleaded for mercy on behalf of these sad Souls & argued for their deportation to the dark Continent of Africa. That Continent will not always be dark. Once it has its children back again – & the Natural harmony of things restored – generations in the future will look to that great yet primitive land & will see Christ's light shining from its depths. I am not ashamed to say that I wept openly at each & every Execution. I took but one pleasure when the Field Marshals of the Militia – albeit tardily – awarded me the Title Captain and that was that; henceforth Lord Albert was the only liar at Northpoint.

Thereafter I continued to work diligently for Coak – but still managed to read & discuss great issues with like-minded people. As Nancy once said – though that sullied ethiopic concubine is the last person from whom I should take counsel – Studdiation is better than Eddication. I watched & I observed & I learned.

The cause of emancipation only got worse & worse & the very arts in which I had been trained were seemingly to become redundant. Then – on the morning of a week after the dreadfull storm – a woman stumbled half-dead onto my land & fell into my arms. She was torn & ragged – her hair a bird's nest & her jacket & dress sundered so that she showed nearly a full breast. Had the pair of them flopped out it would have been more fitting – for this woman augured not one but two new beginnings in my life.

I can barely press on with this Disclosure for my hand shakes. At the memory of her body falling into mine – most surely – & of the gentle milky pap she displayed – surely again. But I tremble more at the memory of what she proposed to me & how the last cloud from my philosophical sky evaporated. That lady – quite unwittingly – brought all my training & experience back to life & uncovered for me the project to which I was born.

'Twas she that introduced me to my Great Work. She who proposed we bring a brood of females from Scotland & mate them with ready-leathered colonial stock. As Mr. Barclay taught me – all breeding must be undertaken through the female line. Soon I had my very own flock to cultivate at Roseneythe. A solid Lowland Scots variety on which to graft the best of the Northern Races. (The Lowlander is a dependable mongrel – he keeps a hung head & a decently lowered eye.)

Why shouldn't the fundaments of my Science be applied to the European as much to the African? The savage it is true – being less developed – is the most easily & soonest distilled. But I have proved the Creating & Managing of bloodlines is no less Successfull in the White race.

My greatest aggravation – as it will have been to all Men of Science & Spirit – is the waywardness of women. The bitch of the Scotch race divides her time twixt psalming & lifting a leg. I should have calculated that few of them could resist guddling tween furzy banks for a great black trout. Tupping a darkie would aye be fine sport for them. No matter. Enough will remain Loyal to my Ambitions to create their New Caledonia.

I must put this pen down – for the shaking will not stop. Trembling still at the memory of the day that body fell into mine & of the gentle milky tit. At how she made my Destiny clear. It trembles too with Anger. Were it not for the slack-pintled tinsel-Laird (ne'er indeed – & mayhaps his Father knew it – was a Cox so falsely named!) & his peering & love of recitations – the success you see around you would have been plain a generation back. The Devil take them both – the onanistic Planter & the schismatic wench Bathsheba.

X

Twenty-three years after George was blown away in the Storm, Elspeth finally gazed on the chestnut-bright eyes and mild countenance of a newborn girl, and recognised at once the combined spirit of George Lisle and her own blithe, younger self. She couldn't quite say why but perhaps because the rain was heavy that night and the wind powerful, because the child was one of the Miller clan who reminded Elspeth of her own sisters and father and aunts, she felt this child was going to be special to her. Or perhaps it was because the colours that night in her dreams – while Bathsheba was being born in a chattel-house – were especially intense and fast-moving. And then, in the morning, when she first saw her, she seemed to know her already. Bathsheba Miller she was christened, but it was Elspeth herself who gave her her pet name, the Rain Child.

The birth followed another great event, less than a year before, in 1853, the grand opening of Lord Coak's magnificent Sugar Manufactory. It had been twenty-five years in planning, taken fifteen years to build and four more to achieve its full, astonishing, potential. Of the most modern design, it produced an extra ton of semi-processed sugar per acre than any Barbadian plantation had managed before. It recovered three-quarters more sucrose and muscovado, and a higher grade of massecuite. It could single crush, double crush, and triple dilute if necessary. Whatever the market demanded. The whole process was overseen by Gideón Brazos, under Mr. Shaw's authority.

Brazos was brought from Cuba, procured together with the machinery design. He was a Spanish-speaking quadroon – neither of which circumstances was agreeable to Captain Shaw. Quadroons were confused and above themselves, and the Spanish language brought elements of Popery and slothfulness. Brazos showed signs of having Hausa blood, an arrogant tribe. The planter assured his factor that Brazos was a slave from a country which still respected the old traditions, and would be transferred to Barbados on the basis of indenture. They needed someone who knew how to run a refinery, who understood the modern techniques so novel to Lord Coak and Captain Shaw. To Gideón Brazos, such crafts were as familiar as the palms of his cinnamon hands.

They also bought a woman in Cuba to be his mate. Shaw instructed Coak how to choose such a companion with care, sending him detailed notes on physical and mental signs to look out for, and questions to ask owners concerning the women's personal history and records. Coak finally selected Golondrina Segunda, a woman in her settled mid-thirties, of reasonably pure Whydah blood. Nearly a decade older than Brazos, a mother already and therefore schooled in the ways of the world. It was decided not to have her accompanied by her issue as they would take up too much of her time, and interfere with her relationship with Brazos.

Since the launch of the factory Elspeth's nights had been disturbed by sudden releases of hissing steam, the distant trundle of carts in the morning, men shouting in English and Spanish, women in Scots. Her days were rearranged to suit the new production. Mealtimes were shorter, concerts truncated or cancelled, and the house during all daylight hours, it seemed, emptied of people. The silence was made all the more intense by the clatter and rumble echoing down the driveway.

The factory brought a renewed sense of industry and increased prosperity to Roseneythe. The pistons pumped away from early in the morning till late at night, eating up wood at a tremendous rate. Carts and drays hauled trunks of trees up the driveway. Coak and Shaw saw to it that all the supplies needed to feed the monster were furnished by the estate itself – Coak's lands bordering a gully thickly wooded with mahogany, fig and jacaranda trees, and what was left of the old Scots birches – freeing Roseneythe almost completely from dependency on the rest of the island. Only the shippers' agents arrived at the gates in the mornings after harvest to transport product to the ports around Bridgetown.

In the time of the factory, Elspeth had less to do while everybody else worked doubly hard. Mary and Diana still referred to her in matters of import, but were adept now at running the big house and the women's lives by themselves. The extra labour created by adding sugar refining to the estate's interests meant that, for a while, the workforce was at full complement. Lord Coak would not hear of his wife taking anything to do with the dusty and dangerous operations that went on in the new building, positioned at the other side of the driveway from the house, near to the estate gates. Lady Elspeth only ever saw the decayed interior of the factory many years after its closure.

The Rain Chile's maturing coincided with the time of the factory. Born when her mother – Nan, the robust but unruly daughter of Mary Miller – was yet to reach sixteen, Bathsheba was prematurely condemned while still in the womb. However, the combined circumstances of the new factory, the clean smir on the night of her birth, and the girl's own delicate beauty, obliterated all previous omens. Nan was accepted back into the community and her daughter quickly became a favourite.

The rain that night fell golden from the evening sky: cold, sparkling drops the colour of fine tawny rum. The great storm had blown everything that Elspeth Baillie had loved – George, the Lyric, her career, her home in Garrison – up into the heavens, where for twenty-three years they had tumbled and spun. Now, in 1854, her hopes and dreams could be glimpsed again in the bright brown eyes of this girl, and heard in the chime of her laugh. Bathsheba was Nan's, conceived of an unknown father, but she was also Elspeth's and George's, a girl who would become, under her ladyship's care, a true grand blanc. The rain-child who would lead them all home, restore the natural hierarchy of things, dropped as silkily from Nan's womb as the rain shower fell from the cloudless sky. A slippery, cold wet child that Diana, who assisted at the delivery, declared was utterly without blemish. Even the afterbirth poured clear and fresh and colourless.

That her father was unidentified was not a cause of much disquiet: Bathsheba was hardly alone in the circumstance and, anyway, no one ledgered fathers anymore. Diana baptised the girl in the traditional way, and spread the word of her exceptional fairness. From the day after her birth everyone helped to protect their girl from the prying eye of the sun. Nan and Diana swaddled her as a babe, then later, dressed her in the lightest of fabrics. Linen, cotton, taffeta. Materials unfamiliar to their own skins, but brought by Lord Coak for his wife from Europe – silk of the finest denier, satin adapted from Elspeth's old costumes. Diana cared for the child as if she were her own. For years after the stillbirth of her own bairn, Diana Moore had lived like a slave-woman: doing all that was expected of her, but joylessly, as one goes about a compulsory task, disinterested. Her deep faith and the kindness and loyalty of Robert Butcher helped her recovery, but it was Bathsheba who returned her to her old, bustling self. The girl had the innate capacity of turning all around her into surrogate mothers, brothers, sisters. Nan was delighted to share her child. The grandmother, Mary, took special care of her darling; Sarah Alexander sang to her and Sarah Fairweather told stories; Bessy Riddoch taught her tricks, Mary Riach helped with numbers. Elspeth's life changed, nurturing her towards her future vocation. Even Lord Coak took a shine to the lass.

His lordship had shipped a piano from Germany some six years earlier to enhance the evening concerts. It was a beautiful if fantastic-looking contraption, so solid and heavy it took six men, taking shifts over an entire afternoon, to haul it from the porch to the hall. Made of mahogany with rosewood inlay and intricate scrollwork, no one had ever seen such an instrument before. Those who had seen any kind of piano expected it to be as long and flat as a dining table with keys attached. But this creature was twice as tall as it was long and, despite its weight, shorn off abruptly at the back.

"It's an Upright," Coak informed them. "Listen to the sound it makes."

Elspeth, who had learned to play concertina on stage as a child, tried it out. It was as loud and metallic-sounding as the factory, making the window casements rattle and bringing people in from fields a quarter of a mile away. Albert had also brought tuition books for her to learn and, while the rest of the community were cutting cane or crushing it in the factory, she worked hard at her lessons – with the sole intention of teaching young Bathsheba. The girl began to learn when she was only five, her small fingers and nervousness at such a massive machine coaxing a sweeter sound out of it than anyone else had managed.

"Look!" cried Elspeth one day, bringing Albert in to hear the girl after only a few months of preparation. "My father would've called her a musicker!"

Albert smiled and patted Bathsheba's brown, tousled hair. "She's no Mozart, let us not be overly indulgent. But she does produce a warmth in her simple melodies."

Elspeth and Bathsheba would spend an hour most evenings, sitting side by side on two dining chairs, making up chords and sequences for which they had no name. They soon gave up on the tuition books and devised their own way of making the upright sing, the little girl sometimes laughing and getting whole runs of notes to sound right, sometimes tiring, refusing to play, or making an incoherent mess of a tune. The woman sat patiently with her, learning alongside her, varying her education by reading her Melville's *Moby Dick* which had entranced Elspeth herself, Captain Ahab a wild admixture of herself and, bizarrely, Shaw. Albert and Diana warned her that the child was too young for such fictions, but Elspeth read it to the end, though often Bathsheba slept through half the narration. Then she would lift the child to the door, calling on Nan or Mary to take her home.

Albert was Elspeth's only calendar during that happy epoch. She had grown used to the cycle of rainy months and long periods of dry heat, within them the pauses for celebrations. The old celebrations of Christmas and Easter merited nothing more than an extra prayer at mealtimes and a bigger jug of rum and mauby; in their stead came the monthly concerts and birthday parties for Albert, and now for Bathsheba. The triple harvests wheeled around her and, like smaller cogs in a perpetual machine, the regular production of refined sugar products, and their weekly delivery to Carlisle Bay. Albert's gradual weakening went barely noticed, shoulders hunching and legs stiffening. His paunch never diminished or expanded, but fell more flaccidly lower on his frame. His hair had thinned, but its colour changed so little, from damp to dry sand. Only his face marked the passing of time. Like an antique looking glass it whitened and dimmed, the reflection from it growing duller. Like the sun at the end of a long afternoon that seems to retreat from the world. She would look round at him when he spoke and, every once in a while, become aware they were both ageing.

On Bathsheba's fifth birthday, he was sixty-three years old. On her tenth, in 1864, sixty-eight. No birthday was ever celebrated for Elspeth, only each tenth anniversary of her arrival. Her parents had never observed her birthdays, presumably because they were in transit or on stage anywhere between Dundee and Ayr. She could only roughly work out her own years. Twenty fewer than Albert. Or perhaps less. Before Bathsheba came, she was in too much of a lacuna, a chasm in time, for age to mean anything. The Scots women seemed to age more rapidly than her: contemporaries became like aunts, nieces like sisters, and then suddenly they were middle-aged, while Elspeth remained less touched – ignored – by time. After Bathsheba, she was too busy to bother with counting. Forty-five-ish passed. Then fiftyish.

Not only Albert's face grew dimmer, but his presence. He travelled less and less, yet was less and less noticed in residence. Captain Shaw, with his lordship always at the ready, hidden away in his office, or near enough in town, seemed more substantial. A midway point between Albert and Elspeth, he was one of those men who got stronger, thicker, more gnarled with age. Handsomer, even, Bess and Susan said. Albert drifted into the background, his energies conducted into the firmament of the factor.

Before she was quite twelve, Diana had begun utilising Bathsheba Miller's abilities in the schoolroom, as an assistant teacher. Equally, the lass was proficient in the kitchen of the big house, and a good worker in the fields and the factory. The women fretted for her health – her slight build and delicate fair skin were not designed to thole the heat and work. So Nan sewed her garments – high collars, low hems and long-sleeved – so tight that not even the heated air could reach her body, let alone the burn of the sun. Despite the girl's leanness, by the time she was fourteen proper she was tall and strong, and sang all day in the fields to her workmates, still cutting and gathering at a rate commended by Captain Shaw himself.

She learned all the tales from the old country that her aunts could remember. She mastered the accounts of hoodies and selkies and the one about the daughters of the sky who returned to their father in his silver palace of cloud. She knew bits and pieces of stories such as the Island of Women and the House of Lir. She sang songs – Want One Shilling and Jock o' Hazeldean – and learned every line of the Lady of the Lake, as taught to her by Elspeth Baillie herself.

Bathsheba stretched and grew until she was as tall and narrow as caneshoot, as brilliant in hue as honey. Her nut-brown hair grew long and thickly. Shaw remarked that she had classic Celtic features. Coak concurred: acorn eyes, skin pale as Rivine daughter of Conor, hazel hair like Loch Morar at dusk. They named her Bathsheba for the town that most had only heard tell of, several miles down the rugged east coast, where dark waves break in dazzling torrents on a slender ribbon of sand. Diana spent extra time on her reading, Bathsheba having shown a lively intelligence from an early age. She liked to draw, and did so with a neat and accurate hand. Lady Elspeth trained her in the ways of the theatre, and the middle-aged lady even began to dream again of the stages of Bridgetown. Perhaps a girl of Baillie family training would yet play to the gentry of the New World.

"Nurse, where's my daughter? Call her forth to me." Elspeth and Mary Fairweather's daughter, Sarah, a nimble and artistic-enough woman in her twenties, would dress in as appropriate costumes as they could muster from the chest of guises in Elspeth's room. Bathsheba would lurk in the kitchen, by the door, waiting to be called.

"Juliet!" cried Sarah, in the role of Nurse. Bathsheba would come running in – always too quickly. If she faulted in any way, Elspeth continuously reminded her, it was in overenthusiasm. A little delay in entering tantalised an audience.

"How now, who calls?"

"Your mother."

Bathsheba would curtsy formally then, although Mr. Shakespeare did not in fact stipulate it, and take hold of Elspeth's hand. Dressed from throat to ankle in soft, creamy muslin, the girl looked like a cloth dolly. Her hands, head and feet popped out of tightly sewed seams and cuffs, her brown hair all the darker for the contrast.

"Madam I am here. What is your will?"

"Nurse, give leave awhile,
We must talk in secret."

Sarah took her turn behind the kitchen door, Bathsheba and Elspeth moving slowly around each other as the maestra taught and the pupil learned. When the Nurse needed to be called to enter again, Sarah was directed simply to open the door and talk from there.

"Thou knowest my daughter's of a pretty age."

"I can tell her age unto an hour."

"She's not fourteen."

The trio had been rehearsing the scenes since Bathsheba was nine. By the time her fourteenth year was in sight – a magical eternity and the blink of an eye – the prentice, as Nan cried her, was much improved.

"'Tis since the earthquake now eleven years;
And she was wean'd – I never shall forget it –
Of all the days of the year, upon that day:"

Although the little scholar's movements were graceful enough, she made too many of them, not quite losing Bathsheba and not quite finding Juliet. She would stroke the piano, mid-scene, or lift up a candlestick, as though she were whiling away an hour of playtime. Elspeth, with only a look, checked her, and her full attention would return to the task in hand.

"Tell me, daughter Juliet,
How stands your disposition to be married?"

"It is an honour that I dream not of."

Elspeth had sworn to herself, since their very first sessions when the lass was no more than four years old, that she would never teach the way her mother had taught her. She would feel none of the jealousy of the older actress towards the promising debutant; would not be a Mrs. Bartleby to this fresh new talent. Rather, she would wonder at and conspire with the girl's growing confidence and expertise. She would encourage daring, applaud inventiveness, push for the girl to take up the whole stage, the entire attention of her public. If anything, Bathsheba was too demure: either not aware enough of the eyes upon her when she sang or recited in front of the whole community, or else embarrassed by their stares. She was still young – the urge to play and display for the world would come yet.

Sarah, never a virtuoso herself, but solid, sure of her lines and moves, made a good third participant in many songs, scenes and little home-written comedy sketches. Her hair was not as brilliant orange as her mother's – a subtler colour of pale stone, the result of a mixture with her English-born father's fairness, nor was her face as unattractive. She spoke out strongly, and her features, if not remarkable, were pleasing enough in front of the sparkling backcloth.

"A man, young lady! Lady, such a man
   As all the world – why he's a man of wax."

XI

It was the factory that nearly killed the special child. At the start of her fifteenth year, the end of a muggy March in 1868, she was doing her duties in the evening – helping Golondrina keep the workshop floor clear, dispensing water and mauby to the women, planters' punch to the men, hosing down the pan that boiled sugar into massecuite – when her long, straight hair became entangled in a piston. There were screams and yells of panic, as Bathsheba tried to pull her hair out of the machine. Nan took her excruciated daughter by the shoulders and ripped her savagely free. A moment later and her skull would have been crushed.

The pistons had torn each and every one of her silky strands of hair, mangling them into the muscovado sugar dust. Everyone crowded round the fallen Bathsheba, lying on the floor, haloed in blood and syrup. They carried her to the big house and to Lady Elspeth who wept and shouted curses.

"How often have I said it – she shouldn't be let near those muckle great machines!"

"She wouldna listen, Mistress. She liked to help Gideon and Golondrina."

"What has she to do with them? Tell them to keep away from her!"

Albert – ever since his factory had been up and running, away far less than before – tried to console his wife.

"I'm sure the girl will be fine. Come away now. I'll call a doctor."

There could have been no stronger signal of the seriousness of the accident than calling in a physician. Not in all the years that Elspeth had been at Northpoint had such an extreme measure been taken. Not when she herself was ailing on her arrival, nor to the deathbeds of Jean Malcolm or Elizabeth Johnstone, or to any of the women's pregnancies, stillbirths or the demise of their children. These cases, and field accidents involving blades and broken bones, were treated by Diana and Shaw and some of the second generation girls who been initiated in such arts by them. In part, no doctor was ever called because there were none between Northpoint and Speightstown. The nearest, Shaw declared, were worse drinkers than the ministers – charlatans, shams, witch-doctors to a man. "You'd be better off with an obeah woman chanting voodoo."

But on this calamitous day a medical man was given access to the Roseneythe Estate. He went about his work quietly and professionally, but lugubriously, and giving little encouragement or hope. He stitched and bandaged the girl but proclaimed it unlikely she could survive such a vicious lacerating. Even if she did, she would be bald, and damaged – in who knows how many ways? – for the rest of her life.

The devouring of Bathsheba's hair had also heralded the end of the Plantation's glory years. Their factory was still the most efficient on the island, but it consumed too much wood – in short supply on the colony – and provoked the envy of other producers who formed a coalition against them, forcing prices down. For twenty years Lord Coak and Captain Shaw had crusaded against the ignorance and fear of their competitors, willing, even, to assist them in modernising their own businesses. The offer was never taken up. By the time of Bathsheba's accident, Coak and Shaw had come to understand their fellows-planters' warnings – scarcity of wood and uncompetitive prices were beginning to take their toll.

The whole of Roseneythe lived for months on tenterhooks praying for Bathsheba to recover. When she finally did get back on her feet, her head was a mass of stitches and scars, deep black bruising, some few hairs growing in ugly little clumps. She wore a headdress like Golondrina Segunda's – brightly coloured sashes – at all times, but soon was insisting on working in the sugar factory again, where the Cuban slave-woman took special care of her, massaging balms made from roots and berries into her wounds. Bathsheba took up her duties, but went about them taciturn and melancholic.

That melancholia seeped into the world around her. The early excitement of the factory had given way to humdrum work and long hours, and with the downturn in the market came a return to harder times. In those months while Bathsheba was silent – exempted from classes, no melodies on the piano or recitations to be heard any more – and still clearly in pain, more letters were written home to old Roseneath by the first generation than had been written in a decade, though no one even hoped for a reply any longer. The games around the chattel-houses, if played at all, were hushed and lethargic affairs; groups of girls seldom walked down to the cove any longer to splash or paddle or swim. With bated breath, everyone waited to see if Bathsheba's quietness was a sign of deeper problems: if she had lost all her talents, all her joy. If, even, her mind had gone completely. Certainly, the girl worked like an automaton, and at meals, although she would answer politely if spoken to, she never initiated conversation. Diana fretted that everything the poor mite once knew had been torn out of her with her locks.

Only Golondrina was optimistic. That lady's English had only begun to make sense in the last few years, partly because she kept her distance from the Scots women, and they from her. She and Gideón Brazos, when not working, kept to their chattel hut, built at the back of the factory. Having her wounds treated there, Bathsheba spent more and more time with the Cubans. In other circumstances the habit would have been decried, but no one wished to upset the girl, and she seemed happy enough in that strange company.

"Let her the time," Golondrina said, in her own version of English. "She will return to herself soon."

Elspeth missed the girl dreadfully. The days became long and unfillable. She still worked and sang with Sarah Fairweather and a few other girls, but she would end her lessons early, or suddenly call a halt to a scene or a song when they were only halfway through.

No further doctors were brought in – for everyone dreaded a diagnosis would confirm their worst fears. All they could do was wait. And that was something Elspeth had become adept at. Her life, it seemed, was lived out like a dance: a series of steps, sudden spins, followed by slow glides, like a Dashing White Sergeant she was one moment in the centre of the piece, the next relegated to the line, clapping on others' frenzy. The world around her would suddenly accelerate for a while – whole months, years, flying past in a kaleidoscope of colours and activity. And followed, always, by interminable, empty days, and nights with slow, shifting colours.

Every morning at sunrise, Bathsheba went with Golondrina to bathe in the cove – Elspeth watching her go from her window – to wash the oils from her head. The saltwater stung maliciously, before the older woman applied her cures. There were still no signs of her recovery. Tongues began to wag, rumouring that Golondrina was an Obeah and a witch.

Then, one day in the fields, a little under a year since her calamity, Bathsheba, carrying a heavy bundle, tripped over and fell. The cloth swaddling her head unravelled, and every cane cutter in the field stopped and held their breath. Not only had Bathsheba's head healed, but the hair had grown back in, and black now instead of brown.

The girl got up from the ground, brushed herself down, replaced her African headdress, and got back to work. Her aunts and cousins, however, and even the menfolk, laid down their machetes and scythes. They stood and stared, and then burst into applause. Her bandanna had unwound itself again and her mother and the girl's closest friends crowded around her, laughing and crying and touching the short strands of black hair that covered her crown in crisp, inky curls.

The commotion reached the attention of the domestic staff, who came running out to see the miracle. Mary Miller, Bathsheba's grandmother, hobbling in recent years, came out from the kitchens and crossed the fields, her vision blurred by tears. Behind her came Lady Elspeth, still strong and quick of stride. Bathsheba was being led towards them from the field, surrounded by jumping, dancing friends, hardly knowing what had happened or where she was being taken. Elspeth caught sight of her and her heart stopped a beat. The girl, her headdress round her ears and chin, and buttoned up to neck, wrist and ankle in coarse, grey field-linen, enclosed in a circle of shouting youths, looked like a saint from an old painting.

"It's a miracle!" shouted Mary, as she took her granddaughter in her arms.

The light was back in Bathsheba's eyes and that, more than the tousled, curling locks on her head, breathed life back into Elspeth, too. Nan, Mary and the girls stood back to let their Lady through and greet the recovered patient.

"Bathsheba," was all she could say. And she stroked the girl's cheek and took hold of her hand.

From the field behind, Gideón Brazos and Golondrina Segunda approached. Then, as was their custom, they halted a little short of the joyous group. The two smallest of their four children stood between them, gleaming dark and mystified by all the activity. Bathsheba went and took a hold of Golondrina's hand, pulling her into the circle. She motioned for Brazos to follow, but he merely nodded and stayed where he was.

"Gola saved me," said Bathsheba to Elspeth. The two older women looked at each other for a moment, a shadow crossing Elspeth's face. The negress looked back at her young, white friend, and Elspeth, following her eyes, smiled again, too.

"Thank you, Golondrina," she said, before escorting the girl into the house.

"It would have happened anyway," Albert said, lying on his bed that night, while Elspeth sat on the window seat looking out into the dark. She was counting her years, wondering how a seemingly single long day and longer night had turned into nearly forty years. She was fifty-five years old – older, much older, than her own mother had been when she left her home country. She didn't look her age – everyone agreed. Elspeth agreed, too. When she looked in the mirror she saw a mature woman, but not an old woman. She didn't feel any different – not in her limbs or in her mind – than she had when she first came to the plantation. Her body was proof that no time had passed at all.

Albert, meanwhile, seemed to be in a race with time. His eyes looked white like a statue's and on the odd occasion when he asked Elspeth to dance or recite for him, he had to use a glass and peer intensely at her. He had developed a marked limp in his left leg, using a stick for a couple of years now. He slept later and retired earlier, keeping mainly to his study during the day, spending only short spells with anyone, even Shaw and Elspeth. Tonight he did not look at her where she sat, but lay staring down towards the end of the bed and the dressing table at the far wall. "I've always said that local knowledge of plants is useful. They cure nothing, of course, but they may speed recovery a little."

"I should have taken care of it myself," Elspeth replied.

"Why should you? She's a fine girl, but she's Nan Miller's duty, not yours."

"It wasn't Nan who nursed her."

"She must have trusted the black woman."

Elspeth nodded and walked to the door, ready to sleep herself. She was annoyed with herself, however, that she had not acted when her favourite child needed her most, leaving it instead to an indentured slave she scarcely knew.

I would have been an unsatisfactory mother, she thought as she undressed. Fate has never given me the chance to do anything. It took away my stage just when I was ready for it. My husband died before he could marry me. His child must have known that I was untried, and that is why she fled. For the first time, she did feel old. Fifty-five years of age, and untested; yet to start a proper life.

Over the next few months Bathsheba's hair grew – but not in the same manner as before. If anything, the matted blackness of those miraculous little stumps darkened further. Instead of the strong straight strands of her childish locks, her hair began to twist and loop around her neck and face in vigorous, dancing curls. What had been her finest feature – her nut-brown hair falling like the sheer face of Ben Mhor – now made her truly magnificent. It was further proof to the doting Elspeth that this child did indeed have something of both herself and George Lisle in her. Elspeth's own hair was darker than Bathsheba's original tone, and George's curled round his temple like Lord Byron's. The convalesced girl left off wearing Golondrina's headdresses, and tied her unruly winding locks behind her head for all to admire. She still, from time to time, suffered aches in her neck and scalp, and so continued with Golondrina's cure of oils. She went on spending evenings with Gideón and his family while receiving her treatment. In time, even the pain disappeared. Some people held Golondrina Segunda in higher esteem than they had before, for the nursing she had so successfully given Nan's daughter. Others spoke more spitefully than ever of wizardry and voodoo.

The wood for the factory was depleted to a dangerous level. The clatter and clunking were heard only once or twice a month now, when wood was brought in, expensively, from neighbouring colonies. The menfolk once more had to seek employment in towns or other plantations. Bathsheba, like everyone else, spent less time in the fields and the factory, dividing her time between the schoolroom, taking walks by herself down at the cove, and being tutored by Lady Elspeth.

The mistress of the house was preparing Bathsheba for her future role as Mother of Roseneythe. No formal decision had been taken, either by the plantation as a whole, or in private with Albert or Shaw. It was simply accepted that Bathsheba —fiercely loyal, friend to everyone, intelligent and respected – had all the right qualities for the role. Shaw, in recent years had spoken often of the new generation and the generations yet to come and, despite, or perhaps due to, the difficulties in business matters, everyone looked to the future. With such a jewel of a girl beside her – trained and tutored under her own hand – Elspeth's thoughts of withdrawing slowly from centre stage at Roseneythe were less painful. The girl could take the burden of her duties from her and her own life would open up again.

The annual celebration for his lordship's birthday in 1871 was coming up, and everyone knew that his last one must surely be soon. The old man ventured less and less out of his room or study and, when he did, he needed the assistance of either Elspeth or Captain Shaw. Everyone hoped that the concert would bolster his spirits, and ready them all for hard times ahead. Bathsheba's first performance in front of the Lyric's old theatre cloth was widely interpreted as the start of a new dawn for Roseneythe. Even Captain Shaw spoke of a new era. It would be exacting, he said, with less wealth than they had enjoyed of late. But they were in good shape: the community was settled, and strong children were growing up around them. Their new world had taken root.

The prospect of hard times did not panic the growing village – over one hundred strong now and nearly a third of the younger generation male. They were well used to struggling for a living – in the older women's cases both before and after their relocation to the West Indies. Their brief success had hardly softened them or made them rich. All that most people had noticed in the time of the factory was that there had been a good deal more work to be done and an extra leg of chicken at the end of the day. The families were all still in debt to the estate, and there were even those men – fatigued by the demands of feeding and maintaining the noisy, dusty machines – who spoke of their relief to see them silenced. The children of that era were growing up stronger and better-fed than their older brothers and sisters, and there had been an observable decrease in unwanted pregnancies and ailing infants. But in the strained eyes and drooped shoulders of their parents the mark of long hours and burdensome work was easily detected. Moiras, Jeans and Marys, who had arrived fresh and strong, if fearful, to the Coak plantation, had shrunk in stature and grown in girth, their necks and shoulders muscled and burnt.

More worrying were the signs of a growing argument and division in their extended family, focused around the recent antipathy between Bathsheba Miller and Junior Wycombe, the eldest son of Nathanial. Until her calamity, Bathsheba had been sister to everyone: there was not a soul who spoke a word against her, nor she against them. She had been a walking balm, her very presence taking the sting out of any dispute. She and her generation were the spirit of the new age, the girls athletic and pretty, the few boys robust and fair, and all apparently deaf and blind to discord or gripe. They were proof that their elders' struggles had finally been worth it. But after the accident and Bathsheba's wondrous recovery – interpreted by all as a blessing from God – the aversion felt by the girl to her childhood friend, Junior, became slowly, and unaccountably, apparent.

Bessy Riddoch was the first to notice the breach. Bathsheba was sitting alone by the side of a field, her energies still not what they used to be, when the Wycombe lad approached her in his usual way, with a smile and a joke at the ready. "Mus' be nice fuh the women, sittin' roun' makin' flower chains."

Bess, bundling cane nearby, had noticed how the younger generation spoke more like island natives. They still used some of the old words, and Annie and Dainty and the Edmondsons swore they still sounded incomprehensibly Scotch to them. To Bess's ears, they could have been born in slavery, half African.

Bathsheba did not even look up at Junior. Bess supposed she couldn't have heard him, it was so uncharacteristic of the girl. The woman had often taught Bathsheba and the other girls how to get a rag out of the boys when they jested with them.

"Show them ye're as fast wi' the mooth as they are. Say, 'Nah nah, I'm workin' at flattening a wee bundle o' cane under ma erse.' Tell them the laddies aye get a'thing cunt o'er bubbies. That'll wheesht them!"

Too many of them had taken her advice too enthusiastically, to the consternation of Diana Moore. Not Bathsheba.

Junior tried again, coming closer to the girl, no doubt thinking, like Bess, that she was lost in her own thoughts and didn't hear him. "Penny fuh them."

Bathsheba looked up at him and her brow fleetingly darkened – a sight unseen since the accident. She said not a word but, looking directly at Junior, got up and walked away, leaving the boy gawping. He looked over at Bess and the two of them understood that something new had entered Roseneythe.

No specific argument was ever heard between Junior and Bathsheba. The lad once or twice tried to call her to account, but she replied she had no idea what he was talking about. Other girls began to shun Junior, and his friends kept their distance from them. Sometimes, the two groups would call bad-temperedly at one another. The parents of each side felt the division growing even between themselves, each blaming the other side for starting the bad blood.

Most would have agreed that a fusing of Wycombe and Miller blood would be a conjoining advantageous for all. Junior was hardworking and, if at times his quipping and banter could smart a little, he was undoubtedly an honest, loyal boy. Bathsheba's friendship with him, actively promoted by the Captain and Diana, came undone, it seemed, when she began spending so much time with Golondrina and Brazos and their family. During her recuperation this was understandable, but when she progressed into sturdy good health, people blamed the black women and coloured man for disrupting a God-given combination.

Shaw set about trying to rid himself of the troublesome Cuban slaves, but it was not so easily done. Slavery, having been abolished by the distant English parliament with no notion of how life was lived to the benefit of all in the West Indies, meant that they could not be sold back to their original country. Roseneythe Estate had cut itself off and had too many enemies domestically to offload the family. Anyway no one had any use for a skilled refiner.

Brazos showed no inclination to buy out his indenture – even at the reduced price Shaw offered him – and raise his family in freedom. The Captain talked openly of the inertia bred into badly propagated mulattos. "The bloodlines have been stirred with a stick. Use a blunt tool, and you end up with the likes of Brazos. Able enough at his work, I'll admit, but too much of a dullard to make his own way in the world. Too attached to the comforts of servitude."

Nathanial had long been Shaw's deputy, so the Captain was pulled into the vortex of the widening fissure between the Wycombe clan and the Millers. The factor, being an instinctive leader, made no public statements about where his loyalty fell, but he could be seen drinking in the evenings with Nathanial and Junior himself, so there was no doubt where his heart lay. The issue of Gideón and Golondrina became entangled in the silent, moody dispute, and those who remained close to Bathsheba, Nan and Mary Miller were associated with the Cubans, while the captain's faction – including

the likes of Bess and Susan as well as the majority of the men –
felt it necessary to declare that Shaw had led them well over the
years and, like him, they had no inclination to defend niggers and
cross-breeds.

Bathsheba, in the lead-up to the grand concert, took to disappearing for long stretches, walking along the cove and out into the
byways beyond Roseneythe. She said she was learning lines Elspeth
had given her.

Everyone was relieved to see that the girl was making an effort
to resume singing and play-acting again. The physical wounds
had taken time to heal; the scar on her spirit would take a little
longer. She worked hard with Elspeth, came back to assist Diana
again, and her old easy temperament was returning. The mysterious schism with Nathanial she took steps to repair, becoming the
conciliator she used to be. If she was to win back the respect of all
the women, she needed to be a mediator again, not a catalyst for
division. Whenever, out for a stroll, she came across Junior or a
member of his cohort, she was at pains to be polite. Putting their
childish spats behind her, Bathsheba set about her apprenticeship
as future matriarch with dedication. She called Junior by name and
bade him a good day with a gentle smile. Anyone could see the lad
was still much taken with her – and that he felt the formality of her
smile more keenly than he had her earlier antipathy.

Everyone looked forward to seeing the debut of their young
favourite. But then, unexpectedly, a new problem arose. After an
evening meal, three days before the concert, Elspeth stood up before
the diners left: "His lordship has requested that Bathsheba rehearse
her piece for him before she takes to the stage." She announced it
with pride, unaware that a proportion of her audience stopped dead
in their steps as they made their way out the door.

"Of course, Bathsheba, I know you'll do wonderfully well. But
Lord Coak is the best judge of performance I have ever known. Win
his approval, and your debut before us all will be wonderful!"

Only on finishing her announcement did she notice the glances
between Bathsheba, Nan and Mary Miller, and a general quietness
as people made their way out the hall. She said nothing, but went

straight to her room, wondering and worrying about the response to a speech she had thought unimportant.

The rumour had gone around for many years that Lady Elspeth was in the habit of rehearsing naked in front of his lordship. Men had sworn blind that, when the lamplight inside the old man's room struck the drapes in a certain way, they could see his wife gesticulating. You could tell, some said, that she was naked. Some said that they had seen her silhouette actually disrobe. Mary Riach, many years ago, insisted that she had caught sight of the lady in the very act when the door was ajar and she upstairs cleaning. Her word wasn't the most dependable as she had been half-blind since coming to the colony, but the story was good for gossip.

Tittle-tattle had always flown around Roseneythe, like hummingbirds brightening up the long hard graft of the day. Quiet Errol Braithewaite had escaped England after murdering a man. Nathanial Wycombe had once stabbed a darkie. At one time or another every man on the estate had been a murderer, thief or bigamist. Bess and Susan, and the younger girls they took out on their jaunts beyond the estate, had orgies with runaways and labourers. Shaw had a secret lover – for a while she was Diana Moore, then Lady Elspeth herself, latterly Jean Malcolm's eldest, mischievous daughter Ada. Everyone dealt in the coinage of gossip and few believed a word. That Elspeth liked to dance around in the scuddie for old Coak had been a favourite distraction for years. There wasn't much scandal in the story. Even if it were true, their patrons were, after all, as much husband and wife as any. And theatrical types, of whom shenanigans were only to be expected.

By the following morning chatter was rife around Roseneythe. "Aul' Coak'll want the Rain Chile t' birl bare nakit."

Bess, coming into the kitchens mid-morning with Mary Riach, the two of them covered from head to foot in cane and dust, pressed Diana on the question. "Is that it, Diana? D'ye think Coak's hopin' for a keek at the lassie's erse?"

"Your mouth, Bessy Riddoch, is fouler than the cutters' latrine."

"What if he does? He'll no' find onything differen' frae the rest o' us."

"Some of us have a modicum of modesty."

Bess laughed, drank a cup of water from the bowl, and made for the door. "Sure, Bathsheba's been trained in the dramatic airts. Is that no' what the whale jing-bang's for? Gettin' a leuk up lassies' skirts for a peep o' their coggies? Settle yersel, Diana. It's no the end o' the worl'."

Dainty, passing, laughed at Dina's stern face. "T'ink we pot ent got no cover?" Laughing, she carried on her way: "Old men like to see young monkey tail – and the monkey have fun wining fuh him!"

Out in the fields, Bathsheba herself was being given unasked-for advice. Victoria Johnstone reckoned it was all a lot of nonsense – Coak and Baillie were decent folk who had never acted out of turn in the past. Sarah Fairweather and her mother were appalled at the very idea – Bathsheba should refuse to go anywhere near the man: rich men have forever used poor young girls in despicable ways. Poor Elspeth would be beside herself with rage, they said, if she weren't too innocent to suspect the truth. Some women and more men stuck up for Albert Coak.

"The aul' coof hardly knows us!" answered Mary Fairweather. "First he was away tourin' the world while we worked ourselves half to death. Noo he lies in his bed. He couldna even name the half o' us."

Susan shook her head and wondered what all the excitement was about. "Gie the mannie a last wee present afore he drops doon deid." What harm could it do? But Bathsheba was in no mood for humour, or for receiving advice. She hardly lifted her head from her work, nor responded in any way to the wise words of cousins, cutters, friends and jokers. When work stopped for a midday break, she did not sit with her group as usual, but scurried off with her mother and grandmother. When she failed to come back on time, Victoria sneaked off in search of her, and came back half an hour later saying the three women were ensconced in the chattel-house of Brazos and Segunda!

What was it in her announcement – a statement Elspeth never thought for a moment would receive anything but a smile or a clap from the around the dinner table – that had so offended Diana and Mary? She was hardly close to either woman, though they were the nearest things to companions she had. Of course, in the day-to-day governance of a house and estate they had had their little run-ins, but nothing prolonged or serious – and nothing she could connect to Bathsheba's rehearsing for Albert.

She looked for a connection with her terrible lapses with Shaw, but could see none. So adept was she at wiping them entirely from her mind, that such unlikely trysts seemed ludicrous rumours even to her own mind. It couldn't be that. What else, then?

Surely no one knew of her recitations for the planter? That their marriage was a little unconventional compared to the lives of the women she had not thought problematic. They must know that gentlemen and ladies often maintained separate bedrooms, and the difference in age between Albert and her would clearly indicate – especially in recent years – that both would need their own privacies. They would know that she visited nightly, sometimes staying for a matter of minutes, sometimes for half the night. But they couldn't have guessed how their lord and lady spent their time. She'd always made sure the drapes were drawn and doors closed. Had there been an occasion where she had forgotten? Even if that were the case, and she had been glimpsed – embarrassing and vexing as the situation might be – what had it to do with Bathsheba?

Surely they couldn't believe that the sixteen year old would be expected to perform that particular duty! The idea made her laugh. It was ridiculous to think she'd let a child disrobe in front of an old man! Poor Albert – he would be horrified. She had been, she reminded herself, not much older than Bathsheba when he first asked her to recite naked. And even then she had thought him an old man. She reflected, too, on Albert's upbringing, surrounded by Salammbo, Anne Bonny and the Empress Catherine at the Royal Naval Hotel. But she herself – Elspeth – was all of those to him. Not that he had the power or desire in him much these last years to have her play those parts.

But it wasn't even his idea. She herself had made the suggestion that Bathsheba rehearse for him. She had wanted to give him his place. It seemed fitting, after all these years of her own Lady of the Lake, that Bathsheba should stand before the man who had begun the tradition – and who she truly believed was still the best judge – and earn his blessing. Becalmed, she felt sleep coming on, the drifting colours appearing behind her closed eyelids. Let the silly women gossip and imagine all they liked, if it kept them entertained. Bathsheba would recite, just as she had trained her, and the concert would be a great success. Thereafter, they could find something else to get their rustic tongues wagging.

XII

Bathsheba Miller, the Rain Chile, had loved Gideón Brazos for as long as she could remember. There was always something special about him. The colour of his skin – the same colour as the weak babies that Diana said died of jaundice or yellow fever. She had noticed it when she was very little. Like cane-leaf, or the bark of the birches Mama used to take her walking to, before most of them were fed into the crushing machines. It made more of an impression on her than the gleaming black of Gola's face. There were plenty of black-skinned people around – working in the fields, passing through to collect the massecuite and crushed cane, out in the roads when mama or grannie took her strolling. She used to worry, when she learned about the yellow-skinned babies, that Gideón might suddenly die too.

Her chattel-house was the last one in the huddle of shacks, closest to the factory. The Millers were Gideón and Gola's nearest neighbours, and she used to play with their little girl, Roseta, though sometimes big people and other girls told her off for it. When her mother and grandmother were working, she helped out up at the factory. Gola had made her a brush out of sticks, a little replica of the one she used herself, and Bathsheba would sweep happily alongside her. Gideón let her roam safe parts of the factory. Especially when it was too hot outside to play. She could come in and make dolls out of broken pieces of cane, or play at sword-fighting with one of his sons. Gola brought them jugs of home-made mauby, or lemonade of her own concoction, flavoured with pineapples or mangoes she took from the diminishing forest behind her home. There was always plenty of sugar. From time to time they even fed the little girl along with their own. They never told her not to tell anyone, but she knew somehow it was better not to.

Mister Gideón was gentle and tolerant with all the children. With them, he smiled a lot and played, though with older people he looked serious and fell quiet. When she was about ten, Bathsheba started working in his factory. Simple tasks, undertaken alongside Roseta and the boys, and Sarah and Junior and her cousins – bringing water to the adults, or ale, or mauby. Clearing up messes. Carting little bundles out to the repository where the carters from the port used to arrive every morning to take away the previous day's work. Or taking rubbish to the dump. Sweeping she had become expert at.

Bathsheba liked her world. She liked helping in the fields, working alongside mama and grannie and all the women who were kind to her, and made her laugh. She liked Lady Elspeth coaxing tunes out of her big booming piano, and learning all those lines – none of which she understood, but they sounded big and important and she could shout them out. Diana was nice, too, and Bathsheba knew she was good with numbers and words, remembering a lot from the ones Elspeth made her read. But most of all, she liked being with Gideón and Gola.

Then came her accident, and her world changed. Not because of her hair. She knew it was different the moment it began growing in, but she thought little of it. She had no memory of getting caught up in the pistons. She had been cleaning a machine – she loved polishing the sleek metal, either shiny bright or strong and black – and then she was in a bed in the big house, feeling sore and sad.

Her world changed further because Gideón and Gola had saved her, but no one wanted them to. She realised there were divisions in her little world. Some people wouldn't talk to others, and they got annoyed if she did. Not Nan or Mary – nobody in her own family. But even Diana got nervous when Gola tried to look after her. And some of the men and boys, like Junior who had been her friend, became angry.

By the time her wounds had healed and her hair had grown in differently, her world changed yet again. She realised she loved Gideón in a different way. Or rather, the old Mr. Gideón had gone, and a new one had taken his place. This one, she suddenly saw, was younger than the previous one, the Gideón she'd known since infancy. Much younger she realised than his own wife, Gola. Bathsheba had been frightened when she was ill and, much as Diana and her sisters and Nan had tried, only Golondrina Segunda made her feel safe; made her believe she would get better. She loved the feel of the woman's strong fingers – black on the back and pink on her palms, like a pair of salmon darting in and out of the water-shadows of her hair. But it was Gideón who coloured her world a protective amber. His voice had the myrrh of Diana's Bible readings in it – an elixitive balm; his amethyst eyes spoke of the hope she needed.

She listened to him talking to Golondrina, fascinated by the spiky phrasing of his Spanish, the breeziness of his Cuban words. She learned phrases they repeated over and over between them. "No importa." "Te cuido yo." "Amiga." Later she learned what they meant: "Don't worry." "I will look after you." "My friend." Bathsheba thought it nice that husband and wife should call each other friends. But she felt little pangs of anger, too.

"You have jealousy, niña?" Gola laughed, and Bathsheba turned away to hide her rising colour and her irritation.

Just before the accident, she started her bleeding – later than all her friends. She had always been encased in gowns and shifts that covered everything but her hands and feet and face, because of her special condition. Diana had warned her not to loosen her robe even when Golondrina was putting the oils on her scalp. But Gola loosened it anyway. Maybe her condition wasn't as bad as Diana and her mama and grannie thought, for Gola said nothing But, even swaddled like that, her new woman's body must have been obvious to all. Gola spoke about it directly.

"Your tetties growing good, chile," she'd say, and even pat them. She also spotted how Bathsheba looked at Gideón. "He's guapo, you think?" She knew what guapo meant, for they often called her guapa when she was in a clean shift.

"I don't know!"

"Course you do, chile!"

Then one day, not long before the big concert, Golondrina sat down with her on the sand in the cove.

"Gideón is my brother."

"He's your husband. How can a husband be a brother?"

Gola laughed loud, little squeals drifting out over the ocean. "He not a brother in that way. Nor neither a husband."

She explained how both of them had been bought in Cuba where slavery was still legal. How she had her own husband back there, but was taken away from him and given to Gideón Brazos. Bathsheba sat in silence.

"Gideón is a good man. I like him right from start, and he like me too. We made our babies and they all fine, fine. But we do not belong here. And we do not belong for each other."

"Why don't you leave?"

"I got my chillen."

"Take them with you."

"To where, chile? No money to get to Cuba. Don't want stay anywhere else in B'ados. Here is good enough. But, ay, I want to see my husban', my proper husban', and the chillen they take me away from, one time before I die."

"When will you go?"

"Never. Probably never."

"Why doesn't Gideón leave? Get a job somewhere. Make money to take you all home? They want him to leave. I've heard people say so. Junior and his father and Bessy and even the Captain."

"He can't go."

"Why not? Because of you and Roseta and the boys?"

"Partly, sí. But more, because of you."

"Me?"

"He love you, chile!" she laughed. "He always love you. He love his own chillen better. But he love you in a differen' way. More and more."

Bathsheba got up and ran as fast as she could along the beach, towards the rock stairs, stumbling up them, while Golondrina Segunda sat on the sand, still laughing.

Later, in their cabin, the younger boys in bed, Roseta eating with the Edmondsons, Bathsheba shared Gideón and Gola's eggs and coocoo mash.

"You take him, el cabrón," Golondrina said when Gideón hugged her. "He too young for me. Wear the hell out o' me. I got to save somethin' for my husband."

Gideón was more shocked than Bathsheba. His cinnemon skin turned dark as though cooked from the inside out. He looked at his wife, astonished. "Cállate, santa. Que está la niña."

Bathsheba understood: he was angry because Gola had raised the subject when Bathsheba was present. But it broke the dam that had separated them. Looking at Gola, the girl saw a kind of love she never knew existed. Not between a man and his woman. She had grown up amongst many strange families. Children of one woman and two, even three, fathers. One wife and two husbands – but that always led to ructions, and she agreed with Diana who fretted about such arrangements. Even if Golondrina and Gideón had been thrown together against their will, to happily push her husband towards another woman, a girl, was outlandish. Yet still the Cuban wife looked at her husband with deep affection. Gideón, when Gola found a reason to leave him alone with Bathsheba, tried to explain.

"She has been good to me. But every night, every minute, she miss her proper man. She love our chillen plenty, but think all the time of how her other chillen are now. Every night, when she is with me – she tell me, fair and honest – that she think of him."

From that night on, Bathsheba, saying she was practising the Lady of the Lake, went out walking with Gideón Brazos.

They loved each other. But they would not make love. Lying down together, despite all of Diana's efforts, was commonplace in Roseneythe. All her friends had done so already. Some had babies at fifteen. Some were married over a year – and some already sundered. But Gideón told her he would not touch her until she was of a suitable age and they had been properly wed – though that was unthinkable.

He was infuriated by being thrown together with women chosen for him by masters and owners, and he swore to Bathsheba that one day he would marry her as a properly respected man should. Bathsheba, with the hot-headedness of youth, had wanted to tell the whole world of their love, and let those who despised them be damned. Gideón argued that could only cause torment for them both, and for others. At best, they would be banished from Roseneythe. She would have to leave her mother and grandmother and all her friends. He would have to abandon Golondrina, and he had sworn that he would leave this place together with Gola and their children.

The Cuban took great risks stealing away from his shack to meet the Rain Chile, Roseneythe's chosen girl, each of them taking different routes through thick copses of fig, palm and jacarandas, meeting in a secluded glade behind the old birch trees whose pale trunks looked like the skin of lovers entwined. From there they walked together, skipping through sea-grape bushes and ginger-lilies, stepping over silver-silk agave, always talking, discovering more about each other, sometimes arguing. She was shocked by her mild lover's undisguised hatred of Shaw, of Coak and the whole Estate. She argued that her mother and the women and their children were not his enemies. As they talked, they slipped together unseen through lianas and scuttled down gullies. When they reached the shore they walked along the sand, safely hidden on the other side of the little islet. Climbing up again, then descending onto the cove, they made their farewells in the cave at the back of the beach.

He introduced new thoughts to her head, questions she had never asked herself. Why was it that the most wretched of men from all over the island were attracted to set up house under Coak's and Shaw's regime? What was it that drew them to Roseneythe? Why did the women feel it impossible to leave, either to return home or seek employment elsewhere in the colonies? Bathsheba contended it was simply because they had made their home here. Gideon countered that they were not free to leave – they owed Lord Coak and his factor debts they would never be able to repay. The system of paying less than you loaned for food and shelter had a name in his land. Enganche: the "hook" from which a person could never release himself. He looked out to sea and spoke of the children who were said to be cast out there at Shaw and Diana's whim: a subject about which Bathsheba's thoughts were too entangled for her to respond.

At the heart of the lovers' variance were the twin figures of Lady

Elspeth and Diana Moore, and Bathsheba could not get her feelings to correspond with his. He recognised that both were sympathetic women, each capable at times of kindnesses and possessing a certain kind of loyalty. A compliance that they profited by. "Who am I to condemn them?" he said, sitting in the cave, looking out at the sun. "I am as weak as they."

On their last walk together before the grand concert, they talked avidly and more urgently than ever coming down through the gully to the shore, along towards their cave. Gideón was worried: Bathsheba was being reckless all of a sudden. In the things she was saying, proposing to him. The concert and the rehearsal were aggravating her, but he was worried, too, that he was to blame for this new impulsiveness.

"We're not ready yet, Ba'sheba. Las cosas are not at their height."

He spoke in a mix of Spanish and English and phrases of Golondrina's translated from the African. Bathsheba followed him in language as she had tried to in everything else.

"What height, amor?"

For months they had been planning their escape. They would steal a boat. Better still, they would commandeer one. The best to be found in Carlisle Bay: they'd creep up in the night, storm it – an army of them! All the Millers and the Fairweather girls and Alexanders, the Edmondsons, Gideón's boys and Roseta, old blind Mary. They'd overpower the crew and set sail for an island where only gentle natives lived.

More seriously, they would find help in Bridgetown. A lawman to win back her mother's and aunts' earnings. They could present themselves at the Colonial Governor's palace, make their case. Or, like the runaways of legend, lose themselves in a hidden glen. Now, before the recital for Lord Coak, they had to take real decisions, make proper plans.

"Ahora no! Too early. You must refuse."

She was tired arguing. Not only with him, but with mama and grannie and – fretting more than either of them – Diana Moore. She couldn't think more today. She got up from the floor of the cave where they had been sitting close together in the dark. Water dropped on her from the cave's ceiling, making her shiver and revealing the pattern of her skin through her wet gown. She took the gown off, the evening sun crouching down to spy inside their secret grotto. Until now, Gideón had always remained seated, marvelling at the beauty of her body, but resisting touching her while she was naked. Now he reached up for her, and brought her to him.

Her lovemaking was urgent and though he tried to slow her down, all the desire for her that he had kept violently in check for so long came flooding out. When they broke apart, glistening, struck dumb, the sun had still not set. They sat against the hard rock, momentarily robbed of their senses, as if God had given them one transcendent moment, then confiscated their powers of speech, hearing and reason. To each the entire world was filled only with the other. When their hearing returned it was the breathing of the other they heard; when their vision became unblurred it contained nothing but each other's nakedness. They tried to speak but couldn't find words. Only a new ache between her legs, and the sweat cooling on her skin brought Bathsheba round.

"What about your promises of marriage?"

He shrugged sleepily and smiled, "I told you. I'm weak."

Shaw would be looking for Brazos, and Lady Elspeth would be sending out for Bathsheba. They had no choice but to return to the problem they had still not solved. The rehearsal for the grand concert would take place the following night and Bathsheba still insisted on doing whatever was asked of her; Gideón tried again to dissuade her.

"What can I do? Hide?"

"You were right, before. We go now. Find fishermen along the east coast to help us."

"No, Gideón. You were right. What about my mother? Gola? Your children?"

Their discussions had gone round and round like this for days, getting them nowhere. Bathsheba got up and sighed, stepped out of the cave, cooling the heat of the evening by stepping into it. Gideón brought out her gown and cowl, to cover up that beautiful, mutinous body. They shared a last kiss under the capitulating sun. So rapt were they by the salt and tang of each others' lips they didn't see the children in the trees, spying on them. Not staring at the preposterousness of the naked Bathsheba, not scandalised or afraid of her, but giggling at the lovers' embrace.

They felt the eyes on them, and broke their kiss. Gideón flinched, ready to run for cover. But Bathsheba held him tight. A girl – one of the Glovers – stepped out, then another girl, next a boy, then one of Bess's grandsons. The children stood and stared until finally the smallest of them smiled. Gideón smiled too, even though this display must mean the end of all their plans. The children stood on the sands, sniggering at the woman's nakedness, and at their cove being blessed by something as ordinary as a kiss.

Elspeth watched Bathsheba return from the cove. She had looked out for her pupil most days, since she'd taken to practising out in the grounds. She had even tried to follow her, hoping to surprise her, on the far side of the hill, or down on the beach. Hold her in her arms, the way she used to when Bathsheba was small, and tell her she was her own daughter. Now Elspeth noticed something different in her gait. Worry, perhaps, at the concert ahead. She remembered how, when George wasn't with her, she herself used to wander the Overtons' gardens at Savannah, imagining her big day, forgetting even the first lines of her recital, panicking, and calming herself, over and over.

Bathsheba was too locked up in herself. It was obvious from the way her head hung down, her feet trailed, how she nervously wrung her fingers. It was a defect in her performances too. Not only in front of an audience, but rehearsing, or in the schoolroom with Diana – a part of her was always held back. Experience would teach her to open up – Elspeth was sure of it. She tried to tell her the wonder of it – the exhilaration an actress feels when her very soul is laid bare before the public. How it cleansed you, cleared away the clutter of the mind, leaving only the role, the words, your presence.

"No one here can understand, Bathsheba," she spoke out loud to herself, watching the girl stumbling in the dark towards the porch below, going in to help prepare dinner. "But you will." You will feel alive. Feel the blood in your veins, your urgent heart. Like a wild beast who has no use for thoughts. Just simply being. There, in front of people, who might as well be all the people on earth. Every hair on your head, every eyelash, each tiny movement of your wrists, legs, lips witnessed, recorded, remembered. The rest of your life you're sleeping; the world hides behind a muslin drape. Then the curtain opens and, suddenly, completely, inescapably, you're alive.

The night before the concert, the big house was in an uproar of preparation. In the kitchen, Susan Millar and Bessy Riddoch tippled as they worked alongside Moira Campbell, Mary Riach, several daughters and two granddaughters. Young men and girls put the large hall in order and set the room up for the concert. The strongest men, under Elspeth's supervision, hung the old heavy cloth at the back of the room.

At eight o'clock the men left the house, as they had done every year, to drink together outside, so that Lady Elspeth could show the women the dress she was intending to wear. She was no longer as tall and slim as she once had been, but everyone agreed she could still carry herself. She had not grown in girth like most of the other older women. Bess and Mary Miller and Martha and the Marys had swollen in the sun like breadfruit swells on the branch. Elspeth, rather, had diminished a little.

This year there were two new costumes on show: Elspeth's and Bathsheba's. Lord Coak had offered to order Bathsheba a new dress, but Elspeth preferred to gift the young debutante an old but never-worn dress she had intended to wear on her first night at the Lyric. A present from George Lisle, it had lain untouched in its original box ever since. Nan and Diana nipped and tucked and remodelled the material – so fine it was apt to tear at the approach of a needle – until it fitted the contours of a woman of an entirely different shape: Bathsheba, taller than even the young Elspeth, less buxom but sturdier at the hips and broader in the shoulder.

This was to be the largest gathering of Roseneythians in their history, invitations being extended to day-labourers, ex- workers, children, and one or two factor friends of Shaw's from neighbouring lands. They would number over two hundred, itself cause for celebration, even if they had not increased quite as much as Captain

Shaw had predicted. Second and third generation Rosies were everywhere to be seen – cooking, hammering, lugging furniture, hanging the old cloth.

It was traditional that, after the house had been prepared for the following evening and Lady Elspeth had displayed her costume, a round of mauby with rum was set up for the women. Elspeth would join them all for a glass, every year finding new ways of toasting the women and girls from the hoard of poems and dramatic lines she knew:

"Here's to the maid with a bosom of snow,
Now to her that's as brown as a berry;
Here's to the wife with a face full of woe;
And now to the damsel that's merry!"

Or, with a mischievous grin and a wink: "To a penniless lass wi' a lang pedigree!"

She would then retire to join Albert upstairs. This year, however, as their drinks were being poured and Elspeth raised her cup, every mind was more concerned at how Bathsheba's first rehearsal would be conducted.

Half past eight o'clock came and went without the girl appearing in the house. As darkness grew, however, and just before the clock in the hallway struck nine, Bathsheba stepped in. She was not wearing Elspeth's dress, but one of her daily work-gowns. She looked simple and clean and fresh; had washed and tied up her hair, the curls kept in place by a splinter of polished driftwood, the sweet smell of cochineal and frangipani around her. She wore earrings and a necklace, gifted her by Elspeth, and bangles made by Golondrina Segunda from cherry stones and petals of dried hibiscus.

She curtsied to Elspeth, but all those present could feel the older woman's disappointment. Why had the girl not worn the dress? Quickly, the guests slipped away, keeping their silence till they were outside the house, where their rumours and theories immediately thickened the blackening night. Diana and Nan left, too – Diana to her chattel-house, Nan to her room below the kitchen – both of them fearful but unable to affect any longer the outcome of the night. Elspeth left behind them, having given Bathsheba a cup of lemonade.

"Finish your drink, my dear. Come when you're ready."

"I'll be there shortly."

Bathsheba remained sitting for a moment, saying her lines quietly to herself before giving herself up for final examination.

While they waited for her to arrive, Albert patted his bed, inviting Elspeth to sit near him. He took her hand, and, though his fingers were dry and crooked, she took pleasure in the fatherly warmth of his weakened grip. He told her that, no matter how proficient this young lass might be in her presentation, no one could ever match the depth and beauty of her own.

"It will sound sweeter on a young woman's lips."

"It will have nothing of the depth. Your art has matured and improved every day of your life, my dear." He sighed, "It'll be like starting all over again – and with nothing like the same certainty of outcome."

Elspeth smiled and kissed his forehead, hearing Bathsheba's footstep in the hall below. He tightened his grasp and asked if Elspeth would be so kind, after the child had finished her attempt, to repeat the ballad for him, alone.

Bathsheba bounded up the stairs, a surprising heaviness in the stride of such a young person. Her knock was gentler and Elspeth called out for her to enter. The older woman was still puzzled that Bathsheba had elected to wear a plain gown instead of the costume that had such symbolic value. The deep pang of rejection she had felt on first seeing her downstairs had subsided a little now, but in its place came an uneasy feeling that Bathsheba's decision had some mysterious implication of its own. Bathsheba closed the door behind her, curtsied, looking a little flushed despite Golondrina's cosmetic skill, her eyes betraying a childish excitement. Albert asked after her health and Bathsheba replied she was well. He inquired if she was apprehensive about tomorrow's performance.

"Maybe a little nervous, yes."

Elspeth plumped up Albert's pillows, then sat in her seat by the window. The old man signalled for the girl to begin. Bathsheba looked lost for a moment, as though the first lines of the long poem had already escaped her memory. Then she stepped back from the bedstead, raised her right arm, and recited in a strong if shaky voice.

"Harp of the North! that mouldering long hast hung
On the witch-elm that shades Saint Philip's spring..."

Elspeth, with a wave of her hand, stopped her before she had scarcely begun.

"Saint Fillan, not Saint Philip, Bathsheba. You know that."

The old man in bed explained that the poet sir Walter Scott was referring to was a Celtic missionary who had converted Scotland to Christianity. St. Philip, on the other hand, is a parish of Barbados. Bathsheba apologised for the fault, but Elspeth remained worried by it – it seemed too simple a mistake, and committed so early in the poem. She wondered if Bathsheba, though seeming contrite, had not intended some deep suggestion by it.

The girl continued, her intonation clear and her delivery so strong and sweet that Elspeth couldn't criticise her. Yet she was aware of wanting to find fault. Bathsheba had learned the entire poem but selected different verses from those traditionally chosen by Elspeth, and she had found her own rhythm and accent, quite contrary to the way she had been taught. In all this Elspeth thought she detected artfulness – hidden messages in the narration of the ballad. The phrase "envious ivy" was given more prominence than it needed, and "to teach a maid to weep" made overly dramatic. His lordship, however, nodded and smiled and closed his eyes, revelling in the music of the words.

"Not thus, in ancient days of Caledon,
Was thy voice mute amid the festal crowd,
When lay of hopeless love, or glory won,
Aroused the fearful or subdued the proud."

Despite Bathsheba's little eccentricities in delivery and move-ment, there was no doubt that Elspeth had chosen her successor well. At certain turns of her head and in particular gestures she saw with clarity the shadow of George when she laughed; and when she was whispering softer lines her expression reminded Elspeth of the young man's serious face as he sat on the shelf beside her the night of the storm. She was all the more convinced that, in a magic beyond her ken, her lover and true husband had somehow entered

Bathsheba's soul. Yet still, something in the recitation disturbed the older woman – maternal pride mixed with bitterer emotions of jealousy and loss.

"The wizard note has not been touched in vain.

Then silent be no more! Enchantress, wake again!"

Elspeth allowed Bathsheba a few more verses and then raised her hand to put a halt to the recital. Bathsheba carried on for a line or two, compelling Elspeth to raise her hand higher still and stare directly into the girl's eyes. When Bathsheba finally fell quiet, her mentor congratulated her and told her she could go. An early night and a long sleep were now the best preparation for her. The girl did not turn to leave, however, but looked towards Coak who lay in his bed, glancing from Elspeth to Bathsheba. She asked if there was not something more he required? Coak appeared confused for a moment, and then he blanched, and looked in panic at Elspeth. Bathsheba put her hand to the ribbon around her neck, and he held his hand in front of his face. Elspeth cried out, "Stop! Leave at once!"

Bathsheba looked as if she were about to speak again and continued to loosen the ribbon at her throat, but then fell silent, and turned to leave.

Once she had left the room, Elspeth sat stunned. When it had occurred to her that people might have known of her private performances she had laughed. Was proud, even, that they knew that someone still liked to gaze upon her. Now she felt foolish and squalid. But what had impelled Bathsheba to provoke the matter, and allude so bluntly to it? Had the girl actually wanted the old man to agree to her nakedness? With just that merest motion of putting her hand to the ribbon at her neck the impudent lass had shone a piercing light on the void that had always marooned husband and wife one from the other.

All their lives Elspeth had considered her presentation of herself to Albert elegant. For the only time in forty years she saw shame in a ritual that had pleased them both. She wondered if Albert had suffered her vanity just to humour her. Only a few moments ago she had felt graceful and strong; still charming despite her years. As she pulled herself up from her window seat and made for the door, she thought of herself differently: used and pitiable. She had not only lost flesh, but sinew and bone, her once young, strong body had shrunk and hardened – not through age but from being imprisoned in her chrysalis – to a nutmeg seed. Albert turned his head away in the bed, mortified by the exposure of both of them.

Elspeth fled downstairs, and out into the night. The air was cool and the breeze light, but the storm that had torn her from her promised future nearly half a century ago still raged around her. It had never stopped raging: the wind and thunder had lodged themselves in her heart and mind. She felt that gale on her face even now; the rain lashing, though the night was mild, as she made her way instinctively down the driveway, towards Roseneythe's gates and Captain Shaw's little stone house. The only way of containing the hurricane was to drive it deeper and deeper inside herself, until it blew and rumbled in the small, hard nut of her soul.

The children's games began at noon. Ropes were attached to cabbage palms and the youngest swung and shouted to their hearts' content. Teenagers, bored by the all the talk of Bathsheba and Lady Elspeth and Captain Shaw, played in the water, using shaddocks and watermelons in perilous ball games of their own invention. Aunts, uncles and older cousins busied themselves in the kitchen, whispers passing between them that Elspeth had been seen entering the factor's home and only returning at dawn. Others said they had heard Bathsheba talk all night in Gideón and Golondrina's hut, and was joined there by her mother. Several parties argued that the girl had been asked to strip off but had refused; that she had acquiesced; that she showed no shame, or was mortified; or that nothing of the sort ever happened.

At nine o'clock Elspeth struck the gong in the hallway of the big house announcing that the evening's entertainment was about to start. She appeared tired and perhaps a little stern, but said nothing that told of any argument or mishap the previous evening. Captain Shaw was nowhere to be seen and the rumours of his rendezvous with Lady Coak had all but died away during the day.

She wore a heavy brocade dress of dark colours, as worn by ladies a little younger in town. Within moments of her disappearing back inside the house people arrived from all directions. They stood outside in groups, talking quietly, until Diana Moore arrived and led the way in. They sat down at tables laden with bowls of fried breadfruit and fresh-cut mango, jugs of mauby and ale, specially brought in for the occasion, sliced eddoes, cakes made by Martha Glover's girls. For the second night in a row all waited with bated breath for Bathsheba Miller to arrive. Lord Coak was brought into the room, supported on one side by Elspeth, Moira Campbell's son taking his other arm. Elspeth lit the candles on the birthday cake when it was brought out from the kitchen to the usual applause. Seven candles, one for each decade. Elspeth had only reached the fifth candle when the door opened. Everyone turned, expecting Bathsheba, but instead watched Captain Shaw and Nathanial Wycombe enter and take seats at the back of the room.

Shaw had never attended these ceremonies, and his presence could only mean turmoil ahead, but there was nothing to be done except to proceed with the concert. Diana, who had always been Mistress of Ceremonies, stood in front of the Lyric's backcloth and announced the evening's proceedings to have begun.

"Take your glasses and rest your feet. There's fine food on its way and entertainment until, as ever, we reach claro clarum!"

Everyone cheered and helped themselves liberally to jugs of ale while Diana introduced each act. Mary Fairweather's daughter, Grace, gave her rendition of "Long, Long the Night", as taught to her by her departed mother. Her sister Sarah recited Lady Macbeth's "Out, damn spot!" soliloquy. A group of children performed infantile songs, "Draw a Bucket o' Water" and "Jessamine". Diana gave a rendition of Burns' "The Cottar's Saturday Night", and Jane Alexander, blushing, "The Flower o' Dumblane":

"She's modest as ony and blithe as she's bonnie,
For guileless simplicity marks her its ain...."

Bessy Riddoch each year suggested ruder verses, never with success, being made to speak some poem in a more respectable vein.

"I'm o'er young to marry yet
I'm o'er young – t'wad be a sin
To tak me frae my mammy yet."

Robert Butcher entertained the room with his whistle-playing.

This year he had recruited James, son of Jean Morton and Ben McGeoch, and two of the newer men, to accompany him on an assortment of home-made drums, and together they managed to lift everyone's spirits with their lively versions of sea shanties and schottisches.

During the band's performance, Bathsheba entered quietly. Those nearest the door caught a glimpse of Golondrina and Gideón taking their leave of her and continuing to stand outside as the door closed. The girl had a long, woollen shawl draped round her shoulders, clasped tightly at the neck, but under it – to everyone's relief – they could glimpse Elspeth's precious old dress. Everyone relaxed a little, stamping their feet to "The 24th May" and "Want One Shilling" in time to the drums and penny-whistle. Diana introduced Errol Sarjant who sang the same wassail songs he sang every year, but he did it in such a deep and melodic voice that nobody minded. By the time Bathsheba was called to take her place before them all of the ale had been drunk and Shaw had allowed the last of the flagons of special rum to be opened.

Walking to the front, her eyes met Elspeth's, and each of them gave the other a little smile. The trick of wearing her dress, but covering herself with the shawl – its subtle tawny and silver hues extracted by Nan and Mary from lily and agave leaves matching the ivory of the Parisian muslin – placated Elspeth. As ever, she had managed to obliterate the memory of a rough night with Shaw from her mind but, also as ever, was left feeling agitated. The incident with Bathsheba and Coak she had calculated, after much thought, was a trifle. The girl had merely loosened her neck ties a little because she was nervous and hot. Now Elspeth just wanted Bathsheba's recital – however she performed it – to be over. If she had criticisms to make they could wait for a day or two until all the excitement had died down.

After a faltering start, Bathsheba found her rhythm and voice and recited her poem admirably.

"Bonnets and spears and bended bows;
On right, on left, above, below,
Sprung up at once the lurking foe."

Her voice raised and dipped, and she strode from side to side.

The older women smiled at her accent – Scottish names mispro-
nounced, phrases sung with Colonial languor.

"From Vennachar in silver breaks,
Sweeps through the plain, and ceaseless mines
On Bochastle the mouldering lines,
Where Rome, the Empress of the world,
Of yore her eagle wings unfurl'd."

Vennachar came out as Venyacuh, Bochastle became Bucyastelle.
Some of her definite articles were pronounced "de" in the local way.
Her staccato vowels and cadenced consonants gave a whole new
tempo and fascination to the tale. The story itself had never been of
great relevance to the audience, not even those born in Scotland,
speaking as it did of people unknown and events unclear to them.
It had always been Elspeth's performance they had enjoyed – how
she strutted and clutched her breast, became apparently genuinely
distressed, and then exultant, whispering one moment, roaring the
next. Bathsheba's dramatic interpretation could not approach the
trained actress's, yet it lulled them into a story that seemed more
personal and closer to them all.

"Like dew on de mountain,
Foam on de river,
Like bubble of de fountain,
Thou ar' gone, and fuh ever!"

She finished on a long, quiet note, and the audience responded
in kind – a moment's lull before their applause. Not the same clam-
our and shouts, the accolades that greeted Elspeth's performances,
but a long, steady clapping. Tears of sentiment welled in the eyes of
the audience while Bathsheba smiled and bowed. Elspeth beamed
warmly at her. Whatever expectations there had been of disruption
and infighting were forgotten as the community relaxed into the
conviviality of the night. Shaw's presence had come to nothing.
Bathsheba's performance had righted any simmering wrongs. The
Captain himself filled folks' cups and glasses with large measures
of rum and the hall sung with chatter and laughter while the elder
women of the tribe went to the kitchen to prepare the main meal.

*   *   *   *

The number of original immigrants who traditionally cooked and served the meal had been reduced from twenty to fifteen – Mary Murray, Jean Malcolm and Mary Lloyd, in 1851, '53 and '67, had joined their deceased sisters, by way of rheums and dropsies, but left behind a gaggle of children and grandchildren. Fifteen could fit into the kitchen more easily than twenty had before. Normally, Elspeth helped too, but this year it was felt that Bathsheba should maintain the tradition of the Lady of the Lake preparing and serving the meal.

The door was always bolted against the revellers outside, for the ladies shed the best dresses they wore for the party and worked in the hot kitchen in their shifts to avoid any staining. The older they had grown the more bawdy their humour had become – even Diana had let her standards fall and laughed at the jokes her colleagues made at one another's expense.

"Is it ony wunner Malcolm will na come near me till he's fou? It's only when he sees double he thinks he has hands enough to gang round me."

"Away wi' you, Jeannie. You're no sae hefty, an' onyway you've still a coggie under your jupes. It's a' they care about."

"I'd fondle ye myself, Jean, if I buttoned up different."

Nan handed Bathsheba an apron to put on over Elspeth's fine dress and her fresh-washed shawl. Margaret Lloyd, her tumbler filled by Susan Millar, started up with a bawdy song from the old country.

"John Anderson, my jo, John
When first that ye began
Ye had a good tail-tree as ony other man."

The women's laughter crashed around her as loud as the old pistons from the closed-down factory.

"But now it's waxen wan, John,
and wrinkles to and fro."

Bessy banged her spoon against the side of the bubbling pot of coocoo mash in time with the song. Susan – her flaxen hair of old turned to white and her angular face thinner than ever – sniggered into the oven where trays of salt-bread were toasting. Mary Fairweather's hair was near as orange as it had ever been, but her plain face wrinkled like dried mango. Mary Riach, blinder than ever now, peered towards the source of the voices and waved her butter-pat in the air. Diana shook her head in disapproval, but couldn't help from smiling, nor stop herself from joining in with the rest of them on the last line:

"I'm twa-gae-ups for ae gae-down
John Anderson, my jo!"

When the laughter had died down, Diana tried to put the company in a higher frame of mind, chanting – for she had little voice for music – as metrically as she could, Burns' toast to the lasses:

"There's nocht a care on ev'ry han'
In ev'ry hour that passes-O
What signifies the life o' man,
'Twere na for the lasses-O?"

But Bessy had another lyric to accompany the same melody.

"Green grow the rashes O
Green grow the rashes O
The lasses they hae wimble bores,
The widows they hae gashes O."

The women laid down their ashets of roasted eddoes and sweet potatoes, pulled themselves up to their full height – in their bare soles and shifts, not much taller than they were wide – and a contest broke out between the differing versions of the song. Nothing personal or angry about the competition, each side trying to out-sing the other. Diana's version, however, did not lend itself to full-lunged bellowing, whereas the coarser edition most certainly did. One by one her followers ran for cover under the all-out attack of their opponents, betrayed the cause and – with a whoop and a rise in lusty loudness – joined the enemy. Diana valiantly struggled on for a stanza or two before seeing the battle lost and with great good humour crossing the divide herself, mumbling the vulgar words, keeping a tolerant smile on her face.

"My heart play'd duntie, duntie O
an' ceremony laid aside
I fairly fun' her cuntie O!"

Bathsheba, at the back of the room, laid down the apron her mother had given her, and began to undo the buttons on her shawl.

It took a moment for Nan to notice but when she did, she let the dishes she was stacking drop back on the table and rushed to her. No one noticed, for Bessy had begun yet another song – "Duncan he cam here again" – and twelve voices joined in:

"Ha ha, the girdin' o' it!"

Their hair wet with sweat, necks bare and shoulders shining with steam from the pots and heat from the ovens, they worked to a quick rhythm. With all the banging of ladles and slamming of oven doors, singing and running from one side of the kitchen to another, no one saw or heard the struggle going on between Nan and her daughter who continued to loosen her shawl.

"He kissed my butt, he kissed my ben
He banged his thing against my wame…."

Nan stood in front of Bathsheba, still pleading with her, her words lost in the din, and holding the now discarded shawl in front of her. But the daughter ignored her mother, and stepped out from behind long woollen mantle.

"And, wow, I got the girdin' o' it!"

The entire crew shouted out the final line and the room was full of the squeal of laughter. But only for a moment. One by one, the women felt the merriment die on their lips. They stepped back from Bathsheba and stared, astonished.

The girl stood before them in Elspeth's dress – no more than a petticoat, as translucent as a wisp of summer cloud, chosen by George Lisle for what it would reveal, not conceal. The women were struck dumb, not because of the girl's near nakedness – with the sweat pasting their own shifts to swollen bellies and heavy breasts, they were every bit as exposed as she – but at the curious pattern on the Bathsheba's skin.

All their lives they had been told it was Bathsheba's sensitive fairness that obliged her to wear clothes covering nearly every part of her. And indeed those parts of her skin that were white had the delicate hue of fresh-plucked lemon. Now they saw the truth. Across her right shoulder, like the leather strap of a carrying-basket, ran a deep black stain. It continued widening down to her breast, over most of her belly, covering her entire left thigh.

Bathsheba held her head up, looking directly ahead, and slowly turned her back to them. The same discolouring, beginning in a light brown but darkening as it drew out, descended from the small of her back across her waist, most of her backside smeared with it. For a moment, the women thought the pattern was on Lady Elspeth's gossamer dress. Perhaps the girl was confessing to ruining it.

"What happened?" Blind Mary broke the silence.

Susan Millar replied that Bathsheba was half nigger.

"Since when?" replied Mary, staring through half-dead eyes.

Between them all, the women had seen or heard of every kind of unnatural birthings – white daughters with pronounced negro features, tightly curled hair set in unblemished skin, or coal-coloured sons with shocks of blond hair. Fully black offspring born to white couples, babes mottled and daubed in various ways. Few of these children had survived. Bairns with pronounced birthmarks had them treated with coconut milk and akkie juice, often successfully. Toddlers with hair deemed too woolly were shaved and their scalps bathed in a shampoo of seaweed, aloe and birch-bark; in a passable percentage the hair grew back in a little straighter. Jenny Campbell was one of the few who rejected all advice and ran off with her lover – a freed slave named Joshua – to Speightstown, and never made contact with the estate again, and was never spoken of.

Bathsheba turned and got on with stirring a pot. The women's stares soon turned from Bathsheba to Nan. Nan of all people – daughter of Mary Miller, with Diana Lady Elspeth's closest associate – had lain with a blackie and kept the debauchery secret all these years! There were a thousand questions to be asked. Was Lady Elspeth herself a co-conspirator? Did Shaw and Lord Coak know? Everyone was too startled to voice the questions. What explanation, if any, had been offered to Bathsheba herself? Who was the father?

"All of you kenned and liked him," said Nan, unable to control the quiver in her voice.

"Did he force himself 'pon ye?"

"He did not."

She said she wished she had had the courage to stand by him and present their child to the world as a wedded couple. "But I seen what happen to ither women and their bairns. My lass might never have been born, or lived past weaning. Her faither tried to get me to fly, but we couldn't think where we might go. He agreed to keep his silence and watched his chile grow from nearhand but in secret."

Nan spoke quietly, as if she were talking to herself and not to fifteen gawking women. Bathsheba's father, she said, never relinquished hope that she and their daughter might one day leave with him and start their lives anew. But Nan couldn't leave the people she had grown up with and loved.

"Ye could hae talked wi' us afore the birthing," came a voice from amongst the women.

"She spoke to me."

All eyes turned now to Diana Moore. Diana – the midwife who ministered potions to stained babies, who mixed concoctions that brought on miscarriages and stillbirths – an abettor to this most unexpected of crimes! She who had worked so closely with Captain Shaw to ensure the health, vitality and purity of Roseneythe; the champion of Shaw's "Method". The enforcer of rules to ensure there'd be offspring aplenty of a strong, white, Christian ilk. The woman who spent her life proselytising on behalf of the factor's ideology, who had trumpeted Bathsheba's purity of body, mind and soul, since the very night the babe was born.

"'Twas a long confinement and painful, during which time Nan influenced me with her arguments. I argued back, saying that, no matter the rights or wrongs of the thing, such a large untruth wasn't possible to hide. Nan swore it was only for a few months until she decided what to do. You'll all remember it was rainy the night Bathsheba was born and the few of you who came near I shooed away. The lass made her way into the world and gave a good healthy scream. She had the face of one of God's favoured angels. When I saw the unfortunate aspect of the rest of her, and Nan's frail state of mind, I agreed to keep the secret for the duration of one month."

That month came and went and soon even Diana became convinced that their trespass might go undetected. "The child entered my heart in some way."

Nan looked over at Diana, with tears in her eyes. "I've thanked you ever' day in my prayers syne that night, Diana Moore."

Bessy Riddoch stepped forward.

"Ye never tholed my dochter's bairn sae kindly, Diana Moore."

Rhona Douglas, seldom heard to speak, did so now: "Nor my ain wee boy."

"Nor my grandbabby's neither, Mistress."

Almost half the women stared at her, anger and hurt aching in their look. Diana looked around them all, and tried to keep her voice steady. So many families she had tried to help – and never sure her assistance was welcome, beneficial or even Christian. Nan drew the looks of the women away from the ashen-faced midwife.

"I was aye frightened by Captain Shaw," she said. "He only has tae look at me, pass my door, glance o'er at me through the cane, and my heart'd tremble near to stopping."

She looked around the assembled women. Susan Miller and Jean Malcolm's faces hardened. Mary's blind eyes moistened. A few other women looked away, or kept peering at Nan as if some explanation of her words could be found in the lines of her face or the nervous movement of her hands.

In the excitement of the evening and the extra alcohol provided by Shaw, the women had forgotten to bolt the door behind them in the customary manner. No one had noticed the door opening, and it was only when Nan proclaimed again that, more than her fear of Captain Shaw, what had kept her at home was her love for all those present, and her respect for Lady Elspeth, that a little gasp was heard. Everyone turned to see Elspeth herself standing there.

All except Bessy who kept her glare on Diana. "Perhaps ye'll inform us now, Mistress Moore, where ye've planked the remains of our babbies?"

There was a pause long enough to hear footsteps coming slowly towards the door. Dogged, insistent steps. Nan quickly threw the shawl over her daughter's shoulders. Shaw entered without knocking.

"What?" he glared at them, his eyes shifting, suspicious and scared. "What secret y'all keepin' here?"

Bathsheba stepped out from behind Nan and spoke out confidently. "Ent no secret here, Captain."

Shaw stood a few steps in from the open door. Behind him, Nathanial and Junior Wycombe, and several more of Shaw's cohort, stared into the kitchen. Bathsheba in her muslin shift stood in the centre, still as a statue. Elspeth was hidden behind the open door, watching, transfixed. She had not understood anything since stepping into the kitchen. The women angry when she expected them to be gay; their backs to stove and pots when they should have been working over them. She heard the words they said but couldn't understand them. Least of all could she make sense of Bathsheba. How different she looked! Not only the peculiar marks on her dress or skin, but the look on her face. She had seen that look before. Last night, as the girl loosened her neck ties in front of Albert.

"Jesus. Look at the state o' yuh," the Captain managed at last.

Elspeth saw him lean towards Bathsheba as though his feet were stuck fast to the floor.

"Away to your house. Wait there for me." He turned to her mother and grandmother, each holding the other's arm. "You two take her back and...' He never finished his sentence. Bathsheba interrupted him – a thing not known in nearly forty years of exile.

"I am leaving. With Gideón Brazos and Golondrina Segunda."

"Leaving?" Shaw repeated, as if it were a word in a foreign language.

"Nan and Mary are coming with me." Her mother and grandmother showed no reaction to the statement. Bathsheba looked around the room: at Margaret Lloyd and Sarah and Mary Alexander. "Who else will come with us?" Her eyes turned to Jean MacNeill. Jean Homes. Young Janet Alexander who cowered near Elspeth by the door.

Moira Campbell kept her head hung low. Mary Fairweather blanched and stared back at her. Eliza and Rhona screwed up their eyes, the better to understand her. Susan and Bess looked at one another. Bathsheba stared into blind Mary's eyes.

"Nobody's going anywhere except you to your house," said the factor quietly. Then he turned and gave out a bellow that no one flinched at, except Elspeth. "Nathanial!"

Elspeth heard movement in the room behind her as Nathanial Wycombe made his way through the bodies there, all standing now in a silent ovation. She watched Shaw turn his head back round, swivelling on his neck, like a puppet's.

"Brazos?" he asked Bathsheba in a tone of mild interest. "You're fucking wi' the Cuban slave?"

"Gideón is my husband."

Then Elspeth felt it: a spasm in her innards. The spear again. She saw her chosen child stained and soiled. Corrupt. Not a smidgeon of George in her after all. Just another peasant; the bidie-in of a stupid, uncultured half-caste. Daughter of some black unknown creature.

"Hoor," she said softly, and no one answered. Nobody moved. Nobody spoke.

"Elspeth," Bathsheba finally pleaded. "Please."

Elspeth broke the stare between them, and looked to Captain Shaw. And she spoke again – in the stage whisper she had perfected for Cleopatra's speech, so that even the back pews would feel their weight.

"Punish them," she said.

XIII

For forty years Elspeth Baillie had not put foot outside the plantation gates; in her mind the rest of the island was still a place devastated by rain and wind and a black, angry sun. For all she knew
the ground was still exploding, had never stopped exploding. The
western seas still stretching out trying to snatch at her. Now the
storm had punctured Roseneythe itself. There was no George this
time to carry her to safety; no Henry to place her out of danger on
a shelf like a child's doll.

Elspeth hardly knew Brazos. He was one of Shaw's and her husband's workers. She must leave them to deal with him as they saw
fit. She was the last to leave the house. "All of you loyal to this
estate now has a duty to perform." She heard, but couldn't see,
Captain Shaw. There were puddles of dim light spattered around –
men with lamps, flambeaux staved into the ground. Several circled
the centre of the action: naked flames placed around Brazos, where
men surrounded him doing something with quiet concentration.

Shaw stepped into view, his face ghostly in the glaur. He walked
amongst the shadows, handing out birch-twigs, like palms at Easter.
He went on talking – about the need to protect their plantation,
their daughters and their way of life. He walked casually back to
Brazos and the men who had Elspeth now saw had been pinning his
arms and feet to the staves which others pounded into the ground.
Shaw was left with the last cane in his hand. He brought it down
viciously on the prisoner's back.

Other men followed his lead and Elspeth flinched at what she
saw – the slow rhythmic slash of canes – the earnest, deliberate
torturing of a silent man – yet she urged them on; could hear her
own voice hissing between taut lips. Beat him. Beat them all. If the
tormentors had turned on each other, if the shadows around her

had leapt into action, attacked one another, mayhem breaking out, it would have been right and fitting. Elspeth longed for crescendo.

Elspeth watched migrant fieldhands, militia men and ex-slaves beat the factory foreman, sluggishly as if their limbs were being worked by some slow invisible machine. Around her in the dark, staring towards the side of the bluff where the strange event was taking place, stood shadows whose faces she couldn't make out. No one raised a voice in complaint. Nathanial Wycombe, she thought, was there, and his son Junior. Perhaps the pleasant young James Baxter. There were women too, following their factor's lead. They stepped up, well-practised in the art of chopping cane, the report of their blows echoing a moment after their strike. Her fellow onlookers stood as if cast in stone, spellbound, arms and hands petrified in the last movement they had been conscious of making.

The thrashing didn't last long. Shaw held up his hand and the beaters stopped beating. The last to stop was a free black man who had been on the plantation since before Elspeth's time, a man she'd barely noticed before. A man like Henry, serenely carrying out his duty. Shaw had to remove the rod from his hand. He gave up his weapon indifferently. Shaw leaned over Brazos and spoke softly to him. Then he straightened up and with a sudden yell, louder and more startling than any of the blows, called out, "Bathsheba Miller!"

No one looked up when Bathsheba's cries came from somewhere behind in the dark. Bathsheba was forced forward, and screamed when she saw Gideón. Shaw said some words which only those closest to the scene could hear. One of the men who held Bathsheba pushed her head up, forcing her to look to her Captain, as he stepped one leg over Brazos' body so that he was straddling the captive between his feet.

"There is a war raging in the heavens, and we each have our part to play on earth!"

As he spoke he loosened the buckles of his braces, like a man preparing to fight hand to hand with a foe. Perhaps that was what was expected of the two men: bare-fisted, bare-chested combat, a direct settling of their quarrel. Shaw spoke again, pulling the braces from his shoulders. "The Enemy was always there to beguile and sully us. This is a great day! He has shown his face, and now we can demonstrate our contempt for him."

He sank to his knees, Gideón still unmoving below him. Elspeth could not fathom what Shaw was doing. He looked like a man squatting lazily in the middle of a quiet afternoon. One of his cohorts next to him untied the scarf he wore around his neck, and handed it to his Captain.

"This man here is a slave. Where he comes from the old disciplines still apply. So we castigate him in the old manner."

Shaw made some motion and heads in front of Elspeth craned to see what was happening, obstructing her view. He gave out a low grunt, then a yelp. Bathsheba screamed; a general gasp went up. When the bodies before her shuffled again, she saw Shaw, still in his shirt but his trews at his ankles, teetering over Gideón and straining. Then the smell of massacuite hit her; the bitter saccharine smell of the dross left after the third pressing; the stench of Shaw refined and distilled to its sickliest. She knew what he had done. She had heard of the punishment before, a common penalty performed by slaver on slave that she had thought was only hearsay. Shaw took his scarf and, like a parent tending a child, cleaned his victim's face.

"What's he doing?" she heard Martha Glover, close by, ask.

A young woman's voice responded: "Tying the gravat roun' his mout'."

"Why?"

"So the nigger mus' swallow the shite."

Shaw stepped off the wriggling, thrusting Brazos and gestured to the tall ex-slave who had undertaken his beating duties so diligently. As he stepped forward, Bathsheba's captors pushed her to the ground. One of them held her head while the other forced open her jaw. Shaw himself undid the buckles on the black fieldhand's braces. It took the briefest of moments for the crowd to understand what was about to happen. One half moved swiftly to prevent the sacrilege, and the other to ensure its success.

The commotion thrilled Elspeth. The looming battle – one group squaring up to another, the insults, the leery dance that precedes a clash – sparked a nostalgia in her. The penny-gaffs and inns of Glasgow and Dundee, the brawling lawlessness – they had always roused her. She used to push against her mother and father as they pulled her away. She listened again now to oaths and curses, watched faces contorted with rage and spite; followed the trajectory of missiles flying over heads, sticks jabbing. The thunder. That deep and dreadful organ-pipe.

As with those dogfights and stouries of old, the posturing resulted in very little. A punch was thrown and parried. Lines of women and men stepped forward, their opposite number fell back. The slurs and affronts grew fiercer as the likelihood of violence receded. It took a goodly time for both factions to tire and wane of their feigning and threatening, disengage one from the other and open up between them an area of neutral ground. Bathsheba's enemies had lost her to her supporters, and therefore the punishment Shaw had intended remained undelivered. His loyal fieldhand stood, braces loosened, trews hanging loose around his thighs.

Bathsheba stepped past him, and wasn't obstructed. She moved towards Golondrina Segunda who stood at the head of her supporters. A man stepped out from behind them, walked over to Gideón and untied him. Gideón got up to his feet, but fell immediately back on his knees, vomiting. Elspeth could not make out more of the identities of either group. All she knew was that Roseneythe had been divided roughly in half, Shaw's group having perhaps the slight majority. He and Golondrina were shouting accusations and blasphemies, the factor's sharp consonants cutting through the Cuban woman's deep, dense vowels, each exhorting the other to leave Roseneythe and never return.

"Tek yuh black-hearted idiocy away from us – before I set the Yeomanry on yuh."

"Ent no law here we breaked. You the criminal, cabrón."

In the penumbra between the bluff and the figs, where only the edges of light from flames and lamps fell, a third group was forming. People aligning themselves with neither Shaw nor the Negress. Five elderly women – blind Mary, fidgeting and nervous, unsure of what was happening; Martha Turner, the tall woman who had been standing by Elspeth's side before the feud had broken out; Moira Campbell, staring at her grandson who stood with Shaw's company; and, at the edge of the little group, Diana Moore. Again Shaw ordered the rebels to pack up and be gone by morning. Moira Riddoch spoke up for them, saying that they were the residents of Roseneythe; that Captain Shaw was no more than a hired hand. He and his cronies were the ones who must be gone before dawn. This exchange seemed to clarify matters for old Mary, who stepped away from Diana and followed the sound of Moira's voice to stand between her and Bathsheba.

Elspeth heard a scraping noise behind her, and turned to see Albert shuffling out onto the porch. He had propped himself between two chairs, leaning heavily on their backs, dragging their legs as improvised walking sticks. The fighting and the smoke from the torches had smudged everyone out in the yard, but Lord Coak was still spruce from the concert. Shaw broke away from his clan and marched towards the house until he stood next to Elspeth and in front of Coak. He was about to speak when the old man held up his hand to stop him. Coak announced that he had heard what had been happening. He spoke in as loud a voice as he could muster, but his thin words snapped in the open air like falling twigs.

"Captain Shaw is my agent and factor. We all owe to him a great deal. His judgement has been sound all the long years he has devoted to the improvement of this plantation and our lives."

Those who disobeyed his superintendency, the planter said, could not remain at Roseneythe. Shaw nodded his gratitude, and began to move off in the direction of his house – the last word on the schism having been uttered. The immediate threat to Bathsheba was over. Coak instructed everyone to return to their houses, too, and think deeply on the decision before them. Regardless of what had happened tonight, there was still a home on his estate for those who submitted to the Captain's authority and his own. There might even be a way for them to parley their differences and come to an accord.

But Bathsheba did not wait for him to finish. She, too, walked up to the porch, then turned her back on Coak to address the company. The sight of such a young woman – elegant gown and pretty shawl ragged and torn by ruffians – presuming to hold forth in front of the entire clan, stopped Shaw in his tracks. Coak attempted to speak over her, but she easily drowned out his voice. "There's no home for anyone here. And there's no going home from here. You've seen this stinking wretch do his worst. Now it's over."

Shaw shouted back that the girl was a whore and half a nigger – she had no right to address anyone. She was the concubine of a Cuban quadroon, the crony of a black witch. He moved towards her, but Bathsheba didn't flinch as he made to rip away the dress that barely covered the secret of her body. So much younger, defter and quicker than he, she merely stepped aside. Nan, however, afraid he would repeat his attack, ran forwards, shouting.

"Dinna lay one finger on her!"

Nan screamed that Shaw was evil. The de'il himself. Other voices joined her, denouncing the Captain. Shaw yelled back that their mouths were as full of shite as Gideón Brazos'.

"Yuh all have a choice to make. Either follow idiot blacks and half-breeds and traitors, or remain loyal servants of the Crown and Roseneythe."

Bathsheba spoke again. "There is no Roseneythe. There is no home. Not here. Out there, there's a whole world."

"Follow the bitch if you're dolts. Those that do – leave at first light and follow the road of vagrancy and confusion. The nigger whore and her dupes'll lead ya'll into chaos. But if you or your chillen wish to see the fruits of our work, reject this band of mutineers!"

Bathsheba waited until he had finished. When she raised her hand to brush back the hair that fell and curled over her face, the black markings on her skin glowed on her underarm in the tapering torchlight. "Stay here and you'll never see anywhere you can call home. This plantation will be your prison. Shaw and Coak and those that follow them will work you till you drop, and keep you mistrusting one another. You've seen tonight what to expect of our bold captain."

She turned and held her hand out to Gideón, standing with her band of followers, head hung in shame, shaking with revulsion. "Down that drive and beyond those gates there are people like us. More and more every day." Gideón, with the help of Golondrina and Nan, came over to her side. She took his head in her hands and kissed his forehead. "Mary. Sarah. Robert. Janet. Bill. Martha. We haven't any estate, or money, not even plans. But we can find lives for ourselves somewhere beyond those gates."

One by one her supporters came and stood behind her. Chastity Murray. Erasmus Lloyd. Jack Edmondson. The young Mary Fairweather. Even some of the fieldhands who had not been long at Roseneythe dropped their sticks and lined up behind Bathsheba, Gideón, Nan and Golondrina. Elspeth Johnstone, trembling in fear. Jean MacNeill's entire family, and Mary Alexander's; the illegitimate son of Martha Glover. Robert Butcher, Diana's husband.

Susan Millar walked up to this newly enlarged group, looked directly into Bathsheba's face, and spat on the ground. She left and stood by Shaw's side. Margaret Lloyd, stumbling with drink, took her place next to her. The diligent black man who had beaten Gideón went and stood behind them. The Wycombes – father and son – were already in place. Mary Murray shuffled over, hiding herself behind a group of militia men and fieldhands loyal to Shaw. Bessy Riddoch took a hold of her Captain's arm. Her daughter, Emma, standing by Golondrina, stared at her as if she had seen her mother for the first time. Bess looked to her, appealing, and said, loud enough for Diana Moore and everyone else to hear:

"Some of us want to bide by the side of our stolen chillen."

Moira Campbell looked to her son who was firmly in place behind Shaw and Susan Millar. She shook her head and took a couple of steps towards her lifelong friends – Nan and blind Mary and Elizabeth – until Susan called out her name, and she looked back at her boy, changed direction and placed herself dutifully between Susan and her son. Thirty-year-old Janet Homes and her husband chose separate paths, she to Bathsheba and he to Shaw. Their daughter, twelve-year-old Peg, followed in her father's footsteps; the girl's friends Margaret and Jamie Malcolm, Sally Morton and Abe Berner followed her trail. Two lifelong friends – Rab Elliot and Jurgen Millar gave one another a thunderous look, and went their separate ways. Annie Oyo had remained the entire time behind Shaw; Dainty chose Bathsheba. The whole community thus severed itself.

Apart from Lord Coak – sitting now on his chair on the porch – the only individuals who had not made up their minds were Errol

Braithewaite and Errol Sarjant, Elspeth, Diana Moore and her husband Robert Butcher. The two Errols hesitated, but finally took sides with Bathsheba. Robert pulled Diana towards the same group, but she stood rooted to the spot. He stroked her hair to alleviate her ordeal. Diana and Elspeth stood alone in the centre of the yard. Bathsheba held her hand out to Elspeth.

"You were always our mother."

"She's mother to us all!" cried out Albert. He turned to her, held his arms out for her to come to him. Shaw spoke out her name. Bathsheba's arm was still extended. But Elspeth turned to neither group, nor to her husband. She kept her eyes on Diana's face, and saw that her oldest friend, Roseneythe's most respected woman, their teacher and scribe, looked lovingly towards Bathsheba's party. But it was Elspeth she stepped towards, and spoke. "Go to them, Elspeth. If I were free, I wouldn't hesitate."

She stepped back again, moved slowly away from Bathsheba towards Shaw's company. Robert – already deep in the ranks of the breakaway group – howled. "Diana!"

His wife, her eyes filled with tears, couldn't look in his direction. "Robert. Who was it concocted all those potions? Who administered the Captain's medicines? Me. Diana Moore. Who wrote up the lists of who should partner who? It was I. I've watched children die. I've watched my sisters bleed and part with their bairns. When the babbies screamed with the burning of the whitening ointments, I kept on rubbing."

There was nowhere for her to live any more, she said, outside Roseneythe. Voices were raised in argument: Nan told her all that was forgiven; Golondrina assured her that she had dispensed as much good medicine as bad. Diana just kept shaking her head. "Do you know why I did it? Because I thought it the surest way home. Not an hour has passed that I haven't thought of the morn I left, my mither and faither too ashamed to bid me fareweel. I've known for years that both of them maun be dead, and our hometown gone forever, yet still I slavishly trod that bitter road." She spoke in the language of her childhood, in the words she'd had before the dominie taught her newer, better ones. She asked her husband to be happy, to forgive her, and she took the final steps to stand by Shaw.

Only Elspeth was left now, her mind numb, shivering as she had not shivered since she had marched through bogs and hail on the way to the cattle trysts of her youth. It was not that she could not make up her mind, but rather that her mind had failed her totally, like an understudy on stage who had forgotten her lines and stood gaping at her audience, unable to move or to think. She heard Lord Coak's voice:

"The boat has touched this silver strand
Just as the Hunter leaves his stand,
And stands concealed amid the brake,
To view his Lady of the Lake."

Bathsheba, her hand still held out towards her mistress, interrupted him and continued the poem.

"A chieftain's daughter seemed the maid;
Her satin snood, her silken plaid,
Her golden brooch, such birth betrayed!"

When Bathsheba stopped, Albert leaned towards Elspeth, so far that it looked as if he might fall from his perch. This house was her stage, he told her in a quiet voice. He was her only true audience. Out there was nothing but poverty. Her father's words might still come true – she could yet be reduced to a whore. Worse, an ancient whore. In this house she would always be beautiful. Always feted, her name remembered for generations.

At the back of her mind she knew that a crucial, simple action was required of her. A crossing of the stage at a climactic moment; a word, a gesture, to gratify an audience. Choose Capulet or Montague; Life or Death. The arguments of the drama had all now been made – follow the mutineers, or keep faith with the king and the prince. But she was unsure of the part she was playing. She felt like the chorus, the narrator of an epilogue, not the heroine.

The two flanks parted without her having made a move. She watched them move off in different directions. Shaw, his hand gentle on the small of her back, guided her the few paces towards her husband. Albert put his trembling hand on her shoulder. Thus escorted on either side, she was led towards the door, footsteps fading behind her.

Our revels now are ended. The words came to her, out of the

past. These our actors, as I had foretold you, were all spirits, and are melted into air, into thin air. In the light of the hallway she moved towards the staircase, at the top of which she thought she saw a figure; a dark silhouette, beckoning her. We are such stuff as dreams are made on, and our little life is rounded with a sleep. It took her eyes a moment to adjust to the light, to see the spectre clearly: handsome young George Lisle, untouched by age and toils, his wound miraculously healed, waiting for her, welcoming her home.

XIV

They left in the heat of the day.

Golondrina and Gideón, their boys and Roseta, helped Mary and Chastity Murray muster a breakfast for sixty or more, of salt-bread and tea and porridge and eddoes. Sandy Glover, four Alexander and five MacNeill brothers and sisters, twelve Morton, Millar and Miller cousins, Börgmann lads with both father and mother, their neighbours the Englund family, Jean Arthur, née Homes, replete with her entire clan, a single Douglas girl, Moira Riddoch and Moira Campbell, the younger Mary Fairweather, Erasmus Lloyd and Samuel Malcolm, old Eliza Morton, Victoria and Bartholomew Johnstone, the Edmondsons, Dainty, Martha Turner, all sat around a blanket spread on the factory floor. Five fieldhands defected from Shaw's faction and joined them before sun-up.

There was a great fervour that they should all stay together as a family. They had grown up, or grown old, together; faced life's advantages and disadvantages as one, and could not imagine being divided. Not again, having been already sundered from half their family. As the morning wore on, however, the impracticability of the plan became clear. One cutter might find work in one planta-tion, one in another; a woman could enter service in one of the great houses, or be fortunate enough to be engaged as a lady's com-panion, and a girl could get a governess's position if she were lucky. They could go to Bridgetown or Holetown, where one or two might find employment in stores or businesses, or to Oistins where a man might find work around the harbour and a woman gut fish. But there was no place large enough for them all.

The MacNeills had cousins on their father's side working on the Oughterson plantation; Eliza's estranged husband might find a place for her with planters in the Parish of St. Thomas. Jenny

Campbell's cousins could go to her in Speightstown where it was rumoured she had a shop and might be able to take some of them on. The fieldhands knew of employers who were hiring in various places around the island. Dainty had had her fill of maid-work, and stated she'd try her luck in Bridgetown. It was eventually agreed, with much sadness and some tears, that they had no choice but to go their separate ways. Great plans and promises were made to never lose sight of themselves as a single family who would one day reunite. The young women and men, filled with ambition, and excited at the idea of making their own way in life, swore blind that they would become successful and own a house one day large enough to accommodate them all.

Gideón spoke of sailing away to an island where people like them could venture deep into the mountains and establish a home where they would be safe from the Shaws and Coaks of this world. The Caribbean sea was full of islands. He had heard of such places from the slaves in Cuba. It was agreed that, should he ever find such a haven, he would summon every last one of his fellow rebels. Bathsheba looked lovingly at him when he spoke this way, but did not add her voice to the devising of the plan. Errol Braithewaite found his tongue when Chastity Murray argued that Roseneythe was their rightful home and, while there was little that could be done in the immediate future, they swore to return one day to oust Shaw.

Gola and Nan let them all make their plans, but quietly went round every individual to make sure they had a realistic destination to aim for that day. Everyone had some notion of a plan – except for themselves. The Brazos family and the Miller family had no idea of where they might be sleeping that night. Golondrina Segunda had no other objective in mind than to join her true husband and first family in Cuba, though none could advise her on how such an immense journey could be accomplished.

By midday everyone, having collected their belongings, reassembled at the factory. None of the loyalists attempted to stop them or interfere with their flitting. They were allowed to dismantle chattel-houses, load crates and carts, and even take three ponies from the stables without impediment. Seventeen entire houses had been taken apart and were now borne on the backs of ponies and on the shoulders of men and women. Others bore little more than two or three sheets tied and filled with the bare essentials for starting a new life.

A few had dressed in their cleanest clothes and held their heads high. Most set out in their daily work clothes, dejection and fear on their faces. It was agreed they would walk as one to the gates where they would make their final farewells. The younger children pleaded to go back to say goodbye to their friends who had ended up on the other side of the breach. Their parents told them to hush. Bathsheba led the exodus out to the top of the driveway. There they stopped and took one last look back at their homes – or the gaps where their homes had stood – and over to the big house.

A group of around twenty had assembled there to watch the sis-senters depart. The two factions looked over at one another – sadness, anger and incomprehension disturbing the hot and heavy air between them. At last one young girl, Jenny Millar's eldest, sitting on the step of the porch, raised her arm in farewell. Several followed her example, holding their hands straight up in the air, motionless. As Bathsheba turned to conduct the party down to the gates, Elspeth Baillie herself appeared at her upstairs window and watched. Robert Butcher was the last to leave. He gave one last desperate call of "Diana!" waited several moments, then turned and trudged slowly out of Roseneythe. A woman mumbled sadly as she turned away from the big house that now they would never know what had been done with their poor little chiles that died. "They were sailed out t' sea, Missy," Robert Butcher said. "You know that."

Less than a mile along the way there was a crossroads and there the rebel party split for the last time. Fifteen or sixteen stood at the head of the road south, about the same number at the western path, the largest group looking mournfully at the hill that would take them towards Speightstown. They kissed and wept and embraced one another, but did not tarry long before setting off along their separate ways. Bathsheba went round each and every one of them, saying it was not too late to go back if they thought that was the best option for their families. As she went, she loosed the hat ribbons of each child – the children who had seen her and Gideón in their embrace on the cove – and kissed their heads. Dark hair and fair, locks that eddied as energetically as her own, and tresses that poured as straight as thatch. She kissed cheeks reddened by sun and toughened by work; pale cheeks, dark skin, some with markings betraying a new mix akin to her own. They looked on her as if they saw a saint, hung onto her clothes as she moved onto the next child. In the silence of the noon sun, the rebels dragged themselves and their belongings in every direction away from Roseneythe Plantation.

Nothing ever dies here. Albert should have crumbled into his grave many moons ago. Shaw still patrols the plantation, or what's left of it, though his bones creak and his arms are too brittle even to snap a dried cane stalk. Diana has been condemned to a dotage of solitary prayer, like a whimpering Romish nun. There are black-belly sheep, running wild since Francie stopped shepherding them, that should have fallen hooves-up years ago. Looking out her window, Elspeth spends her days watching the loyals struggle vainly against wild, insurgent cane. She feels she herself has become a wretch like the obeah women whisper of: dead, but walking. The figs have stretched their bony fingers all the way up to the big house, and scratch at her windowpane in the night. If things go on like this, she and Albert and Shaw and Diana will live to as be old as them, their fingers as skeletal, hair like fig-beard, immortally stranded.

She had taken to wearing red. Two years after the Disruption, she ransacked her wardrobes and cupboards, the linen stores below stairs that Mary and Nan used to regulate, and rid herself of anything in another colour – India shawls, jackets, shoes, bodices, camisoles and knickerbockers, corsets, hose, stockings and petticoats; she separated out all the pinks, blush hues, damask, cerise, even purples and puce, every shade from peach to the deepest crimson, and had Annie Oyo burn the rest. The yellows and saffrons, blacks and navy, royal and saltire blues. The cream-tinted clothes that Lord Coak had loved to see her wear and divest herself of – magnolias, ivories, the exquisite oyster-shaded Irish underlinen she used to love most. Nothing but a sunset-sky of reds. From time to time – maybe twice a year – Albert would ask her to come and perform for him. She never went. She hardly saw the man from one month to the next. He lay in his bed or, with Junior's help, hobbled to his study to sit at his desk and write business letters that were never sent. On one occasion she returned to the arms of Shaw – this time in her own room, next door to Albert, where he must have heard them toil breathlessly to throttle some life out of Shaw's old body and her lethargic soul.

Annie Oyo, now very elderly and nearly bent double, saw Shaw come out of her Ladyship's room in the morning. She waited until he had clumped down the stairs and said at the open door to her mistress: "When yuh ent got horse, yuh mus' ride cow." Since that morning, Elspeth's and the Captain's paths seldom crossed.

Diana, as busy as ever, she saw frequently around the house. Elspeth spoke to her as little as possible. There were still a few births – a new clutch of Jeans and Marys, Alberts and Roberts. New names, too: a Flor, a Susannah, a boy baptised Turner; a Preston. More often, she counted down the dead: Susan Millar and Nathanial Wycombe of Yellow Jack. Martha Morton. Eliza Riach, at only two years old. The stillbirths and miscarriages. Bessy Riddoch left one morning, four years after the rebels, with an American salesman, who had been on the plantation for a morning only.

Once, dressed in her ruby pelisse, pink skirt and nut-brown demi-broquins, none of which matched or even fitted, she passed Albert's office, the door of which was left ajar. He sat at his locked escritoire, peered out at her through thickening spectacles and cataracts, and asked: "Why do you dress this way?"

"So that the Devil or God might see me. One of them has forgotten to kill us."

She never ventured beyond the porch, instead she wandered around the now endlessly quiet house. On the other hand, the dream of colours and shifting shapes that had seldom left her sleeping mind in all those years, seemed closer, intimate. Anyway, sleep evaded her; when she did, finally, nod off she was awake again within an hour or two. Walking up and down stairs, only Coak wheezing in his room, pacing round the big rooms downstairs and the kitchens, she sang to herself and remembered old lines and songs. On one of these rambles she discovered a door she had never seen before. A latch, on the floor, at the back of the largest pantry. Elspeth pulled it open and found stairs leading down into the basement. A dunnie. It hadn't even occurred to Elspeth that such a place might exist.

The following night she took two candles, lit one, and descended wooden steps that looked as if they had barely been touched by any feet. The sight that greeted her was extraordinary. She touched, and recoiled from, damp, slithery tubers which, she realised, must be the roots and lianas of the fig trees that grew in the grounds above. They had managed, over years, to creep down into the building's foundations, forcing their way through four-foot thick walls. They plunged right through the ceiling and down into the earthen floor, lodging themselves firmly in the ground, and seemed now to be growing upwards again. The crypt of Roseneythe was a subterranean forest. Elspeth wondered if these growths and limbs were the only things keeping the house standing. Apart from them the dunnie was empty, and seemed never to have been used, though she wondered if it wouldn't have been the natural place for people to have hidden during the great storm.

It became her favourite place to roam when she could not sleep. The basement was like a shadow of the house above, the shapes of the hallway, kitchen, dining hall and rooms etched in wet stone walls. A photographic negative of the living house above. One night, some months after she first discovered this new haven, she turned a corner into a small enclave, though she couldn't think which room above it mirrored. But someone had been in this underworld before after all – for there, in the corner, was an old cupboard, its wood damp with rot and the door hanging off its hinges. She pulled the door open. Inside, a jumble of broken nibs and torn sheets of paper. They tumbled all over the many shelves and out through a hole in the back, the cupboard having been eaten away by damp. She picked the papers up and they felt like yesterday's porridge in her hand. Most, she saw now, were sealed documents. Hundreds, perhaps thousands, of letters.

All were addressed to Roseneath Parish, or thereabouts, in Scotland. She rummaged through the heap at her feet: the majority were in Diana's neat hand. Others were scrawled in first attempts at scribing; some had no address at all but had been carefully and lovingly sealed. She pulled at another tottering column of clammy envelopes. These were written in hands she did not recognise. Elspeth found one that was dry enough to survive the breaking of the crude seal.

Diana, child, why cannot you respond? What has become of
you all? Daily we petition ministers, magistrates, and merchants
connected to Lord Coak, for some clue as to your fate. No news
has reached these shores of any shipwreck. We have travelled to
Glasgow, spoken with ships' companies, with harbour-masters and
excisemen. They foreswear that no disaster could have occurred.
We presuppose therefore that you arrived safely at your destination.
Then what? What befell you? We have implored constabularies
in Edinburgh to take some action, to compel this Coak to provide
news of you. We have communicated with the Colonial Office.
None, it seems, possess any power to track you down, or pursue your
employers. We are at the very end of our wits. Most every night we
pray together in the Kirk, even those who have not bent a knee or
intoned a psalm for many a year. God is the only power we can now
appeal to.

We trust, though it's hard to keep hold of the faith, that you have
not forgotten us; that your new lives take up all your minds and
time and soul. In our hearts, we beg your forgiveness. Though it was
the most painful day any of us expected to suffer, the day we let you
go from our homeland, we truly believed in the righteousness and
benefit of the deed to you, our daughters. Do you fault us for our
decision? Is that why you keep this terrible cruel silence? We thought
some of you may return to us, or some of us go to you. Never, in the
darkest of our nights, did we dream that you would be divided from
us eternally, and so wholly.

Pray God there is some obstacle in your new territory that will
shortly be resolved and we can hear once again the words of our
beautiful, beloved girls.

This separation, Diana, is ageing myself and your mother; your
brothers have become dour and resentful. Many have already given
up hope and left the Parish. There is labour for men and women in
the great towns of Paisley and Glasgow. We cling on to our lives here
in the fading confidence that we will yet hear word of you; learn of
your fate, your lives.

The world here is silent without you. Answer us at your earliest opportunity, before broken hearts result in broken bodies and spirits.

Your ever-loving father and mother,
Jack & Janet Moore

XV

The next morning she got up and dressed in front of the mirror. Tarnished and skewed as it was, its silvering faded, Elspeth reckoned she could still recognise the shape she remembered. Her belly had distended, but only a little. Her breasts hung only marginally lower than they had done. The autumn leaf of her sex had the first frostings of a Galloway November. Her shoulders – though it was hard to tell in the bulging reflection – appeared straight enough. The hair on her head matched her crotch, its colour untouched by the cochineal and seaweed dyes other women of her age needed. She washed herself, dressed, put on a brocade coat, picked up a bundle of the letters she had taken the night before, went downstairs, and walked down the driveway beyond the porch.

She reckoned it could be no later than five o'clock of the morning. No one had seen her leave. A fresh wind blew off the sea. The ground was damp underfoot. She was glad she'd had the sense to put on the coat and her nut-brown boots. She needed to walk. That was all she knew.

Putting one foot after another, not thinking of where she might be bound, she kept at first to the path curling beneath its umbrella of jacarandas. As she went, rhythmically, the letters secured in an inside pocket of her coat, she looked over towards the fig trees which she now knew were secretly tunnelling their way under the entire estate. Coming up the bluff, she stopped and looked out to sea. It was a fresh morning. The waves churning up the surface; a strong sea-breeze keening in and long, billowing clouds scudding fast overhead. Rain in the air, snell, like old memories.

Just over the brow of the hill a smaller, coarser path left of the main one headed downwards, roughly towards the bay below. From her bedroom window she had often seen Diana disappear over the hill and, with only her head visible for a few seconds more, turn right. This must be the path she took. Elspeth was in no rush; detours and bylanes were welcome. Earlier than she expected to she felt the splash of sea-spray on her face and hands. There was a fair old wind coming off that ocean this morning. Getting nearer still the spray became colder, its drops bigger. More like smir than sea-mist. The path became ever more irregular and hard to negotiate even in those sturdy boots. Once or twice she went over on an ankle, or lodged her toe in a hollow. As she approached its end, the path coming to a halt at the rocky side of the inlet, she discovered another even smaller track. Not really a track at all, just a ragged line where feet, or perhaps wildlife, had left a mark. She ventured a little up it, her boots already soaked through. Still it was a path, of sorts, and she was in no hurry.

There must have been a high tide last night. Elspeth knew nothing of such things, though she had, from time to time, seen the sea, from her window, come in further than usual. That must be why the spray was so cold. And why, too, the ground so gouged up and muddied. Among the guddle of sand and mud and wet, loose earth, her eye caught a little mound of white. She took one more step. Skulls and bones. Muddied and broken, lying next to coconut husks and plump, burst breadfruit. Scores of bones; little skulls in the glaur. Diana Moore and Shaw's secret graveyard. She was aware only of the thud of the tide and the hiss of the wind. Then the ground around her feet began to whiten. She felt the smir turning harder, striking her skin like hailstones.

She stared into the open grave. The sea-spray and drizzle played in front of her eyes like moving shadows; like dew rising from damp heath. They curled around in the ditch and she thought she could see blank faces, wide empty eyes, glimmering through the mist and puddles, like fog trapped between Scottish hills. Little hands. Ripping themselves one by one from their tomb into the dull air. Crying out into the ocean and dissolving into the morning haze.

The distance from Roseneythe to Bridgetown, she had heard say, is over twenty miles. How long had it taken her to walk that distance, coming in the other direction? She had never known. In her ruined boots, paper scratching at her from inside her coat, she climbed back up the track and took whichever road presented itself to her. Did she have to circumvallate the entire island or cut through its centre? No matter: she was a winter damson-leaf, fluttering red and ruddy on the breeze. She walked away from Roseneythe every bit as insensible as she had walked once to Northpoint. The road below her feet, and the neighbourhoods and countryside around, trundled past unnoticed. She combatted the pain in her feet, the leadenness of her step, by trying to calculate her age. No calculus, however, could lead her to an outcome of under sixty. She walked for no more than what she judged half an hour at a time, resting against trees, or sitting on stones, between whiles.

The air warmed under the risen sun and lightened her footsteps. She was out beyond the gates before she had realised it. On a solid, hard road and climbing slowly up a broader, gentler hill she looked down again at the sea, much further below now. The sea had calmed itself. Looking inland, there were fields and houses and woods on all sides. Barbados appeared huge. In her mind she had thought there was nothing, just Roseneythe and Bridgetown, connected by a ghostly thread of road, strung over a clutter of destruction. But the cane was green, nodding sympathetically in the breeze; the houses were solid, safe. Little roads led off into mysterious lives. Thawed now, her limbs looser from the exercise, her spirits rose, and she walked proudly, draped in her red ensign. She saw other travellers along the way, surfacing to view like they were emerging from the sea. Blacks, in the main, and shades of brown. At each meeting agreement was quickly reached as to what a wonderful morning it was turning out after all. She accelerated her pace, coming down through a place signed Greenridge, past Archer's Bay and Stroud Point. When she was tired or hungry she knocked on doors and asked for food and drink. As often as not she was offered both. Poor people, quiet people or talkative; some white, most black, nearly everyone opened their doors to the mad old woman in red, in too heavy a coat, free of baggage for a journey.

As she sauntered down around the west coast, by Nesfield and Boscobelle, then back to Fustic and Littlegood Harbour, she recited to herself:

"Harp of the North! that mouldering long hast hung
On the witch-elm that shades Saint Fillan's spring!"
Or sang: "I'm twa-gae-ups for ae gae-down
John Anderson, my jo!"

She was offered lifts – to the next town, to the city itself – on the backs of carts, in white men's fancy carriages, on the tops of piles of beetroot – but refused them all. She spent two nights sitting, sleeping under fulsome trees, and one night accepting the hospitality of strangers.

From them and from wayfarers whom she fell in with along the road, Elspeth heard different views on abolition and emancipation; different memories to Shaw's of slave revolts. As a woman alone, never offering any explanation for her travels, she was offered plenty of advice and warnings. Be careful down by St. Philip's – there's been disturbances there. Folks exchanged news and blather. A family called Edmondson set up farm not so long back just over there. A Miss McNeil is offering piano lessons in Baxter's Road – and cheap too. Some fella called Prescod was radicalising the whole island. If she's passing she should stop in at Campbell's rumshop just by Speightstown. Had she heard there was a lady now writing for *The Liberal* newspaper? Jean Alexander it says here, in black and white. They say she's from abroad. "An' what I say to that is, higher monkey climb, the mo' she show tail." Elspeth harkened to none of them, remembering her father's advice: "Dinna put your shovel in if you've nae dirt tae lift."

When she was finally left in peace Elspeth spoke – the sun plunging into the sea, dousing its fire – to George. She asked him – directly, business-like – if he really would have married her? If he would have thrown away his fortune and his name, for love. There was never any answer. She never expected one. George would not have wedded her. Better, he'd have set her up in a fine house in Garrison. She would have pursued her career – with his help instead of Albert's. She would have received her lover on clandestine visits and laughed at his stuffy life in St. Michael, at his plain and tiresome, gentle-born wife, while she gadded about Bridgetown, took trips to the theatrical cities of the New World. She would have had other lovers. And still, despite it all, she would have ended up attired in red, walking somewhere. More away than towards.

In the morning, a young girl – a quadroon, Elspeth reckoned – companioned her a bit of the road, talking incessantly. About her work as a domestic, the good plantations and the bad. Halfway through her ramblings Elspeth became aware that she was telling the tale of a man from a town called Castries who told of another man, from Barbados, who had arrived in an island called St. Lucia. "They say he had two wives," the coloured girl blethered, "one black, one white, and a family of one girl, two boys, and a babe-in-arms." Elspeth had no idea why the girl started telling this story – she didn't seem to care if it interested Elspeth or not. She only looked to Elspeth when she came to the point of her story. "The white wife, well the fella from Castries say he saw her suckle the babby." And here the girl cupped her breasts and her laughter pealed through the morning air. "Yuh know what she had? One white pap and one black."

At Freshwater Bay she had her first glimpse of Bridgetown – just a few roofs and spires from atop a little incline. It had not been her intended destination but she supposed, like Rome, all roads lead to Bridgetown. There was a main road that would take her directly to the heart of the city. But there was a smaller one that seemed to hug the coast but must surely take her to town eventually. She felt the papers in her pocket and remembered that her expedition did have a purpose.

She took the seaward road, looking out at the water the Alba had once slipped through. When she thought she was within an hour of town she sat down with mangoes she had picked up from the ground and a loaf of bread a stranger had gifted her, and took out the letters that had curled and dampened next to her breast.

Once more I write to you from out of the dark. Nigh half a century has passed only to find myself alone on another dark morn writing again to you.

As I prepare to embark on the last journey of all, the picture that remains with me is of a young woman scribbling with her quill while her beloved parents lie awake and wait for her to leave.

I see her so well and the details of that morning are not so far removed from my present condition. The sun is not yet up, my room encloses around me and I have not the energy to even light a candle.

In the gloom I can see chestnut hair falling over this pen and tears discolouring the paper, yet what hair remains to me is turned to ash and my eyes have for many years refused to moisten.

O, my dearest mother and father, I have grown so hard and brittle. My hand is cramped into a fist from writing countless letters, signed in my own name and in those of girlhood friends – friends who grew to despise me.

Did I not understand your lessons, father? I learned fealty and obedience – to think and act without presuming to question God's Will. With that wisdom, I was sent away, and hoped to return a better and profitable daughter. I failed.

My whole long, bitter, life, since that melancholy morn – the burn gushing by our cottage while I lifted the latch with the first ray of sun – has been nothing but defeat. I fear that my punishment will not end yet, that where I am bound is a place of eternal retribution.

I have been deceived. By a Lord of the Realm and his lady wife, by a Factor of the land and a Minister of the Kirk. In turn, as the Devil requires, I have deceived those who trusted me. I have collaborated with our tormentors. Throughout it all I have written loyally to you, mother and father – full knowing since near the beginning you received not one word of mine. Letters from nowhere, my words blowing back at me on the sea's cool wind.

I have no information as to where you went or how you lived. I know nothing of the world in which you died. The youngsters here, three generations removed from our home, still dream of old Roseneath. I continue blithely with my skilful misleading. I see no harm in providing them with a dream, a spiritual home. This is the only craft I have truly mastered. God knows there is little enough in their lives to lift the spirit.

How many years are you dead, mother? How was the end? Do not weep for me, for I know we cannot be further sundered. You will not rise to heaven, nor I descend to Hell. My damnation is knowing there is no damnation. I loved you. I never stopped loving you, and that love has been the undoing of me.

Your faithful daughter, Diana Moore

Elspeth Baillie recognised nothing of her city of dreams.

This must be the sea she frolicked in with Virginie and Isabella and Derrick and George. Across its waves, beyond the corpse of a sailor sacrificed for her, lay Greenock and mountains and moorland, and perhaps yet still, a troupe of Family Players pinching a living.

Somewhere, over there, the Ocean View had stood. The gamblers would still be gambling in one of the newer establishments of the foreign city in front of her that veiled the old one she had known. Where the Lyric had stood, or Savannah had been, she had no clue. Nonie's lodgings were at the back of the town, furthest from the coast, but the streets laid out before her made no sense. She had paid so little attention to the town that should have been her home, had taken no notice of what ships were in the port and how the buildings were or the lie of the land. But she remembered the heat in the air, the power of the light, and how the sun prickled gently on her cheeks, unhunching her.

Now there were mean little hotels next to grander ones, the Seamen's Mission, rumshops and boarding houses. She turned away, having seen all she had come to see. Like the end of a theatrical performance: having been Juliet or Cleopatra for a few nights running, the last curtain call is taken, and the actor returns to earthly reality; to the dullness of an existence where no great love, or murder, or tragic death is required. Juliet shrivels inside the breast, Miranda seeps away like candle-smoke, and the truer tragedy of life without accolades or drama insists on its proper place.

When evening fell, she followed a sign for Parris Hill and watched the sun go down behind the tall sugar-cane.

"Be not afeard. The isle is full of noises,
Sounds and sweet airs, that give delight and hurt not."
It must have been autumn, for the trees were dropping their leaves like undergarments. Coming down the hill she met the sea and stopped.

"The clouds methought would open and show riches
Ready to drop upon me , that, when I waked
I cried to dream again."

She took the letters from her coat, and noticed for the first time that among them was Shaw's Essay. She placed it and the women's epistles on the wash, like children's paper boats, and watched the tide suck them out. Words. Words on water. She wondered as she watched them sail away – black scrawls on white parchment – what happened to words once they were spoken. They lived in the air, becoming ever fainter but never dying. The very air she was breathing at that moment was full of all the words she and everyone she knew had ever uttered.

Perhaps Fate had chosen red for her own twilight – she had no comprehension of her own mania for it. If the other women – those who had not left and never would – had been turned slowly into fig-trees, ruddy, stout, and dry like vines, rooted and immobile, then Elspeth Baillie was a flame tree, the pride of Barbados, blowing red to the end of her days.

I gave Martha Ruddick a copy of Jean Alexander's book the day before I left Barbados.

"An old aunt," she said, "used to tell about something that happen when she was a chile. Be about 1910. Two women came out o' the blue, stopped by for a few weeks. The older was white and silver-haired, the young 'un a dark-skinned picky-head, but they tell unna they was mother and daughter. Mrs. and Miss Armstrong."

Martha said these women claimed no connection with Roseneythe, having arrived in Barbados from a distant island and choosing to pass some time here on account of the famous beauty of the place, and the solitude and serenity they found. The daughter spoke uneven English, her sentences peppered with Spanish words. The estate rarely had visitors, but it was proud of its hospitality. From the moment they arrived, the Misses Armstrong were made welcome and comfortable, and the ladies in return demonstrated a willingness to learn about their hosts. They sat and listened to stories, barely talking themselves, but nodding their heads encouragingly at anyone who spoke with them.

"Keen artists they was. Apart from one li'l suitcase between them, all they brought was easels and watercolours." They wandered around the grounds sketching, in pencil or paint, the woods, the fields, the house, and the bay. Especially the bay. "The mother, my auntie say, drawed that cove every single day she was here."

They also painted portraits. As people spoke to them and told them their stories they would ask permission to draw while they listened. So, while Beatrice Johnson or Jemima Lode sat talking of the old days, retelling tales about Nan Miller and Rhona Douglas, and the last sad days of Diana, and Junior Wickham spoke of Captain Shaw and Lord Coak, the women would listen and smile and nod, and paint unobtrusively.

Martha poured me a glass of mauby in the room where the portraits still hung. "These be the pictures they left behind."

"Was the mother Bathsheba Miller?"

Martha shrugged. The strangers, according to her old aunt, built a little cairn of stones down by the cove. "It still there – least till the developers come, and rub everything out."

247

I went to the window and looked out at the bay. Plans had already been made for Northpoint Bay Holiday Complex. The cove will be a water-hazard over the fifth hole of a manicured golf links. The figs and jacarandas will be gone. There'll be luxury chalets instead of wooden chattel-houses. "I just keep a still tongue and a fuzzy eyebrow," Martha said.

"What became of Elspeth?"

"Nobody knows. No grave marked out to her here. Some say she die in Shaw's cabin. Some that she become a procuress down Baxter Road way. My auntie swore she die on the road 'tween here and town. Elspeth Baillie be like salt in sauce. She's everywhere and nowhere."

Martha joined me at the window. "We've had enough of this place. Everywhere you look you feel the crack o' the factor's whip and the taste o' bitter planter's punch in your mouth. Everyone wants to go home, don't they? Like you doing today, sir. No place like home."

I asked where home would be for her and the Rosies now. "We're still a long way off. But folks are waiting. Cousins up by where you come from, mister. People still lookin' for we back there."

Author's Note

This story was conceived twenty-one years ago when, working for UNESCO in Barbados, I met my first "Redleg" (properly, poor white; and the "Rosies" are entirely of my own making). I have accumulated far too many people in that time to say a proper thank you and sorry to. But certain names should be mentioned: Cheryll Seally in whose various homes I worked, and who introduced me to Jill Shepherd (famous for The Redlegs of Barbados and her rum punches), Fiona Morrison Graham for the RLS Award to write this book (sorry, I wrote a film), Dr. Gavin Wallace for the grant (sorry, I wrote another novel) and Lydia Conway for cajoling me into writing Barbado'ed which got this fiction going again.

Redlegs became a kind of personal travel book. Written over various trips to Barbados, and; in Grez-sur-Loing, Sanlucar, and Pamplona, as well as my family home when my elderly mum was living alone. Both she and the home have gone now. By chance I finished the novel in Japan visiting my daughter. A generational novel indeed.

Less thanks to the various people who tried to make me change the book in ways I wasn't equipped to do and which the book itself didn't like. But a heartfelt thanks – and sorry – to my ever-patient family. And to Rosemary, Ana, Carolyn, Bruce, and others who believed I might write something worthwhile sometime (even if this isn't it).

But my greatest debt is to Mike Gonzalez and Allan Cameron. Mike, for years of advice and friendship and for his continuing belief in this book. Allan, of Vagabond Voices, for his passion and unstinting commitment and, together with Janice Brent, for the gift of an extraordinarily meticulous and astute editing process. Mike and Allan gave me the confidence to finally publish; without them Redlegs would never have seen the light of day.